That was one of the things she'd most loved about him; Colton or not, he wasn't above apologizing.

"I shouldn't have made such a big deal out of a passing comment," she said.

"And I shouldn't have accused you of. . .what I did."

She nodded, accepting the sincerity she heard in his voice. "I guess the past isn't so far behind it can't jump up and bite."

For a long, silent moment T.C. watched the horse, who was back on his feet now, shaking to get rid of the dust he'd picked up.

Then, without looking at her, he asked quietly, "Did you mean it? About. . .wanting me?"

Honesty was the very least of the things she owed him. "I've never, ever stopped wanting you."

His eyes closed. The silvery light made his lashes stand out as a dark, thick sweep above his cheeks. He turned then. Looked at her straight on. "You'd better get inside, Jolie. Or we're going to start this dance again."

"Then let the music begin," she whispered.

* * *

The

COLTON FAMILY RESCUE

BY
JUSTINE DAVIS

MILLS & BOON

First Published in Great Britain 2016
By Mills & Boon, an imprint of HarperCollins*Publishers*
1 London Bridge Street, London, SE1 9GF

© 2016 Harlequin Books S.A.

Special thanks and acknowledgement are given to Justine Davis for her contribution to The Coltons of Texas series.

ISBN: 978-0-263-91946-2

18-1016

Our policy is to use papers that are natural, renewable and recyclable products and made from wood grown in sustainable forests.The logging and manufacturing processes conform to the legal environmental regulations of the country of origin.

Printed and bound in Spain
by CPI, Barcelona

Justine Davis lives on Puget Sound in Washington State, watching big ships and the occasional submarine go by and sharing the neighborhood with assorted wildlife, including a pair of bald eagles, deer, a bear or two and a tailless raccoon. In the few hours when she's not planning, plotting or writing her next book, her favorite things are photography, knitting her way through a huge yarn stash and driving her restored 1967 Corvette roadster—top down, of course.

Connect with Justine at her website, www.justinedavis.com, at Twitter.com/justine_d_davis, or on Facebook at Facebook.com/justinedaredavis.

Chapter 1

"You made him smile again."

Jolie Peters glanced up at Mandy Allen as she paused by her prep counter. The server never failed to pass on little tidbits like that, and it made her job—and the fillips she'd added to it of her own volition—worthwhile.

"Thanks, Mandy."

It was a simple enough thing, an extra swirl of the house's famous barbecue sauce on the rim of the plate was standard presentation, but it was Jolie who had had the idea of doing it in the initials of their regulars. And the staff was always careful to give the plate the right orientation so the customer couldn't miss it.

"And Mrs. Sandoval really liked the monkfish. I told her you suggested it, because she likes lobster, and she said to pass along her thanks."

Jolie's smile widened. "Thanks. I really appreciate hearing that."

And she did. It would have been easy enough for
Mandy to have implied the suggestion was her own, but
the woman was scrupulously honest.

"Peters!" She turned at the call from Martine Amaro,
the woman responsible for keeping the back of the house
running smoothly, which she did with the efficiency of a
twenty-year drill sergeant. "Garza is here. You're done."

"With two minutes to spare," she muttered as she
headed to the employee room, pulling off and dropping
the crisp white apron and cap into the laundry cart on the
way. Because heaven forbid she should run into overtime.

She immediately apologized silently to the woman
who was in charge of keeping things moving. Not only
had she hired her when many wouldn't, but Mrs. Amaro
had been more than fair, had allowed her to adjust her
hours to be in keeping with Emma's day care, and when
there were leftovers to be doled out, she made sure a portion was saved for Jolie even if she was off shift.

She wasn't getting rich, but she was getting by. Her
apartment was in an old building and not in the greatest
area, but it had been renovated recently enough. Her car
was a decade old but reliable. Most important, her daughter's day care was close enough to walk to for lunch, well
staffed and utterly trustworthy. Between the cost for it
and her rent, she had little extra, but she was content. She
had, after all, come a very long way.

"See you for a moment, Ms. Peters?"

Uh-oh.

The reaction to Mrs. Amaro's words was instinctive.
Things had been going well here, and she thought she
was all right, but nothing in her life had ever stayed right
for long, except Emma. Jolie had been here nearly a year,
but she never took anything good for granted. She never

expected anything good to last. Because in her experience, it never did.

As she walked toward the office, her mind was racing. If she lost this job, what would she do? She was finally at ease, if not happy with her life. It had been a long, difficult trek to get to that point. Was it now going to blow up in her face? She'd been honest about her past, so at least there was nothing there to come back and bite her. She—

"Sit down," the older woman directed.

Jolie sat. She tried to fight down the tension rising in her, but it was hard. She'd spent so much of her life in one scrape or another that she couldn't help thinking she had—unknowingly this time—wound up in another one.

"Relax," Mrs. Amaro said, and smiled. She did it so rarely it took Jolie aback. It changed her entire face, made the stern, brusque woman seem kind and approachable.

Jolie let out a breath. "I was afraid I was in trouble."

"Quite the opposite. You're doing good work."

The last of her tension drained away, replaced by a warm relief. "Thank you."

"In fact," her boss said, "you're getting a raise."

Jolie nearly gaped at her. This, she would never have expected.

"Courtesy—" Mrs. Amaro's smile widened "—of the governor."

She blinked. "What?"

"He appreciated that you put his initials and campaign logo on all the plates at his fund-raiser back in July. The head of catering staff told him it was something we did for our regulars. The governor promised us his next function, and suggested whoever had thought of it should get a raise."

"I...wow."

Although she admired the governor and appreciated his graciousness to the staff, she had volunteered to work the prep for that fund-raiser mainly because the extra money would pay for Emma's day care for the rest of the month. True, it had taken some time and practice to get the logo right, but she had liked doing it. And she was surprised the busy man had even noticed, let alone taken the trouble to say something.

"Thank you," Jolie said. "Thank you very much."

Mrs. Amaro dismissed the gratitude with a palm-out gesture, but she was still smiling. "Thank the governor."

Jolie couldn't help smiling back. "I'll just drop in this afternoon and tell him." When the woman's smile became a grin, she added, "But thank you, too. You've always been more than fair to me, and you've understood about Emma, and I appreciate it so much."

The grin changed to a thoughtful expression. Then the older woman said softly, "I was where you were once. A young mother, alone, scared, trying to get myself off a wrong path."

Jolie's breath caught in her throat. It was hard to imagine Martine Amaro as anything other than in control. "I didn't know."

"Not something I advertise," she said rather gruffly. "But you're doing well. And I think you will continue that way. You know what's important, setting an example for your little girl."

"It's the only way I know to show her how to be," Jolie said, feeling her eyes begin to sting. She fought the tears. She would not break down, not now, when things were looking so rosy. Or perhaps that was why she was getting emotional.

"You've been fighting so long you don't trust anything good. I get that, too."

Someday she would love to hear this woman's story, but she knew this wasn't the time or the place. There was one thing she felt she had to know, though. "Your child?"

The smile Martine Amaro gave her then warmed her to the core. "He's twenty-three and already a licensed contractor, and I couldn't be prouder of him."

"And he of you, I suspect," Jolie said.

"As Emma will be of you. Now, get on with you. Go buy yourself something nice."

Jolie laughed, warmed even more by the hope that those words would be prophetic.

Something nice? she wondered as she headed out toward her car, pushing her dark hair back as the breeze tossed it. It had been a very long time since that possibility had been within reach. But maybe…something nice for her and Emma? The girl loved it when they wore matching things, so maybe something like that.

As she drove the short distance, she thought about taking Emma out for dinner to celebrate. They did it so rarely it was quite the treat for the little girl, and she always behaved immaculately; more than once Jolie had been complimented on the child's behavior by total strangers.

She realized she was smiling. Realized with a jolt that what was making her smile was happiness. A feeling she normally didn't experience unless she was with Emma.

The old alarms went off in her head. *Don't trust it. Don't trust anything.*

She'd had a very short learning curve on trust. Except it had been more like a roller coaster since her parents had died, one with more downs than peaks. The first real peak had been Kevin Oberman, Emma's father, who had convinced her he loved her and vanished the day after she'd told him about the plus sign on that little stick. The second had been the day she was hired at the Colton Ranch. Which had led to the third.

And that one, the biggest one, followed by the longest drop, she tried never to think about. And when she couldn't stave off the memories, she let them come in the nature of a reminder, pounding home a lesson learned the hard way.

Don't trust.

She'd trusted with all her heart just once. It had been the biggest mistake she'd ever made. Even bigger than Kevin, because at least that had resulted in the child who was the sole highlight of her misbegotten life. The one person she loved without reservation, and who loved her back unstintingly.

But those trusting, halcyon days on the Colton Ranch, when she'd briefly but so very sweetly let herself think she'd found the treasure she'd coveted since her own childhood, a real family, seemed long ago now.

But the lesson learned was harsh and close and real, and she would do well to keep it that way. And to remember not the sweetness she'd had so briefly but the bitter ending. In fact, she would do well not to think about T. C. Colton at all but to remember every vivid, painful moment of that last meeting with his parents. Whitney and Eldridge Colton had presented a united and brutal front, and she'd been helpless to stand against them.

Now, she thought with no small amount of pride, they might find her not quite so easy to push around. Setting that example Mrs. Amaro had talked about. She wanted Emma to be a different kind of woman, and the only way she could see to ensure that was to be what she wanted her daughter to become, to show her the way.

Showing Eldridge and Whitney Colton they'd been wrong about her was just a bonus.

And T.C.?

"No," she muttered under her breath as she pulled in to the back of the day care, where it was easier to find a place to park. "Not going there."

She never let herself think about that part, that he had let her go, hadn't even come looking for her. True, she'd never answered his calls or texts—that had been part of the deal—but she'd thought he might at least be curious enough to look. And she knew him well enough to know that if he decided to look, he would find; he was not a man who gave up easily. Unless he wanted to.

He never even missed you. He'd probably replaced you by the end of the day.

The old lecture played like a worn-out loop in her head. She could accept that. What she couldn't accept was how he had let Emma go, too. She would have sworn he loved her. He'd been hesitant at first, unused to babies, but tentatively, he had begun to interact with her. She would never, no matter how hard she tried, forget the look on his face the first time he'd lifted the child above him and made her break into a rain of delighted giggles. His smile had matched the baby's, and in that moment she'd believed in forever.

I can take it, she thought. *But how could anyone not miss a child as sweet as my Emma?*

No, she knew she'd done the right thing. For all three of them. His actions—or lack of them—afterward had proved that. He'd probably been relieved, since he'd made no effort at all to change her mind.

She hastened inside the day care, greeted the administrator in the foyer with a nod and a smile, and headed for the pickup area in the front of the building. Her first sight of Emma, as always, drove all the negative thoughts out of her mind. The little girl shrieked with joy when she spotted her, and ran to her with arms raised.

"Mommy, Mommy! Look what I painted!"

The child waved a large piece of heavy paper at her. Jolie looked at it dutifully. After a second's scrutiny of the splotch of green and blue, she smiled. "It's the park," she said.

Emma was delighted she recognized it. "See the tree?" she asked, pointing at the slightly crooked shape that leaned toward the water, rather isolated and alone.

"I do."

That park was why she'd taken that apartment despite the neighborhood, even though it was a bit over her initial budget. Having the park with the pond right across the street was worth it. She didn't have to drive to give Emma room to run and play, and what she saved in gas money probably evened it all out.

And now with the raise, they would be fine. She hadn't thought of all the ramifications of that extra money coming in. She gave Emma an even wider smile and the girl giggled.

"What's this?" Jolie asked, pointing to a blotch of several colors on what was apparently supposed to be a fluffy white cloud.

"A rainbow," Emma said seriously. "It's not borned yet."

Emotion welled up and nearly spilled over at the child's simple words and beautiful imagination. "I love you, Emma Peters."

"Love you back, Mommy. Can we go now?"

"We can. I have a little treat in store for you tonight."

Emma's eyes widened. "Really?"

It tugged at Jolie's heart that a treat was so rare it astonished the girl. Maybe it could be more often now, she thought as she took the girl's hand and they headed back to where she'd parked. Emma clutched her painting as they stepped outside and the wind threatened to steal it. Visions of it blowing away with Emma in hot pursuit made her grimace. There wasn't much traffic back here; the only person she saw was a woman on foot walking past the back door of the boutique shop next door, but you just never knew.

"Why don't I hang on to that, and you go get in the car?" she suggested, hitting the button that unlocked the doors.

"'Kay."

Jolie took the painting with her free hand, keeping her eyes on Emma as she ran to the passenger side of the car and pulled the back door open.

"Jolie? She forgot this."

The call came from behind her and she turned her head to see one of the day-care monitors in the doorway, holding out Emma's favorite headband, paint stained from being used to hold her hair back while she was creating. Jolie glanced back, saw Emma was safely in the car with the door closed. Just in case, she locked the doors before she walked back to take the headband. The woman smiled as she handed it over, and waved to Emma before going back inside. Jolie stuffed the headband into her pocket, wondering if the paint was there forever, or if it might wash—

Somewhere nearby, a car backfired, and she felt a split

second of satisfaction at the maternal instinct that had told her not to assume cars wouldn't be around.

Emma screamed.

Jolie whirled, running before she was completely turned around. She could see her. Could see that she was looking out the side window, staring at something in great distress.

There was no one else around. She reached the car. Saw that Emma was apparently unhurt. But still staring. Jolie turned around.

The woman she'd seen behind the boutique was lying on the ground. Blood was pooling around her. It took a moment for Jolie to process what seemed impossible. And when she got there, her breath jammed up behind the knot in her throat.

That hadn't been a car backfire.

It had been a gunshot.

Chapter 2

T.C. Colton leaned back in his chair, staring out the floor-to-ceiling windows at Dallas. He could see the Reunion Tower to the right, past the edge of the hotel complex built around it. He smiled as he usually did when he spotted it, remembering the first time he had, when he'd asked his father why they'd built it to look like a shifter. It had taken Eldridge a moment to realize it did indeed look like the stick shift on his car, and the old man had laughed.

Because it looks out over the place where the movers and shakers work, son.

Worry over his missing father spiked through him yet again. He tamped it down. He couldn't let chaos creep in today; there was too much to do. Right now he envied his brother Zane, who as head of security was able to keep himself busy outside this building by visiting all the various Colton holdings for spot security checks. Here, things had gotten shoved aside in the initial panic after the senior Colton had vanished, and while Colton Incorporated was built to run efficiently no matter what happened, the distraction of every Colton at the top was beginning to show.

Not, he thought ruefully, that having Fowler distracted was a bad thing. At least he hadn't left any messes for T.C. to clean up. That he knew about, anyway. Yet. But there would be something. There always was. There were many things not in his job description as executive vice president of Ranch Operations that had become his responsibility, and cleaning up after his ethics-challenged half brother was one of them. He couldn't seem to help himself; if there was a devious or underhanded deal to be made, or a manipulative scheme to be hatched, Fowler Colton would find it, or come up with it himself. They'd clashed about it too often to count.

"You know if you put half that energy into honest dealings, we'd be right where we are, but I wouldn't have to run all over town placating people and paying off the ones you've screwed over."

"But it wouldn't be nearly as much fun, little brother."

Fun.

Not something he strove for in his work. Oh, he enjoyed what he did, and truth be told he didn't mind putting out fires. It was what intrigued him about his work, the various problems that cropped up and how to best solve them. Even Fowler had to admit his approach worked; T.C. hired good people and then trusted them, offering help if needed, but leaving it to them if they said they could handle it. Something his brother freely admitted he would never be able to do.

"I never trust anyone outside of family, T.C. And sometimes not even them. Especially not even them."

He'd have made a hell of a politician, T.C. thought sourly. It was all like a game to Fowler, a game he was the best at. And that he took great glee in winning. He truly did have fun with all his machinations, and nothing pleased him more than triumphing over someone who was fool enough to be honest in his dealings.

Whereas T.C. hadn't really had fun in...four years.

The memory shot through him the way it always did when his guard was down. He'd been fixated on his worry about his father and his weariness with his brother, leaving the door open for the thoughts he dreaded most.

Jolie.

And the worst—or best—of the memories, that moment when he'd given in to an urge he had never expected, to take the only-months-old baby he was still nervous about even holding, the baby who was looking up at him so solemnly, and swing her up above him so she could look down for a change. It seemed to have thrilled her, and she had broken into a peal of delighted laughter. He hadn't been prepared for that, and certainly not for how it made him feel. Something deep and primal had sparked to life in him in that moment, an urge to protect, to nurture, to keep this beautiful bit of human life safe forever.

And then he'd looked at Jolie. Standing there, watching them. There were tears streaking down her face, but the glow in her beautiful gray eyes was pure joy. He'd known in that moment that it was right, righter than anything had ever been in his life. They were his, and they would build a life that would be rock-solid and Texas strong.

A month later, they were both gone.

She'd thrown them away and, as his mother so coldly put it, taken the money and run. Just as she'd predicted when she first realized her son had taken an interest in the lowly cook's assistant.

"She's a gold digger, Thomas. All she wants is Colton money," Whitney Colton had said, after storming into his rooms on the second floor of the ranch house. Which he'd always thought was a singularly inaccurate name for a place that looked more like a mansion of the antebellum South.

"You know people said the same thing about you, don't you?" he'd snapped back at her. He'd scored with that one; he knew it by the color that rose in her cheeks and the anger that flared in green eyes so like his own.

"And I've proven them wrong for twenty-five years now," she retorted sharply.

Yes, he'd scored, but in the end he'd lost, because she'd been proven right. Jolie had jumped at the first chance at a chunk of cash. A big Colton payday must have been her goal all along. He'd fought the knowledge, right up until his mother had shown him the cashed check, with Jolie's signature unmistakably on the back.

It had been the most painful learning moment of his life. He never, ever wanted to go through something like that again. And it only got worse when he started to wonder if it had been only the money, or if it had been him, too—if he had somehow failed her. So he kept things light, dating occasionally but never seriously, throwing himself into his work with a new energy, and in the process helping create the smooth-running machine that was now Colton Inc.

Which was a damned good thing, he told himself now,

since everything else was in chaos. And the last thing he should have been doing was sitting here dwelling on useless, painful memories. And it irritated him that they were still painful, after all this time. He'd assumed he'd be well past it now. Maybe you never forgot the first time you really crashed and burned.

With ruthless determination, he shoved it all back into the compartment it had escaped. His father was missing, his nasty half sister Marceline wanted him declared dead so she could get her grubby hands on her inheritance. That had been a family fight he didn't ever want to revisit, ending with Marceline putting forth the question he reluctantly had to admit had merit; if their father had been kidnapped and was still alive, why wasn't there a ransom demand?

And then there was the very real possibility that not only might Eldridge be dead, but someone in the family had killed him.

A tap on the door spun him away from the view he'd no longer been focused on. His assistant, Hannah Alcott, stepped into the office when he called out an okay. Holding a sheaf of papers in her hand, she strode briskly toward him, her energetic stride belying her age, which T.C. knew to be nearly sixty. Once his father's executive assistant—and, T.C. suspected, at least partly responsible for his father's steering away from his more unethical turns—she had nearly quit when Fowler took over the reins of Colton Inc., saying bluntly that she wouldn't deal with his methods. T.C. had tried to intercede, and been unexpectedly flattered when Hannah said, "You're the only one in this place now that I could work for."

And so she was here, and his life had instantly become easier. She was efficient, smart and utterly trustworthy.

"Are you happy over here?" he asked as he took the papers she held out. His office was—purposely—on the other side of the building from his brother's, and smaller, and the adjacent office for his assistant was also smaller.

"Yes, Mr. Colton." Her tone was formal, but there was a note of respect that had been lacking when she spoke to Fowler. His brother would have been surprised at how much that meant to him. Respect of underlings, as Fowler put it, didn't matter as long as they followed orders.

"Thank you for accepting the offer. You've made my life easier."

"Thank you for making it. I didn't really want to leave."

They were still feeling their way, and although it felt odd to T.C. that he was referred to deferentially as Mr. Colton by a woman a generation his senior, she seemed to prefer it that way. And what Hannah Alcott wanted, she also seemed to generally get.

"I don't think I've ever said that I admire you for standing up to Fowler the way you did."

She looked at him for a moment, quietly, steadily. "Someone needs to. And I'm here because you are the only other one who has."

T.C. supposed Fowler would say he was ridiculous for being so pleased at words from a "mere executive assistant," but nevertheless, he was.

"May I ask you something?" she said when he smiled.

"Only if you promise to stop asking if you can ask."

She returned his smile. "Why didn't you have an assistant before?"

He gave a half shrug. "I figured I needed to know how to do it all before I asked somebody else to do it."

"And that, Mr. Colton, is another reason I'm here." Briskly turning back to business, she gestured at the papers she'd handed him. "The Wainwright papers are on top, and the analysis you asked for is in the folder."

"Already? You are a gem, Mrs. Alcott."

"I am."

He couldn't help smiling again, rare enough in these days of worry and mystery that he appreciated it. "I should give you a raise."

"You already did. I'm quite sufficiently compensated, Mr. Colton." But she was smiling as she left the office.

He realized after she'd left that one of the reasons he liked her was that she imposed a sense of order on things, and amid the current chaos, that was no small accomplishment. She—

The door opened once more, and Hannah leaned in. "Hurricane Fowler headed this way," she said.

He grimaced. "Thanks for the heads-up."

"Five minutes?"

He gave her a grateful look. "Ten. I'm feeling strong today."

She nodded and backed out once more.

His brother at full force was not how he'd wanted to spend this afternoon. He needed a back door, T.C. thought, not for the first time. He even considered a dive into the adjoining bathroom, but knowing Fowler he'd barge in anyway. He smothered a sigh and braced himself. It was easier, knowing that in ten minutes Hannah would remind him of some urgent piece of business that had to be attended to immediately. It felt cowardly to him, but sometimes it was the only way to deal with the steamroller that was his half brother.

There was a thud as the door was shoved open; the formality of a knock was usually absent when Fowler was involved. He felt—and acted—as if he owned not only the entire building but everyone in it.

"I know who killed Dad!"

T.C. stood up; he'd expected some business-related demand, or another lecture on his lack of bloodthirstiness on the Wainwright deal. T.C. believed in healthy competition, and the occasional solid partnership; Fowler believed in wiping the competition off the field.

"We don't know," T.C. reminded his brother, "that Dad's dead."

"Never mind that. I know who did it."

T.C. groaned inwardly. *Great*, he thought. *Here we go again. It's not enough that Mother accused Alanna of all people. Now Fowler's got some other crackbrained theory?*

"I presume your glee means you've found another suspect for them to chase after besides yourself and Tiffany?"

"Oh, yes."

Foreboding sparked in T.C.'s chest. Fowler was *too* gleeful. This was more than just some harebrained idea to throw suspicion off him and his self-absorbed, money-conscious girlfriend. T.C. waited silently, refusing to rise to the bait, denying Fowler some of the pleasure he seemed to get out of making people jump to his tune. Irritation flickered in his eyes.

"You're so cool now, but you won't be. Not when I tell you who it is, who I saw right here in town, not an hour ago."

He'd been right. This was more. And it was aimed at him. "Just get it over with, Fowler. I have a busy schedule."

Fowler folded his arms across his chest and smirked.

"I've already called the sheriff, so don't think you can stop that."

T.C. frowned. "Why would you think I would want to stop you?" He wanted his father found, and while he doubted whatever wild claim Fowler was making now would prove true, he also felt every avenue should be explored.

"Because you're a pushover and always have been when it comes to her," Fowler said, in that nasty tone T.C. had learned meant he was about to spring his trap.

The foreboding exploded into full-blown apprehension. "Her?"

Fowler's smirk widened. He was clearly taking great pleasure in this.

"Jolie Peters."

Chapter 3

Jolie clutched her still-weeping daughter close, rocking her, cooing at her, trying to soothe her. The police were being kind, but as grim as she would have expected them to be, dealing with a cold-blooded murder. The Central Business District had its own dedicated police. They knew the area inside out and were coolly, briskly efficient. If she wasn't in such shock, Jolie would have been impressed.

And if it wasn't for Emma, she might feel safe.

"It's all right, honey," said the uniformed woman kneeling before them as they sat on the edge of the police unit's front seat. Jolie had purposely put their backs to the bloody scene. The sight of a woman who just a couple of hours ago had been alive being put in a cold, dark bag and loaded in the back of a van was not something she wanted added to Emma's already horrible images.

The woman's voice was soft, gentle, and Jolie liked the way she looked at her for permission before she reached up and brushed her fingers over the child's tearstained cheek. "Maybe you'll remember more later when it's not quite so scary."

"I'm sorry," Jolie said, "but she's too upset."

"Of course she is. Who wouldn't be? And just knowing we're looking for a woman helps a lot."

"You believe her?"

The other officers had seemed to doubt Emma's account, which Jolie understood, given that the girl had been practically hysterical. Although she seemed to be calming down now. As if the quiet, adult conversation going on over her head was soothing her. Jolie's gaze flicked to the woman's face and saw she knew that and was doing this intentionally. She glanced at the name tag over her left pocket, which read T. Wilcox.

"I have a three-year-old boy, Tyler," she said, "and I know when he's making things up. I trust you do, too."

Jolie gave her a grateful smile. "I do." She glanced at the people both in uniform and civilian clothes clustered around where the body was, at last, being removed. "But I'm not sure they believe her."

"It's not that they don't believe her, it's that she's able to give so little to go on. And no one else saw a woman in the area. Plus, a crime like this isn't usually the way a woman would go about a murder. But I heard John Eckhart caught the case. He's a good detective, one of the best. He'll—"

"Liddy," Emma said suddenly.

Jolie looked at the child on her lap. "What, honey?"

"Her eyes were like Liddy's."

Officer Wilcox looked at Jolie, clearly puzzled.

"Lydia," Jolie explained. "She's an anime character Emma loves." Her brow furrowed, and then she smoothed back Emma's tousled hair. "Do you mean the color, honey?"

"Green."

"Well, now," Officer Wilcox said with a wide smile. "That's brilliant, Emma."

The flicker of a smile curved Emma's mouth. Wilcox was obviously a very kind woman. Jolie gave a brief, silent thanks, as she always did, to Art Reagan, the beat cop who'd pulled her out of a morass of trouble and helped set her on a better path. And who had kept her from forever being wary of anyone who wore the uniform and badge. It was he who'd gotten her the job at the Colton Valley Ranch. He was distantly related to Bettina Morely, the cook there, and she'd given Jolie the chance on his say-so.

She felt a sudden burst of longing, something she hadn't felt—hadn't allowed herself to feel—in a very long time. A longing for the safety and happiness and hope she'd felt for that idyllic and painfully short time. Right now especially for the safety. And for the man who'd made her feel that way, that she—and her little girl—would be safe. She wanted more than anything to feel that way again.

She yanked her frazzled brain off that fruitless path.

"Do you know who she is?" Jolie asked. *Was*, she amended silently, grimly.

"Can't say yet." Officer Wilcox looked up, assessing her.

"What?"

"Just thinking…"

"What?" Jolie asked again. When the woman hesitated, she added, "My little girl has witnessed an awful crime, and was threatened herself."

"Might have been worse, if you hadn't gotten there so quickly."

Jolie didn't need the woman to remind her the killer could have broken a car window and gotten to Emma. That her little girl could have been killed right then. She suppressed a shudder and went on.

"You know what witnessing something like this could do to her," Jolie said. Probably leave her with an indelible, lifetime, horrible memory long term, and likely nightmares and skittishness or worse short term. None of which she wanted to say aloud in front of Emma, for fear it might plant the ideas. But she was guessing this officer would understand that; she seemed a very perceptive and insightful sort. And she was a mom. "If she can deal with that, I can deal with whatever you're thinking."

Officer Wilcox glanced over her shoulder to where the van was finally pulling away. Then she looked back at Jolie, rather intently. "She was about five foot eight, I'd say a hundred and twenty-five pounds. Long dark hair. Gray eyes."

Jolie's breath caught as it registered. She went very still as her gaze shifted to the departing van. Her arms tightened around Emma, enough so the girl made a little sound of protest. She made herself ease up, tried to suppress the shiver that went through her.

Five-eight. A hundred twenty-five pounds. Long dark hair. Gray eyes.

Wilcox could have been describing her.

"She came back for more money, of course."

T.C. barely heard his brother's gloating words. He was

staring out at the city he loved, the city he'd thought Jolie long gone from. In truth, he'd half suspected she was long gone from Texas altogether. But perhaps he should have known better; he'd been Texas born and bred just as she had, and the blood of Texians ran in her veins just as it did in his. They might succeed elsewhere, might even flourish, but there would always be a part of them that longed for this unique, amazing place.

"I told the cops she has a huge motive. I'll bet the old man turned her down when she came at him for more money, and she killed him."

T.C. knew Fowler wanted him to react, so he kept his mouth shut.

"As if what Mom and Dad gave her back then to stay away from you wasn't enough. Greedy little bi—"

"Shut the hell up, Fowler."

He knew the instant he said it, it was a mistake. And Fowler proved him right by practically crowing. "Ha! I knew it, you fool. I knew you'd never gotten over that little slut!"

T.C. spun around to stare at his brother. When he spoke, his voice was as cold as a rare Texas snow. "It's going to take you longer to get over the bones I'm going to break if you don't get your ass out of here."

They were nearly the same height, but T.C. was younger, stronger, and tougher—those parties Fowler tended toward, not to mention the overindulgences, softened a man—and they both knew it. They'd been involved in enough brawls growing up, and a few after that, that there was little doubt who would be left standing. Besides, Fowler no longer got his own hands dirty. He paid others to do his dirty work for him.

Like someone to kidnap, or even kill, his own father?

T.C. tried to quash the thought, but at this point he had few illusions about his family, in particular his ruthless brother.

"Really?" Fowler said in that superior tone he adopted when someone called him on his obnoxiousness. "Resorting to physical abuse now?"

"It's more honest than your kind of abuse," T.C. said, knowing he'd won the instant he heard the shift in attitude. In a moment Fowler would raise his nose and sniff, as if of course he was far above such tactics. When it happened, T.C. nearly laughed aloud. His brother was nothing if not predictable.

Fowler left without another word. T.C. sat back down, and the sound of the desk chair shifting seemed abnormally loud in the quiet after their outburst.

In typical Fowler fashion, he left the office door standing open. T.C. stared at it, thinking he should get up and close it, but in that moment even that simple action was beyond him. And then Hannah was there at the doorway, glancing in only long enough to roll her eyes expressively before pulling it shut for him. A thought jabbed at him; given Fowler's penchant for revenge, the passive-aggressive kind, he wondered how he was treating Hannah. He'd have to ask, because he doubted the assistant would complain. He was going to give her that raise, whether or not she wanted or needed it, T.C. thought.

He turned back to the windows, to the view he'd been contemplating before his brother burst in. It looked no different. There had been no change in the buildings, the reflections of the Texas sun on the glass edifices, the orb on the tower was still there.

And yet it felt entirely different.

How could the knowledge of the presence of one person among the million-plus that populated Dallas proper change everything? How could the thought that Jolie was here now make even the bright Texas sun seem different?

Why was she here? Had she ever even left at all? Could she have been within reach, even, as he went about his life, went about Colton business? Fowler said he'd seen her, and he rarely left the Central Business District unless it was for some party or function, and T.C. would have known about that. No, his brother liked to stay where he could tell himself he was an uncrowned prince of industry, with frequent jaunts to Austin to walk the halls of power, as if he needed to prove to himself just how much weight the Colton name carried. But he hadn't made one of those trips for a couple of weeks, and he'd obviously seen Jolie recently.

Maybe even today.

Damn, he should have asked him where. But that would have given Fowler more satisfaction than he was willing to provide.

Besides, what did it matter where he'd seen her? It wasn't like suddenly finding out she was still here changed anything. Fowler might as well have seen her in Antarctica. She'd still taken money to abandon him and what they'd built together. She'd destroyed their future. In the end, to take the money and run had been her choice. She hadn't even loved him enough to tell him face-to-face.

And she'd taken sweet, precious little Emma with her.

Emma.

She'd be…four years old now. Halfway to five. He tried to picture the sunny little girl who had so captured his heart. What was she like? He had little contact with small children, so his only measure was trying to remember what his little sister Piper had been like then, when he was seven and she four. She had chattered, made wild leaps of imagination and pestered him with the question "why?" about seemingly everything, but that was about all he remembered.

"The old man turned her down when she came at him for more money, and she killed him."

No. Not Jolie. Not the woman whose laugh could light up an entire room. Sure, she'd had a rough start in life and had gotten tangled up with some unsavory people, but she'd changed all that. For Emma, she'd remade her life. She would never intentionally hurt anyone. She just wouldn't.

Would she? Could he really say this when she'd done just that, and for the most venal of reasons—money?

He spun the chair around, turning his back on the city that held the one woman he'd never been able to let go of.

"Don't wanna go sleepy time."

Emma mumbled it against Jolie's side as she sat on the wide window seat in the study alcove that served as the girl's bedroom in the small apartment. The nearly full moon shone in through the large window, something the girl normally enjoyed, but not tonight.

"I know," Jolie said. She could only imagine what kind of nightmares the girl might be afraid of, and rightfully so. She'd thought of keeping Emma with her, but had had second thoughts that that might plant the idea of her having bad dreams, or worse, not being safe in her own bed.

"What if I see her?"

"Then I'll be right here."

"You won't let her get me?"

"Never ever."

That seemed to comfort the girl. She snuggled closer. "I don't like her. She looked at me mean."

"It's all right," Jolie began, automatically soothing before the sense of the child's words sank in. Until now, it had always been the woman was mean-looking. But this…

"She looked at you?"

"When she saw me. In the car."

The killer had seen Emma? Knew Emma had seen her? Jolie had to steady herself. "Did she come toward you? Toward the car?"

Emma nodded. "But I wasn't scared, Mommy. 'Cuz you locked the door. She couldn't get me. She ran away and you came."

Jolie hugged the girl even closer, her mind racing but her heart outpacing it.

"Did she ever actually touch the car?" she asked, some vague idea of fingerprints stirring in the tiny portion of her brain that wasn't flooded with panic.

Emma shook her head. "She ran away," the girl repeated.

She could have killed my baby! She had a gun…why didn't she just shoot…thank God, but why didn't she… Emma is small. Maybe she couldn't see her…that's why she came toward the car…if I hadn't come back when I did…why on earth did I leave her alone, even for seconds…? Never, ever again…

The horror was building rapidly inside her, and mixed with a healthy dose of self-condemnation, she knew the child would sense it at any moment. She already seemed to be waking up rather than winding down for sleep. Jolie fought down the roiling emotions. "Put your head on the pillow, sweetie."

Reluctantly the child did so. "Sing me the song," she said.

Jolie's breath caught. She hadn't asked for it in a while. How odd—or perhaps not—that she asked for it today, the same day her own foolish brain had been so full of the man who had first sung it to her, surprising Jolie with his deep, beautiful voice gone soft and sweet as he sang—wonderfully, she thought—the song of all the pretty little horses to the babe in his arms.

She often wondered if Emma remembered, too. If she remembered him. Or if somehow the song had just lodged in her memory and she didn't associate it with anyone in particular; she just liked it.

Her own voice wasn't nearly as good, or as strong, as T. C. Colton's, and she hated the way singing it brought him so close in her mind, but tonight she wasn't surprised it was what Emma wanted.

She tried, although she was shaken. She managed enough that her daughter relaxed into sleep. Grateful, both that Emma had gone to sleep and Jolie was able to stop the song that brought such painful memories, she stayed put for a long time. Finally she stood, but she knew her focus would be on Emma all night, in case the child did have those nightmares she herself feared.

She called the police, getting a weary-sounding woman who was nevertheless polite, and if not comforting, at least reassuring. The woman would forward along the information—that the killer had seen the only witness—to the people handling the murder case first thing. She also took down Jolie's address, assuring her they would keep her location on close patrol check.

Far from sleep, she busied herself around the small apartment, gathering dirty clothes for washing, putting her day planner—the one she clung to for several reasons, including the man who had given it to her—in a desk drawer and assembling Emma's lunch for tomorrow. If she had the choice, the girl wouldn't go anywhere near the day care. But Jolie didn't want to make things worse by freaking out and have Emma sense it and become more frightened herself. And she had to work, so she had little choice.

"I wasn't scared, Mommy. 'Cuz you locked the door. She couldn't get me."

A shudder went through her. She felt the crash coming and quickly put everything away. She returned to the living area, where she pulled Emma's favorite item, the big bluebonnet-blue chair, over toward the alcove where she could hear easily. She sank down into the cushioned softness, only then letting it all wash over her.

For a long time she simply sat there, shaking. She felt as if the ceiling fan were turned on, although it wasn't. She thought of getting up and checking the thermostat, but she knew what she'd see. It might be October, but this was Texas; it was hardly cold. The chill was in her, not the room.

Emma. Her precious baby, the only thing that really, truly mattered in her world.

She drew her feet up, curled her legs under her and settled in. She wasn't going anywhere tonight. She would doze here. She didn't want to go too deeply asleep in case Emma awoke, frightened.

She only wished she had a way to turn off her tumbling thoughts. But it was impossible to avoid the harsh reality; her little girl had witnessed a green-eyed woman kill another woman in cold blood, and the killer knew it. Jolie wondered if this would leave her child forever terrified of green eyes.

A vision of other green eyes, those belonging to the man she had hoped to spend her life with, drifted through her tangled mind. Funny how eyes that were so cool and dismissive in his mother, Whitney Colton, could be so different in him. His gaze had been sometimes amused, sometimes thoughtful, occasionally angry, but always powerfully male. And never, ever cold in the way his mother's had been the day she had insisted Jolie was nowhere good enough for her son, and ordered her off Colton Valley Ranch.

She yanked her thoughts out of that well-worn track, even as she acknowledged the irony that thinking about her daughter seeing a murder was the only thing powerful enough to do it.

That, and the fact that the victim bore a distinct resemblance to herself. Although that was merely an afterthought to her. Everything was, except her little girl's safety.

At last she slipped into fretful sleep, and it was she who had the nightmares, images of the lifeless woman whose name she didn't even know, lying in a pool of blood, staring at the cloudless sky. In the dreamworld, she could only move in slow motion, as if she were underwater, despite her desperation to get to her daughter. When she finally got to the car and opened the door, Emma turned to look at her. She was also drenched in blood.

Emma screamed.

Jolie jolted awake. For a split second, not even a breath's time, she thought she'd dreamed it.

Emma screamed again.

Jolie erupted out of the chair and headed for her daughter at a run, ready to soothe her child from the nightmare she'd probably had. In the next instant, some-thing snapped in her brain and time slowed to a crawl.

There was someone there. All in black. He had Emma. Was dragging her toward the window he'd somehow got-ten in through. The child was kicking wildly. Screaming when she could twist her mouth free of the hand cover-ing it. The black-clad shape froze as light from the other room slashed across the floor. Something in the black-gloved hand glinted.

A knife.

The sight propelled Jolie into furious action. She ran, hard. Lowered her shoulder and dived at the black fig-ure. All three went to the hardwood floor.

"Fight!" she cried out to Emma. Just as she'd taught her, the girl doubled her kicking, elbowing and clawing. She caught Jolie once by accident, but Jolie didn't care. She was too focused on wrenching the would-be kidnap-per off her little girl.

The would-be kidnapper who was, she realized with a little shock, a woman.

Simultaneously the woman pulled free, releas-ing Emma. Jolie had the ski mask she'd been wearing clutched in her hand. But before she could get a look at her, she was gone through the pried-open window. All Jolie could say for sure was that she'd been female, and maybe blond.

"Mommy!"

Jolie rolled over to Emma, and scooped up the terri-fied child. "It's all right, baby, it's all right."

But it wasn't. She knew it wasn't. Because there was only one person that woman could be.

The killer. And she was after Emma.

Chapter 4

T.C. tapped a finger on the steering wheel. He was accustomed to Dallas traffic, and used it to work through the things on his plate for the coming day so he could hit the ground running when he finally reached the office.

But today he was spending more time pondering his restless night. He'd gone to his rooms at about ten, planning to do a little reading before bed, but hadn't been able to focus. He'd finally given up and headed for the kitchen and some of Mrs. Morely's incredible pecan pie, hoping the rare indulgence would soothe his scattered mind, but he had veered off when he realized just thinking about the pie and its maker made him think of Jolie, and he didn't want to go down that rabbit hole again. Then he'd had to dodge the dining room, where his mother was apparently deep into a late-night session—because of course she couldn't do it in the clear light of day, he thought sourly—with another one of her psychics. He didn't know if she was foolish enough to actually believe in them, or if she just thought it might throw off suspicion that she had had something to do with her husband's disappearance.

And that's a hell of a thing to think about your own mother.

He had pondered just going back to his rooms. He knew it wasn't really food he was looking for, it was peace of mind—enough to sleep. And that seemed out of reach, as it had for most of the three months now that his father had been missing.

Besides, he'd been in no mood to walk past Fowler's room, not when he and Tiffany had been having passionate and very noisy sex when he walked past their door coming downstairs. Hearing that again was something he'd prefer to avoid. Leave it to Fowler to be as loud as possible, as if he wanted everyone to know he was getting laid. But Tiffany was just as loud, although he suspected that was her flattering Fowler as much as anything.

He wondered if the woman would ever manage to harangue Fowler into a ring. He thought his brother truly cared for her, at least as much as he was capable of caring for anyone other than himself, but he kept holding her off. However, Tiffany had a plan, and becoming a Colton was the goal. Was she determined enough, cold-blooded enough, to pull off the old man's disappearance in the hope that Fowler would be shaken enough to take the plunge? It was hard to believe Her Whininess, as he and his sister Piper often called her, could be that clever, but maybe…

He hated feeling this way about his own family. But he hated even more thinking about his brother's noisy sex, because it made him think of Jolie, who had always been rather quiet about it. But her heated whispers, the expression on her face, the amazement in her beautiful eyes as they made love, had been all he'd needed.

"Stop it, damn it," he muttered under his breath as heat and need shot through him, making his entire body clench. Only Jolie had ever done that to him, only she had had the power to send him into overdrive with a mere thought. He stared at the delivery truck ahead of him as if it held all the answers.

By the time he reached the Colton building, he'd managed to force his unruly mind to stay on the things he needed to deal with today. Once at his desk, he went quickly through the plan Hannah prepped for him every morning. The format she suggested had seemed odd to him at first, but now he didn't think he could function without it. Her method of prioritizing, and noting in advance which items could be time-shifted and which could not, had increased his productivity markedly, and he rarely disagreed with how she had weighted things.

Well, except when she slid in something like suggesting he attend a dinner function, an evening at the symphony or some other formal affair. He'd rather spend a day doing the dirtiest of work in one of their oil fields than tux up for one of those things. He'd leave that to Fowler, who could con the feathers off a peacock and leave them glad he'd done it. At least, until reality set in.

He was midway through his email inbox when Hannah appeared in his doorway.

"Mr. Colton?"

Something in her voice, an undertone of…what, he wasn't quite sure, made him look up quickly.

"What is it?" He stood up quickly. "Something about my father?"

She looked immediately apologetic. "No, I'm sorry, nothing about that. But there's someone here asking to see you."

He opened his mouth to say he didn't have time for unscheduled appointments today, then shut it again. Hannah knew this perfectly well, since she'd drawn up his agenda for the day. He also knew she would normally smoothly redirect anyone who wanted to disrupt that schedule without what she deemed a good enough reason. And he'd rarely disagreed with her on that, either. So something had made her think this was worth making an exception for.

"All right," he said, not even asking who it was.

He saw a glint in her eyes that told him she knew exactly what thought process he'd just gone through. "Thank you," she said, and he knew it was for trusting her.

"You've never made me sorry."

She smiled. "I'll bring them in."

Them? he wondered as she turned to go. He reached down and closed out his email program, because he'd had a confidential communication open. He looked up when he heard footsteps in the doorway. Didn't even hear Hannah quietly close the door. Could look at nothing else but the woman with the little girl in her arms.

Jolie.

He only realized how long it had been, and that he'd forgotten to breathe, when he at last had to suck in a long, audible gulp of air. Crazily he could hear Fowler's voice in his head, chanting as he always did, "Never let 'em see you sweat."

In this case a cold sweat, rising not out of exertion but

pure, emotional reaction. Fowler had forewarned him, and yet he was still stunned.

Jolie.

And Emma? Could that girl with the tousled blond hair and the finger caught between white, even teeth as she stared at him really be her? Could this be the baby he'd held, made laugh, thought would be his daughter?

Of course it was. Look at her eyes—they were Jolie's eyes, wide and thickly lashed and that gray shade that could go from silver to stormy in the space of a moment. She was wearing jeans embroidered with a cartoon character he didn't recognize—not his forte at all—and a T-shirt that matched the bright green thread in the design. She had a small Band-Aid on her neck, and he nearly smiled when he saw it had the same cartoon character on it.

"I'm sorry," Jolie whispered.

His gaze snapped back to the woman. God, her voice. That same husky, low voice that always sent a shiver down his spine and had once had the power to stir him no matter how distracted or tired he was.

Judging by his body's instant response, it still did.

"What?" *Oh, brilliant, Colton.*

"I'm sorry," she repeated quietly. "We didn't have any place else to go."

His brow furrowed. She'd managed to stay completely gone for four years, but now she showed up saying she —and Emma—had nowhere else to go? This made no sense.

"I would never have dared to come to you, but it's for Emma."

His gaze shifted to the child, who was staring at him with what appeared to be fascination. He knew she couldn't possibly remember him. She'd been barely six months old when Jolie vanished out of his life, but she was looking at him now much as she had done then, although with more awareness.

"What?" he said again, almost blankly, aware no one who'd ever dealt with him in the business world would ever believe this was really T. C. Colton, the man with the reputation for quick, incisive thinking.

He saw her glance at Emma, then back at him, without speaking. It took him a moment, but then he realized she didn't want to talk in front of the girl. He felt an odd reluctance to do anything about that, but finally he reached for the office intercom. "Hannah? Do you feel up to a little babysitting?"

"That cutie? I'll be right in."

Jolie hesitated, looked doubtful. He guessed she was reluctant to let the child out of her sight with a stranger. He said the only thing he could think of to reassure her of Hannah's utter reliability. "She has three grandsons. I think time with a girl would delight her."

Somehow they were the right words. Jolie nodded. Hannah came in, and Emma went to her willingly enough, after an encouraging nod from her mother.

"We'll be right outside, not a step beyond my desk," his assistant assured Jolie. "And in that desk," she said to Emma, "there are some very interesting things. Would you like to see?"

When the door closed after them, T.C. looked at Jolie again. "Afraid you'll have a sugar high to deal with. Hannah has quite the candy stash."

"She deserves a treat. It's been a horrible couple of days."

He raised an eyebrow at her, but she didn't go on. For

a moment, he was torn between wanting to know why she was here now and why she'd left then. He scoffed inwardly at himself, still a fool, wishing there was a valid reason beyond a check with a lot of zeros on it.

He waited, letting the silence pressure her. And finally, without the diversion of the little girl, he was able to look at her more carefully.

She looked exhausted. Her eyes were reddened, whether from a sleepless night or tears or both, he couldn't know. She looked thinner than she had, the sweet curves he'd so lusted for slightly lessened, and he felt a sudden urge to feed her to get them back.

"I thought about going to the ranch," she finally said, "but I know your mother would try to throw me out under the best of circumstances, and this is hardly that. I'm sorry about your father."

As a Colton, he was used to everything about the family being general knowledge, and something like the disappearance of the family patriarch was still headline news, even after three months.

"Try to?" He gave himself an inward shake; why, of all things, had he fastened on that?

Jolie's mouth—that wonderful, soft mouth—curved up at one end in a soft, almost pleased smile. "She might not find it quite so easy to bully me and send me packing this time."

His eyebrows shot downward. And suddenly his brain kicked into gear.

She's back for more money, of course.

He'd barely heard his brother's gleeful words. He'd been too startled by his news that Jolie was here. But he would have discounted them anyway; Fowler was desperate to get the spotlight off Tiffany, and if doing so meant throwing someone else—anyone else—to the wolves, then so be it.

"She's a gold digger, Thomas. All she wants is Colton money."

His mother's words echoed in his head.

Maybe it takes one to know one?

Yes, she had stuck it out, but that didn't necessarily mean it hadn't started as a strictly mercenary arrangement. He had few illusions left about his mother.

"I would hardly call a payoff in six figures bullying," he finally said.

Her gaze shot to his face, and he saw some of the old fire in her eyes. "What would you call threatening a baby?"

"What?" She'd startled it out of him this time.

She started to pace the office, and when she spoke it came out as if rehearsed. Or as if she'd been thinking what she would say to him for a very long time.

"It wasn't enough for your parents to tell me I was ruining your life, that I had no place in it, that I would never, ever be good enough to be a Colton. I already knew that anyway. And I knew you knew that, and you wanted me anyway."

"I never thought that." The words came out sharply, because they were true. He'd known that because of her past Jolie carried around some pretty strong feelings of worthlessness. He'd had it all figured out, how he would help her get past that, that one day she would really, truly believe how crazy in love with her he was. But she vanished before he ever had the chance.

She kept pacing, the words coming out in a rush. "I'm not talking about what you believed. I'm talking about what I believed. And deep down I believed every word they said was true. But I still said no. I told them I loved you, and I was staying."

He drew back slightly. "You did?"

"Yes." Her mouth tightened. She stopped, turned, looked at him. "That's when your mother brought out the big guns."

"She has them," he said neutrally, although it was difficult under the steady gaze of those gray eyes. But he knew well enough, his mother used her weapons on him often enough, imperiously wielding her power as the Colton matriarch to get her way.

"She told me if I stayed, she would make my life a living hell. With a few potent examples."

He hadn't actually thought about that. He'd known his mother didn't approve, didn't think Jolie was good enough—although he'd never been certain if she'd meant good enough for him, or good enough to be a Colton—but he hadn't thought it through to how she might express that disapproval had Jolie stayed. He knew too much of his mother's ways to take that lightly now.

"And then," Jolie said, stopping in front of him, a mere two feet away, meeting his gaze levelly, "she promised to do the same to Emma. To make her life hell, to make sure she always knew she didn't belong, she wasn't welcome, she was unworthy and despised."

T.C. went very still.

"And to top it all off, she dropped some very pointed hints about children having accidents on ranches all the time."

He couldn't imagine even his mother threatening that. Emma had been a baby, helpless, innocent.

And your father's a frail old man, and you're wondering if she killed him.

"She wouldn't have done it," he said, but there was enough uncertainty in him to make the words less than convincing.

"I couldn't take that risk. Not with Emma."

He was shaken, he couldn't deny that. Told this way, what his parents had done seemed much more nefarious. And the threat to Emma, then only months old, was more than a little disturbing. And made him wonder again, just how far would his mother go to get what she wanted?

"And the money?" Jolie said, her voice fierce now. "I took it so Emma would have chances I never did. It's in a trust fund, for her. I've never touched a penny of it, and I never will."

T.C. stared at her, a little awed at that ferocity, of the depth of her love for her daughter. He'd known it before, or thought he had, but at this moment she took his breath away.

But then Jolie Peters had always taken his breath away.

His own reaction, the swiftness of his response to her, as if the last four years had never happened, unsettled him. And that made his voice sharp when he grasped at something—anything—as distraction. "Why are you here now?"

Something flashed in her eyes, and her expression went from fierce to frightened in the space of a split second. He saw her take in a deep breath, as if she needed it to steady herself.

"Someone's trying to kill Emma."

Chapter 5

She'd never put it in words until this moment. And now that she had, Jolie felt an icy chill go down to her bones.

Someone was trying to kill her precious girl.

And, she realized as T.C. stared at her, he didn't believe her. As easily as if they'd never been apart, she read him. "Have I ever been prone to hysteria?"

"You weren't, no." The implication that things could have changed in the past four years was clear.

"Still not." She took a deep breath, then plunged ahead. "Emma witnessed a murder."

She saw his eyes widen. Those vivid green eyes that had melted her with a glance.

"I think you'd better sit down," he said after a moment, gesturing toward the leather couch in the sitting area of his office. It had changed, she realized belatedly. The entire office had been redone since she was last here. Even the desk had been replaced. She wondered at that; he'd always cared little about the trappings, it seemed unlike him to just redecorate on a whim.

"New couch," she said as she sat, wondering if it sounded as inane to him as it did to her. "Among other things."

He didn't sit beside her. He sat in the big, matching chair positioned at a right angle to the couch. The chair was a subtle statement of who had the right to private real estate in this setting, the reminder of who was in charge in this domain. As if anyone could ever forget.

But he'd never done it to her before, in the few times she'd been here.

He stared at her, his expression almost grim. It hit her then, a memory so hot and strong it nearly sucked the air out of her lungs; the day she'd tried to tease him out of here, to get him to take a break from preparing for some upcoming high-powered negotiation with an Angus breeder in Kansas. They'd ended up making love on his desk, urgently, and then again on the couch, long and slow and sweet.

No wonder he'd gutted the place.

And she guessed she knew now how he'd handled her abrupt departure.

"Talk," he commanded.

She didn't quibble over his tone, or the sharp order. He had every right. It took her a moment to get started, although she'd thought of nothing but how she would explain all the way here; it had helped keep her mind off the terrifying knowledge that someone had actually tried to grab Emma. But once she had begun, it came pouring out in a rush.

And rather confused. But he didn't stop her, or ask

questions, and she knew he was more than capable of taking her rather scattered account and putting it in order. It was one of the things that made him so good at what he did, better even than his half brother Fowler, who was the more famous—and infamous—Colton of the two. As president of Colton Inc., Fowler loved all the trappings and used them to aid in his wheeling and dealing, while executive vice president Thomas simply did what needed to be done to keep things rolling. She had little doubt which of them Colton Inc. would miss more.

"She tried to do a sketch with the police artist," she said when the story was finally out, "but she's only four. She couldn't describe much more than her eyes. Then last night it was dark and she was terrified." Her fingers were knotted together and resting on her knees, the only way she could stop them from shaking. "But it was a woman. It has to be the killer."

He just looked at her, in that quiet, assessing way he had. She made herself go on.

"I know it's crazy, asking you for help. But with you, at the ranch, is the only place I've ever felt completely safe. And I know you loved Emma, once. So when the police asked me if there was someplace safe I could take her..."

He still said nothing as her voice trailed off. She steeled herself, and sat up a little straighter. She saw something flicker in his eyes then, as if something had shifted in his clever brain. But still he said nothing. And even knowing it was a tactic, knowing he used silence as a tool, she felt compelled to fill it. And to give him the acknowledgment he deserved.

"I know you hate me, and you have every right. Nothing, not even your mother's threats, can change the fact that from your point of view, I took money to leave. But this is for Emma—as was that, not that it makes any difference to you—and I'd do a lot more than beg to keep her safe."

"Would you."

It wasn't a question, and Jolie belatedly realized how her last words could be interpreted. She felt her cheeks heat but told herself at least he'd finally spoken. But then she had a sudden vision of him demanding sex in return for his help, of him taking out whatever anger at her remained, ruining forever the sweet memories that were all she had left of that brief, too-brief time in her life when she'd thought she'd truly found her place.

"So you really think I'd do that," he said, his voice harsh.

She looked at him, realized she'd forgotten he read her as easily as she read him, and that he'd guessed what she'd been thinking. The sex part, anyway; she doubted he could guess at how much those memories tormented her. She made herself hold his gaze, and it was one of the hardest things she'd done since the night she'd left him.

"No. You would never use that to punish, even if you wanted to." Her mouth twisted. "Besides, you can't want me anymore."

"Oh, I want you," he said, his voice so harsh now it made the admission more a threat than anything. "But, lady, I can't afford you."

The words she doubted had ever been spoken by a Texas Colton in decades echoed in the space between them. But she knew how he meant it. And for the first time she had an inkling of what her departure had cost him emotionally.

"I'm sorry," she said again, meaning it fiercely. "Sorrier than you can ever know. But I couldn't make her live like that, under your mother's hatred. I took the only chance I would ever have to make sure Emma would never grow up like I had to."

"So you made your little deal with the devil."

She blinked. "These are your parents we're talking about."

"Exactly."

Her brow furrowed. He'd never been blind to his parents' quirks, but he'd never been this critical. It struck her as especially odd now, with his father missing. But she didn't want to go there, so she said nothing.

"Where have you been?"

He sounded as if he'd fought asking, so she considered her answer carefully. "Here."

"You never left Dallas?"

"Only for a while. I went to school. Came back. Had a couple of jobs, worked my way to where I am now."

He looked at her over steepled fingers. "Which is?"

She gave him a sideways look. "I work at a hotel." She decided not to tell him at the moment that her hotel could be seen through the big windows of this office. Or that she'd hesitated taking the job for that very reason.

"Doing?"

"Sous-chef. Mainly I work in one of the restaurants, although I'm on the banquet staff, too."

She waited, thinking silence could work in both directions, and that she could do it, now that she was a little calmer. And if answering these questions would get him to help her keep Emma safe, the cost would be little enough.

"Stayed in the kitchen, then."

He didn't say it the way some did, his mother in particular, who had a way of using the phrase "kitchen help" that had set her teeth on edge.

"It was what I knew."

"Use us as a reference?"

That cut, and she knew he'd meant it to. He would never belittle her job, he respected honest work. But what she'd done...

She pulled herself together inwardly. She'd done what she'd done, she'd thought it her only option at the time, and she couldn't change it. She'd apologized, both for coming here and for what had happened four years ago. He deserved that. And she would beg, if she had to, for Emma. But she wouldn't grovel at his feet. She would find another way.

"If I'd been braver, and smarter—and less scared for my daughter—at the time, I would have demanded a glowing reference as part of the deal." She got to her feet. "I'm sorry to have bothered you, Mr. Colton."

"Leaving so soon?" He didn't even react to the formality. She realized she was getting a taste of what negotiating with him must be like.

"This was obviously a mistake." She grimaced. "I thought I was past making them this big, but obviously I was too scared by last night to think straight."

His jaw tightened. She wondered if it was in outrage that she'd had the nerve to even begin to think he might help her. She wouldn't blame him if it was.

"I can't change what happened, but I am glad to have had the chance to apologize and explain. I know it makes no difference to you, but it does to me."

She turned and walked toward the door. Her heart was sinking, and she felt panic hovering anew. Mrs. Amaro, she thought desperately. Perhaps she would watch Emma tonight while Jolie went back to the apartment and gathered some things. She didn't want the girl to go back there, wondered if she would ever feel safe there again, even if the killer was found.

And then they would go…somewhere. She didn't know where, but somewhere safe. She would think of something.

She had to.

Chapter 6

T.C. watched her go. He was so angry at himself he said nothing. Well, angry at his body, anyway, for the instant, fierce response to her. If he'd had half that response to anyone else, he'd likely be married and have produced the precious grandkids his father kept nagging him about.

Had kept nagging him about.

And that unwelcome thought made him realize that after that first moment, he'd never once thought of Fowler's accusations.

"Jolie."

She stopped, half turned back to look at him. He steeled himself and ignored the flash of hope he saw in her eyes.

"Have you seen my father?"

Her brow furrowed. She seemed genuinely bewildered by the question. "Of course not. I would have told you, first thing. And the police. I wouldn't have forgotten that, no matter what that woman did last night."

Out of what he told himself was idle curiosity, he asked, "I thought it was too dark to see?"

"It was. That's why I can't say for sure she was blond. It could have been the light."

"Then how are you so sure it was a woman at all?"

"I could tell when I tackled her."

He drew back slightly. "Tackled her? You tackled an armed assailant?"

"Of course," she said with a frown. "She had my little girl."

And a knife, T.C. thought. Jolie might not have had the strength of will to stand up to his mother and father four years ago, but as a mother, she was clearly a tigress.

He wondered, only briefly because the images the thought caused were beyond disturbing, if the would-be abductor was indeed this killer, why she hadn't simply killed the child—the witness—in her bed? Why try to take her? Had she intended to just kill the girl, but panicked when she was caught in the act? Had Jolie interrupted a murder?

And why was he even wondering, when he was not involved? He was so not involved, he insisted to himself.

When he said nothing more, she turned back and opened the door to the outer office.

"Mommy, look!"

The little girl's voice was excited, happy. She appeared in the doorway, a large piece of paper in her hand. It appeared to be a drawing of some kind.

"The nice lady gave me markers. An' a big piece of paper. So I could draw a picture."

"Bless her for putting a smile back on your face," Jolie said softly.

"It was a dog," the child said, pointing. "But it got too big. So it's a horse."

"I can see that."

T.C. watched this exchange with every effort at detachment. He failed miserably. Memories of the baby he'd held—rather inexpertly—who had smiled up at him and cooed, reached out and touched his cheek with seeming fascination, threatened to swamp him. And then he again noticed the Band-Aid on her neck, finally connected it with the story Jolie had told him, and nausea roiled his gut.

"Can I show your friend?" the little girl asked.

"Emma, no, I—"

It was too late; the child was already running toward him, confident, happy, the nightmares behind her for the moment. His first thought was what a good job Jolie had done with her daughter. His second was utter panic.

"See?" Emma plopped her slightly crooked drawing down on his desk. He saw the bits of red, black and green on her hands, which he guessed corresponded to a couple of smudged spots he noticed on the drawing.

"I...yes."

"He's eating grass. 'Cuz that's what horses do."

"Yes, they do," he said, wondering if he sounded as awkward as he felt. The girl was busy explaining all the features of her drawing, and he caught himself just watching her rather than the paper she was pointing to. He could see traces of the baby he'd known, in the round cheeks, the sunny blond hair, the gray eyes. Her mother's eyes...

"And he's got big spots."

T.C. focused suddenly on the drawing. His first thought was that it wasn't actually too bad, even if it consisted mostly of squares and circles cobbled together over four stick legs, the animal was recognizable as a horse, although crooked and out of proportion. But she'd caught details that surprised him, like the slope of the pasterns and the presence of hooves. Wasn't that a bit advanced for a kid not yet five years old? Maybe Hannah had helped her a bit, he thought. She'd been quite the horsewoman in her day, and still rode regularly.

He looked back at Emma. The child's brow was furrowed in concentration. "I saw a horse like that."

He smiled despite himself, and looked back at the drawing. And belatedly it hit him.

Flash.

He stared. Coincidence, surely? The green highlighter grass and the lopsided red pen square he guessed was a barn, that could have come from anywhere, but a piebald paint horse? She'd only had markers to use, so a black-and-white horse wasn't unexpected, was it? He doubted Hannah's collection ran to shades of brown.

But that didn't change the fact that his own personal mount, the horse he rode most often at the ranch—and had ridden when Jolie and Emma had lived there—was a black-and-white pinto.

"It does look like Flash, doesn't it?" He hadn't even realized Jolie had returned until she spoke, from barely two feet away. "I don't think she could really remember, she was so young, but who knows? She's a very bright girl."

Could she really still read him so easily? With an effort he managed to say evenly, "And not a half-bad artist. I was expecting stick figures."

"The lady helped a little," Emma said honestly. "How their feet go."

Oddly T.C. felt relieved at this confirmation of his guess. "Not quite a child prodigy, then."

"Thank goodness," Jolie said, echoing his relief, rattling him yet again. "Bright I can handle. Genius would be something else altogether."

"She's…" He didn't know what to say. Polite? Charming? Enchanting?

"Yes," Jolie said, proudly. "She is."

Emma picked up her drawing and looked at it with childlike satisfaction. "I was gonna draw the mean lady. Like the policeman wanted. But I don't want to."

And just like that the elephant in the room trumpeted, and T.C.'s stomach knotted at the thought of this child in danger. He'd been able to dodge this when the child wasn't right here in front of him, had been able to focus instead on her mother, and how much pain she'd caused. But now, with that sweet, innocent face right here, with those wide eyes, still trusting despite what had happened, the thought of something happening to her was more than he could take. Helplessness was not a feeling he was used to or tolerated well, and he'd had more than enough of it in the last few months.

He might have lost his father and been unable to do anything about it, but he could do something about this.

Telling himself he simply couldn't leave a child—any child—in danger when he could help, he made a rare, snap decision.

He stood up. "Come with me."

Jolie blinked, probably at the edge in his voice. "What?"

"You asked for help."

"Yes, but—"

"Don't quibble now."

"Mommy?" Emma asked, very clearly uncertain.

T.C. moderated his tone as he looked down at the girl,

who was clutching the drawing in one hand, the other firmly in her mother's grasp.

"It's all right, Emma," he said gently; whatever his feelings about her mother were, no reason to frighten the child any more than she already was. "Would you like to see a real horse that looks like that?"

He heard Jolie's quick intake of breath but kept his eyes on the little girl, who suddenly smiled at him, a wide, dimpled smile that made him a different kind of helpless. And there she was for an instant, that tiny being who had once giggled at him with delight, filling him with emotions he hadn't even had names for. The memories, the hopes, the plans for a future that included this child flooded his brain, and even the pain and anger of Jolie's desertion couldn't overwhelm it.

Emma nodded enthusiastically, then looked at her mother. "Can we, Mommy? Please?"

He lifted his gaze to Jolie. Found her staring at him.

"It's what you came for, isn't it?" he asked.

Slowly she nodded. "But I thought you…"

Her voice trailed away, but not before he heard the doubt, and an echo of the fear he'd heard before. She'd known that five minutes ago his answer was no, that he would have let her go without a second thought, after what she'd done.

All that had changed the moment a sunny, innocent little girl had plopped a childish drawing on the desk where he did work that helped shape this city.

And he gave Jolie the one answer that trumped all the others.

"For her," he said softly.

Chapter 7

It was amazing how different, how much better it felt, just to be doing something. Although to be honest, it was T.C. who was doing it, she felt as if she were simply riding along in his wake. And right now she was willing to do that, because she knew better than anyone what he was capable of accomplishing. How many hours had she spent while Emma was in the children's section at the library, doing internet searches on him, reading about his progress up the Colton ladder? How many voices she knew and respected—including the governor, who had complimented her—had said they'd much rather deal with the tough but honest and straightforward Colton than his brother Fowler?

She'd finally weaned herself off the compulsive research—it hurt too much. Telling herself she'd had no choice only carried her so far. And no amount of rationalizing changed the bottom line: she'd abandoned what they had for money. And T. C. Colton was a bottom-line kind of guy.

"Did you drive here?" he asked as he led them toward the elevator after stopping for a brief conversation with the apparently unflappable Mrs. Alcott. Telling the woman to cancel appointments, rearrange his day?

"No. My car's at home. The CBD officer dropped us off here when I asked him to."

He gave her a sideways look. "You've been with the police all night?"

"Since it happened."

"I took a nap in the big man's office," Emma said happily.

Jolie laid a hand on her daughter's head. "Yes, you did. The lieutenant was very nice, wasn't he?"

"And Mom," T.C. said, eying her, "got no sleep at all, I'm guessing."

"I slept before."

"Mommy slept in the big chair, so she could see me," Emma confided. Rather inanely, Jolie was glad she'd never spoken to the child about him, the way she was now burbling about everything.

"I'll bet she did," he said. He gave the child his full attention when he spoke to her. She liked that. Most adults talked over her, not realizing Emma was exceedingly bright and understood more than they expected. "She wanted to be right there if you needed her."

"Mommy's always there when I need her."

He shifted his gaze back to Jolie. He spoke quietly. "All anyone needs to know."

They were in the elevator and headed down before

Jolie's weary brain got around to wondering where they were going.

"What…?" she began, then faltered, unsure of what to say. She'd asked for his help, after all, and he'd miraculously agreed; she shouldn't be questioning him.

"We'll pick up what you need from home, for both of you, for a few days," he said. "Leave your car there, so it's not obvious you're gone. Then we'll head to the ranch."

"Oh."

"Second thoughts" was hardly the description for what she was feeling as he took charge. She was up to at least a dozen reasons why this had been a bad idea by the time the elevator doors slid open in the subterranean parking garage. No one was going to welcome them, the opposite in fact. His mother would probably pitch a fit laced with high drama, Fowler would sneer and that nasty Marceline would be cutting and cruel as always. Another half brother, Zane, was much nicer, and although the big man was intimidating, Jolie had always thought of him as fair. But then, she'd always thought his full brother, Reid, had been a good guy, and he'd left the Dallas Police Department in disgrace over a year ago, after some corruption scandal that had ended up with his partner dead. She'd been too busy at the time to follow the case, had in fact avoided it once she realized it was truly Reid Colton involved; the last thing she needed was more in her head reminding her of T.C.

No, the only Colton sibling she'd really bonded with had been Piper, because Piper, adopted by T.C.'s parents after her mother's death, knew what it was like to come from nothing and to always be the outsider. But even Piper would probably hate her now, for what she'd done to her brother, adoptive or not.

"Maybe...maybe this isn't such a good idea," Jolie began, but stopped as a car pulled up in front of them. A uniformed valet got out of the light blue SUV, a young man who looked fresh out of high school.

"Vacuumed, gassed up and ready, Mr. C," he said, leaving the driver's door open.

"Thanks, Jordy. How's your dad doing?"

The young man smiled. "Lots better, thanks, Mr. C. He said to thank you for the barbecue."

T.C. grinned at the kid. "When I was in the hospital last year, that was the thing I missed most."

"Him, too." Jordy walked around and opened the passenger door. He also opened the back passenger door, and Jolie saw with surprise that there was a child's booster seat already strapped in. She flicked a glance at T.C., who only shrugged.

"Hannah is very efficient."

"Obviously," she said. "But you have these just sitting around, waiting?"

"Mrs. Alcott said to take it out of her car," Jordy explained. "Her grandkids are off somewhere. Here you go, princess," he added, smiling at Emma, who smiled back in obvious delight.

"That was kind of her to even think of it." Jolie smiled at the young valet. "And thank you for getting it in right. I always have trouble."

The young man grinned. "I've got five little brothers and sisters. I know car seats."

Jolie smiled, but still checked the fastening herself once Emma was inside. Then she got in herself. The valet smiled back, then tapped his forehead in a salute toward T.C. and turned and left, whistling cheerfully.

"Nice guy," Jolie said as T.C. got into the car.

"Yes. He's a good kid. Even if he does want to be a rodeo star."

She gave him a sideways look. "Is there a kid in Texas who hasn't wanted that at some point?"

"Not that I know of."

He said it lightly, and as if he didn't remember at all telling her that being a professional calf roper had once been his highest ambition. That had engendered a lengthy discussion of the various rodeo sports, from bull riding to barrel racing, and the strength and skills required for each, which had morphed into a discussion of his dream to someday breed top-drawer cow horses.

And she realized belatedly that her protest about this perhaps not being the best idea was long past, and here she was going along as if she'd never had those second, third and many more thoughts.

He put the car in gear, and in moments they were at the driveway out onto the busy street. He gave her a questioning glance.

"Where are we going?"

She couldn't seem to find any words, least of all the ones that would get her out of this situation she was now regretting she'd gotten into.

"We live at Cliff Park," Emma piped up from the back seat.

Jolie nearly jumped. T.C. said nothing, but she thought his focus had suddenly sharpened. Her first thought was to hush the child, but then she wondered what she had expected. Emma was merely following her mother's lead, so she had no reason to mistrust this man. And for all the "be wary of strangers" lessons she had given the girl, it had to be clear to even the four-year-old that this man was not a stranger. And before her mind could leap to all the ways in which he was not a stranger, she looked away from him. She didn't want to see the expression on his face.

"It's changed," she said. "There are parts that are still bad, but our neighborhood is much safer."

She stopped, realizing she was talking about the place where Emma had nearly been kidnapped, or worse.

"It's what I can afford and still get to work in less than an hour most days." She sounded surly even to her own ears. She tried for a more even tone. "And my place has been redone. It's really nice."

"Jolie."

It was the first time he'd said her name. She suppressed the little shiver that went through her. "What?"

"I didn't say anything about where you live."

"You didn't have to."

She heard him take in a deep breath. "If we're going to get there, I'm going to need more than just the neighborhood."

"Oh."

She gave him the address. And was startled into silence when, as he pulled out and merged into a brief break in the traffic, he tapped a button on the steering wheel and a disembodied voice said from above her head, "Select name and action."

"Call Manny, mobile," he said.

"Calling," the voice answered helpfully.

"Is he talking to the roof, Mommy?" Emma whispered, loudly.

"He's making a call, honey, so we should be quiet."

Probably a business call, perhaps to someone he'd had to shunt off to handle this, she thought guiltily.

"Rodriguez," came the male voice through the speaker.

"Hey, Manny."

"T.C.! Where the hell have you been? You don't call, you don't write, you son of a—"

"Easy, buddy. You're on speaker, and kick."

Kick? Jolie wondered.

"Sorry. Hey, I got the tickets. Beautiful."

"You won that bet, fair and square."

"Dam—darn right I did. So, what's up?"

"I'll catch up later, but right now I need a favor."

"You got it."

To Jolie's surprise, he rattled off their address she'd just given him.

"Hey," the voice answered, "I just saw that. Southwest graveyard had an attempted kidnap there last night."

"Exactly. I'm on the way there with...the parties involved."

"Gutsy lady. She tackled the suspect head-on. And gave us evidence. That ski mask may not lead us to the person if she's not already in the system, but it'll nail her down when we do find her."

The unseen man's words warmed her despite not having any idea who he was.

T.C. said nothing except "Can you make sure it's clear?"

"Beat car should be in the area. They've got it on close watch. But I'll make sure and get back to you."

"Thanks, Sarge."

She studied him as he drove in the ensuing silence. Her thoughts were tumbling anew, questions rolling over and over in her mind, but she wasn't sure where to start. Or if she should start at all. After all, he was helping, he didn't owe her even that much, let alone explanations of every move he made.

"Sarge?" she finally asked, thinking that at least she had a vested interest in knowing who this was.

"Manny's a cop with Dallas PD."

"You make bets with cops?"

His gaze flicked to her for an instant, then back to the busy road. He was avoiding the freeway, she noticed, and sticking to Houston as they neared the Trinity River Greenbelt.

"Football."

"Maybe we should have taken the Landry, then," she said, referring to the freeway named after the famous football coach in a weak effort at a joke after her instinctive defensive reaction at having to tell a Colton she lived on the edge of a place once known for its crime rate.

"We'd be going five miles an hour," he said.

She couldn't argue that, so instead asked, "Kick? Also as in football?"

"No, K. I. C.," he spelled out. "It's something Manny started." He glanced at Emma in back, then back at her. "You can figure it out."

She thought for a moment, about what he'd interrupted when he said it, like a warning. And then she had it. "Kid in car," she said.

"Yep."

She thought about all the circumstances when police might need an acronym like that, and none of them were particularly pleasant. At the same time, she appreciated the tact of it. Back when she'd spent some time sitting in the back of police vehicles of various sorts, from the hideous night when they'd come to say her parents were dead to the time when she'd gotten caught shoplifting food out of a grocery store and taken the long ride to juvie, they'd taken little care in what they said in front of her.

"Where did you just go?"

He asked it softly, and she wondered what had shown in her face. Conscious of Emma in the backseat, she answered, "Just thinking about the night someone who dresses like your friend said I was going to be a regular."

He got it, as she'd guessed he would. "You never told me that."

She turned in her seat to look at him. "You're helping us at the drop of a hat, out of the blue, after what I did, and after four years of...nothing. I figure you deserve whatever answers you want."

They lapsed into silence as he negotiated some traffic. Emma was also quiet, and Jolie knew she would soon recognize familiar places. She thought about reassuring the girl, but decided not to say anything that would plant the thought that there was anything bad about going home again. Time enough to deal with that if it happened.

"Why were you in the hospital?"

He gave her a sideways look. "What?"

"You told the parking guy you were in the hospital last year." Usually if a Colton ended up in the hospital, it was big news, and she'd seen nothing. She'd stopped looking by then, of course, but sometimes it was hard to miss.

"Oh. Broken ribs."

"Ouch. What happened?"

"Little territorial dispute between a couple of long-horns."

So he still actively worked the ranch. It didn't surprise her, but it did please her. Not that she had any stake in how he lived. Or any right to an opinion, for that matter.

He slowed as they neared her building. And Jolie realized belatedly he hadn't been using GPS at all, nor had he asked her for anything beyond the address. How had he known so exactly where to go? Not like the Coltons hung out in Cliff Park. Or did the Coltons just consider the whole massive city of Dallas their oyster, and thus know it all?

She nearly laughed at her own thought. Nobody could commit an entire city of over a million to memory.

He flicked a glance at her as he pulled into the driveway. The stone lions that figuratively guarded the front of the building, one of the reasons she had chosen this place—Emma loved them—sat impassively staring out at the park and the small lake across the street.

"I'm in the back, and there's a back door," she said.

He nodded and continued driving toward the back corner of the building before stopping.

Unable to resist, she asked "How did you know right where to go?"

He gave a one-shouldered shrug. "I've looked over some maps of the area."

"I've looked at maps of a lot of places, but I haven't committed them to memory."

He let out a breath. "We've…been involved here a bit."

"Involved?" It hit her then. "In the rehabbing of the neighborhood?"

"Yes."

The quirk of fate bit deep. And she knew the answer before she even asked the question. "Let me guess…including this building?"

"Among others."

"How'd you get your brother to agree to that?" Fowler had little interest in helping the less fortunate areas of the city.

"I showed him the results we got in Uptown."

She should have figured Colton Inc. would have been

involved in the shift from questionable to upscale of the Uptown area of Dallas. And that success would be impossible to argue with, even for Fowler Colton.

"I thought you were in charge of the ranch?"

"I am. But I keep up with the other projects. We all try to, so we can step in if necessary." He grimaced. "Dad's orders. He always thought Fowler might tick off the wrong person one day."

And instead, Eldridge might have.

She guessed that thought was behind his expression, and there seemed no point in bringing up the obvious. So she stuck with the topic at hand.

"Do you really think the same can happen for Cliff Park?"

"I do. It's going to take a lot of time and effort, but it can be done."

She believed him. If he said it could be done, it could. Her faith in his judgment—except perhaps in women— had never wavered. But she didn't know whether to be glad or not.

"My rent's going to go up," she said rather glumly as she opened the car door. He got out as well, and she could feel him watching her as she opened the back door and got Emma. The girl was looking at the familiar building as if she wasn't quite sure how to feel.

"Make sure you bring some jeans, Emma," he said to the girl conversationally. "You'll need them if you're going to ride a horse."

The girl's eyes widened. "Really?"

And that, simply all thought of what had happened last night seemed to vanish, and the child couldn't wait to get in and grab her things.

"Thank you," Jolie said to him when they were inside and the girl ran ahead to their door.

"Figured she might be a little wary, after what happened."

That he'd even thought of it made her feel oddly tight inside. But she shouldn't have been surprised. T.C. had never been the kind of man to blame an innocent for someone else's actions.

Not even when the woman he loved—or thought he did—walked out on him for a stack of cold, hard cash.

Chapter 8

The rehabbers had done a good job, T.C. thought.

But Jolie had done a better one. She'd made the small apartment a charming, homey place. Cool blues and greens predominated, good choices for the Texas heat. None of the furniture appeared new, but it was all well cared for, and if the pieces didn't match, they at least fit. He liked the effect, with each piece unique.

And he liked the way the wooden floors gleamed, and the small but updated kitchen sparkled, the stone counters gleaming like the new appliances. It was tidy and efficient, as was the whole place.

He especially liked the painting of a huge expanse of hill country Texas bluebonnets that adorned one wall. It evoked everything he loved about this one-of-a-kind state he called home.

Emma had apparently inherited her mother's tidy tendencies, for the only toys he saw were a doll carefully placed on one of the two upholstered chairs, and a pony with an improbably bright-colored mane and tail. A large stack of children's picture books sat by the chair occupied by the doll. He had a sudden vision of Jolie sitting there with Emma on her lap, reading those books to the child. It made his gut knot, in the same way it used to when he would hear her telling the baby a story as she went to sleep at night. A story she was far too young to understand, but Jolie didn't care; she wanted her daughter to love to read when she got old enough, and she'd told him once that it started with loving stories. T.C. got the point, even approved, but he had suspected it had been the lulling sound and safety of her mother's voice that did it. She—

His thoughts cut off when he spotted the boarded up window in the alcove off the living room, realized that was how the woman who tried to grab Emma had gotten in. And suddenly he was questioning the wisdom of coming back here at all. The sight of the broken window right above the window seat where the child apparently slept somehow made it all vividly real in a way Jolie's forced calm during her recitation of what had happened had not.

"I should have just sent someone to get what you needed," he said, his jaw tight.

Jolie paused in gathering clothes from the drawers beneath the seat, while Emma named each item as her mother placed it in her small backpack. She shook her head as she met his gaze.

"No," she said. "One stranger in our home is enough."

"Hardly the same intent."

"Still," Jolie said, turning back to her task.

He'd forgotten that about her. Forgotten she'd grown up with so little that she'd tended to be protective of what she had. Forgotten how much he'd wanted to heal that part of her, until she never worried again about not having enough, or losing what she had.

Except when she was throwing it away. Selling it out for cash.

Was it true that she'd never touched the money? Once, he would have sworn she wouldn't lie to him. But that was before he'd realized their entire life together had been a lie.

"She promised to do the same to Emma. To make her life hell, to make sure she always knew she didn't belong, she wasn't welcome, she was unworthy and despised."

He looked at the little girl, listened to her chatter as she tried to convince her mother she really, truly needed all her ponies with her, so they would know she still loved them even if she was going to see a real one. Where would she be now, this charming child, if Jolie had stayed and his mother had followed through on her threats?

Could his mother really do that to an innocent child?

He grimaced inwardly at the absurdity of wondering if his mother could be that cruel to a child when he was also wondering if she was capable of murdering her husband of nearly thirty years.

"I know it's not up to Colton standards."

Snapped out of his thoughts, T.C. shifted his gaze to Jolie, who had come to a halt beside him. He saw the set of her jaw, saw her arms folded in front of her, knew she was ready to defend herself and her home.

"I'm not Fowler, Jolie," he said quietly. "I like it."

"Oh."

She didn't relax, but he could sense the fight ebbing out of her.

"And I really like the painting."

"So do I. It spoke to me, so I used it as inspiration."

He realized then that the colors in the painting were echoed in the room. That was the kind of thing Jolie had always excelled at, and he never even thought of. His mother had called in one of the most expensive decorators in the country when she redid the ranch house years ago, and the result didn't have half the life and warmth this little apartment had. And if Jolie wasn't lying about not touching the money, she'd likely done it on a much, much smaller budget.

And his mother chose art that went with the décor. It would never occur to her that it could be the other way around.

"Where did you get it?"

"A friend painted it."

A friend? He caught himself looking for a signature on the canvas, not admitting even to himself that he was hoping to see an obviously female name. What did he expect, that she would still be alone? That she'd never gotten over him and was pining away for what she'd so callously thrown away?

"I was ruining your life... I had no place in it... I would never, ever be good enough to be a Colton."

Funny how his parents' version of what had transpired had been so different. According to them they'd merely had to wave the check in front of Jolie and she'd jumped at it, because it was what she'd been after all along. They'd neglected to mention the coercion and threats.

His mother, he thought grimly, had some serious explaining to do.

Emma came over to them, one of her clearly beloved
ponies clutched to her chest. But T.C. didn't miss her
glance over at the broken window. He'd only distracted
her from what had happened, not erased it.

"What about when dark comes?" the child asked.

T.C. crouched down so he could look her in the eye.
Eyes so like her mother's, wide and a silvery gray. "We
won't come back until it's all safe and fixed here," he said.

The girl looked relieved. "Is it safe there?"

"Good question," Jolie said, startling him. He glanced
up at her, realized she was thinking of what had apparently happened to his father. Which made her concern
quite valid.

He looked back at Emma. At her wide, innocent eyes.
Made a snap decision. "Where we're going is. Nobody
goes there but me."

Emma smiled at him. His heart gave a little leap in
his chest.

"Kiddo, go get your purple sweater," Jolie said. "You
might need it."

T.C. straightened up as the child darted back to what
obviously served as her room. Jolie was staring at him.

"Just where are we going?"

"You came to me," he reminded her. "Are you going
to decide now you don't trust me?"

"Just wondering if you had payback in mind."

He drew back slightly. Studied her for a long moment,
saw the trace of fear hidden behind the determinedly
cool expression.

"I'm not Fowler," he said again. "Besides, I'm not
doing it for you."

The look she gave him then was the saddest thing he'd ever seen. "I know. Believe me, I know."

He didn't know what to say to her, so he switched to business mode. "Do you have someone coming to fix the window?"

"The landlord does." She gave him a sideways glance. "Does that mean you?"

"Not anymore. We turned it back to a local management company." He left it at that. "You should bring anything of value."

She gestured at the tote bag on the chair next to the doll. "What there is is in there."

He said nothing about the fact that it was so small. And he knew without asking there would be no jewelry or other things with intrinsic value in that bag. More likely mementoes of Emma, and the few things she had of her parents.

He glanced around the small apartment again. She had come a very long way from the orphaned kid she'd once been. And she was clearly determined that her daughter would have a better life than she'd had.

Emma came running back, the rather bright purple sweater Jolie had requested in her hands. His gaze snagged on the boarded-up window once more, and for the first time it really hit him what Jolie must have felt like, the panic and horror she must have felt. It would have immobilized many people. But she had done what needed to be done, risked her own life to save her little girl's.

He looked back to where Jolie was folding the sweater more neatly, to fit in the small, battered suitcase. The same suitcase she'd arrived at the ranch with, and prob-

ably left with that night that seemed both an eon ago
and yesterday.

He might not be sure of anything else, but he knew
one thing. Jolie would always do what needed to be done
for Emma.

Chapter 9

Emma fell asleep in the backseat, and while she was glad the girl was sleeping after the long night, Jolie found she missed her chatter and humming. The silence in the car stretched out uncomfortably.

At least, Jolie was uncomfortable.

"How are Piper, Reid and Zane?" she finally asked.

"Fine, getting by and in love." His tone was clipped, on the edge of sharp. She doubted it was only because of the traffic he drove in every day and was quite used to.

She supposed she didn't deserve any more details than that. Now that action had been taken, now that she felt safe, her emotions had calmed enough for her to consider other aspects of her decision to come to him for help. Such as what he must have felt when she waltzed in out of the blue, to borrow a phrase his mother had often used. Whitney Colton had usually said it in the most scandalized tone she could manage, and usually in reference to anyone trying to unrightfully intrude on the Colton world. Which most certainly had then—and would now—included her.

She'd known that, but she had come to him anyway. If she was as honest as she tried to be with herself, she had to admit she'd also known what would happen. He would see to the heart of the problem, take charge and make things happen. It was what he did. It was who he was.

She was glad Piper was well; his adopted sister had always been nice to her, perhaps because she could easily have ended up living the kind of life Jolie had lived, if the Coltons had not adopted her. As for Reid, the firing of a disgraced cop after the death of his partner was news anywhere; when it was Dallas and the cop was a Colton, it was the biggest of news. And not the kind of headlines social-climber Whitney Colton would relish. Jolie wondered if she was making Reid's life the living hell she'd once promised to make Emma's. Probably not, since he was a "real" Colton. The news about half brother Zane surprised her, though; she'd always found the big, dark-eyed head of security for Colton Inc. more than a little intimidating. She must be quite a woman, whoever she was.

"I saw an article about Alanna's horse program for kids in trouble," she said, feeling oddly as if she should account for not asking about his half sister, by his father's first wife. "It had a photo of her, so I know she's doing well."

"She is. She's in love, too."

Jolie stifled a wistful sigh.

"Is Ellen still with you?" She'd felt a particular kinship with Ellen Martin, the cook who was also a single mother, although her daughter, Daisy, was much older than Emma. She'd always admired the woman's unfailingly sunny disposition in the face of...well, anything.

"Yes. Daisy's still horse-crazy, and that's caused some adventures."

She had the feeling there was more to the story, but it felt awkward to pry. It was no longer her world, after all. Silence reigned again, and she was steeling herself to not feel pressured into breaking it when he said, "I notice you didn't ask about Fowler or Marceline."

She gave him a sideways glance. "Fowler's on or in the news almost every day. All of Dallas knows how he is at any given moment."

One corner of his mouth twitched, as if he were stifling a smile. To her amazement, he also let out a stifled sound that might have, cut free, been a laugh.

"And my other charming half sister?"

"The less I say about Marceline, the better."

This time it was he who gave her a quick glance before turning his attention back to the road. "Such restraint."

"You are helping us," she pointed out. "Doesn't seem wise to speak ill of your sister."

"I doubt you could come up with anything I haven't already thought myself." His tone was very dry. "Although she has been acting a bit odd, even for her, lately."

Odd on top of nasty? The idea made her shiver inwardly. "Still thick as thieves with Fowler?"

He shrugged.

"Odd coalition, that," she mused aloud.

"They have a lot in common, each hating a stepparent."

Jolie bit back the first thing that rose to her mind, that at least they had stepparents, and while neither Whitney nor Eldridge Colton was the warm, cuddly type, they at least weren't physically abusive.

There was a slowdown as a stalled car ahead knotted up traffic behind it. Overheated, Jolie guessed; the October weather seemed to be echoing the blistering temperatures of September. She was almost glad; it gave her the excuse to stay silent as T.C. quickly dodged off the road onto a side street. Never let it be said a Dallas Colton didn't know his city.

When they got back on the road to the ranch, the traffic was lighter—no doubt thanks to the clog they'd avoided—and they picked up some speed. Jolie was remembering all the times she'd purposely avoided this trip, despite the temptation to at least drive out to the big gates. But somewhere in her mind she'd had the fear she'd end up in jail for trespassing, whether she actually set foot on Colton property or not.

And now she was headed directly there. Could even T.C. protect her? She wasn't worried about him keeping them safe from the killer; she knew he could. But keep her—and more important, Emma—safe from his family? That she wasn't so sure about.

She would, she decided, take what abuse there would be. His mother could heap whatever she wanted on Jolie's head and she would quietly accept it, as long as she left Emma alone. She could take it, for as long as it took for the police to find the killer.

At least his father wouldn't be there to torment either of them.

The moment she thought it, remorse flooded her. His father was missing, possibly dead. In her view probably dead, because it just wasn't part of Eldridge Colton's makeup to be cowed. He might be old, and not in the best of health, but he was still the patriarch of both the Colton Valley Ranch and Colton Inc., and he would not go quietly. And it had been months now, with no word. It seemed obvious to her, but she wasn't about to say anything. If T.C. still had hope his father would be found alive, she wasn't about to dispute him.

But her guilt over her unkind thought drove her to speak.

"It must be hard, not knowing. About your father, I mean."

For a moment, he didn't answer, and she thought he wouldn't.

"What's hard," he finally said, "is wondering if someone in my family has something to do with it."

She blinked. "With…his disappearance? Do you really think that?"

He flicked her a quick glance before making the turn onto the road that would finally get them straight to the ranch. "You, of all people, find that hard to believe?"

"I don't," she admitted, "but I would think you would."

He let out a sound that could have been a wry chuckle. "Well, you were always honest."

"Yes," she said. Then, more pointedly, she repeated it. "Yes, I was. And am."

She saw his expression change, his brow furrow. And she knew he'd gotten her meaning, that she'd been honest about what had happened four years ago, about the threats made to Emma by his mother.

It wasn't until she could see the start of the long front drive, leading to the huge, black iron gates with Colton Valley Ranch emblazoned across them in gold, that she realized if he was seriously considering someone in his family had something to do with his father's disappearance, then surely he must be doing the same about what she'd told him. She hadn't expected him to believe her about his mother's threats, but maybe, now—

He drove right past the turnoff.

She couldn't help herself, she looked down the drive, then at him. He'd never even glanced at the road that led to his home.

Irrationally fear spiked through her. Where was he taking them?

The crazy ideas that flooded her mind told her more than anything so far just how terrified she'd been—and still was—for her daughter. This was T.C., not some serial killer or abductor. She was the one who had assumed they would go to the ranch, the place she'd once thought of as a haven of safety. And it had been, until Whitney Colton had tumbled to the fact that there was more going on between her youngest son and the kitchen help than just a casual flirtation or hookup.

Ask, she ordered herself. How hard could it be to just ask where they were going?

She couldn't make herself say the simple words.

She had to stop reading thrillers, she thought. Her imagination was going into overdrive, filling her with insane possibilities. What kind of craziness was it that had her calculating how to get into the backseat, free Emma and roll out of a moving car?

It was all she could do not to turn in her seat to look back at the turnoff to the ranch. As it was she stared at the expanse of grassland they were driving alongside, trying to remember just how far the Colton Valley Ranch stretched. Then it occurred to her that they, like most of the really big ranches, had satellite locations scattered over the state, providing the extra land that raising beef required. Maybe they were headed to one of those.

It suddenly occurred to her that there were probably many places on all those thousands of acres where you could bury a body—or two—where they would never be found.

And the man driving this car probably knew where every one of them was.

Chapter 10

"Worried?"

He read her easily, even after all this time. He'd seen the way she'd looked at the drive to the house as they'd gone past. Nor had he missed the sudden new tension in her face as they kept going.

It was a moment before she answered, in a tone that told him he'd succeeded in making her bristle. "Should I be?"

"Maybe I do want that payback."

She appeared to be considering her answer carefully. He waited. He was good at that.

"Even if you did," she finally said, "and from your point of view, I would understand that, but you would never hurt Emma."

Well, that took the wind right out of your sails, didn't it, Colton?

On the heels of the thought, he felt a little churlish.

After what she had been through, she had every reason and right to be wary.

And Emma. Most especially this was about Emma. It was hardly surprising that Jolie was as spooked as a horse that had stepped on a rattler. She might have only dropped back into his life a couple of hours ago, but he already knew, as he had four known years ago, when it came down to it, Emma's welfare ranked far above her own.

He slowed as they came up behind a slow, lumbering flatbed truck loaded with building materials. The truck was new, and the driver was smiling as he waved them around. T.C. smiled inwardly. He liked the signs that his state was doing well when so many weren't, liked that people were prospering. And he liked that Colton was a part of all that.

"It's good to see people working, isn't it?"

Her quiet words snapped him back to the tiny world inside this car, and served him up a reminder that she had shown she still read him as easily as he'd moments ago read her. The thought unsettled him.

"Speaking of working, where are you, specifically?"

For a moment, he thought she might not answer, and he wondered what was so difficult about the question.

"The Balcones," she finally said.

He blinked. Turned his head to look at her, longer than he should have, vaguely aware he was lucky the road ahead was empty for a stretch. She'd been working at the relatively new hotel he could quite literally see out his office window?

"For how long?" He thought it came out fairly even, considering. But she drew back slightly, so he guessed she'd heard something of the emotion behind the query.

"Just over a year. Since they opened."

A year. She'd been practically within his sight for over a year. Hell, he'd even been in there a time or two in the last year. The new restaurant they'd opened had quietly built a reputation in a competitive market, and had rather quickly become reliable enough in quality and service to gain a spot on Dallas's list of the top fifty places to eat. He'd found the place subtler than many, the food delicious and the presentation less ostentatious than others, and it ranked high on his list of places to take associates who didn't need the flash or the trend. And that Fowler wouldn't be caught dead in such a quiet, unpretentious place was a huge mark in its favor in his book.

He knew he was dwelling on all that to avoid the obvious question hammering at the door of the small compartment in his brain where he kept all things Jolie. But it finally broke through and appeared as if in neon; had she been there when he had been? Had he eaten food she had fixed, or plated? Had she been that close, the distance between them measured in feet, not miles, and he hadn't known?

"Why there?" Those words weren't anywhere near even, but he couldn't seem to help it.

It was a moment before she said, her tone dry, "They hired me."

He smothered the urge to glare at her. But his hands tightened slightly on the steering wheel. He heard her make a small sound that might have been a sigh.

"I'd worked with the woman who runs the back of the house before. She gave me a chance back then, even though I was fresh out of school."

That startled him into looking at her. "School?"

"Culinary school. I took some courses. Got a certificate, couldn't afford the full program. But it was enough that she gave me a shot. And when she left to start at the Balcones, she offered me the chance to go with her."

"And you took it."

"She believed in me when no one else did. I would have done more than just changed jobs."

"Loyalty," he said, almost under his breath.

He hadn't meant it as a dig at her lack of loyalty to him, but he sensed her stiffen. He'd actually been startled enough that he'd put their past back in that compartment again. And puzzled at his own reaction; Jolie was smart, capable and talented, and knowing her history he shouldn't be surprised she was also tough enough to succeed in a rather cutthroat industry.

"I did hesitate," she said. "I wasn't sure I could handle the…proximity."

There was no mistaking her meaning; she hadn't been sure she wanted to work that close to the Colton building.

To him.

"But you managed to overcome your distaste."

That he had meant as a jab, and he saw her flinch.

"It wasn't distaste," she said, a tremor in her voice that made something tighten up even more in his gut, which in turn irritated the hell out of him. "It was pain."

"You're the one who bailed on me," he reminded her.

She turned her head, looked at the little girl sleeping in the backseat. Then she turned back, meeting his gaze and holding it levelly. She said nothing more, but then, he supposed no words were necessary. Emma's well-being trumped everything.

Apparently the relatively civil conversation inspired her to ask what he guessed had been her main question all along.

"Where are we going?"

They were miles past the CVR. drive now, so it wasn't surprising she was concerned. He wondered if she realized they were still paralleling the ranch; most people who didn't grow up in the life didn't realize just how much land it took to keep a cattle operation going.

He, on the other hand, being in charge of the entire ranch operation, knew every damned square foot of the place.

"What if I said California?" he asked, wondering why he felt compelled to prod at her; they'd talked about visiting there, she'd been curious to see if the Pacific was very different from the gulf. He'd wanted to take her there, or anywhere else she wanted to go, and had happily been making plans to do just that the day she walked out of his life.

"Then I'd say I underpacked," she answered, her tone almost nonchalant. That tone irked him even more, which in turn compounded his irritation.

He was over it, wasn't he? Sure, it still rankled a bit when he thought about it, but he didn't let himself do that very often. Okay, so maybe he wasn't completely over it, but it wasn't like he dwelled on it every waking moment, as he had in the beginning. And he'd been to California, twice now, and with a determined effort he'd managed not to even think about her while there. Much.

"You came to me for sanctuary, so that's where we're going."

"Should I assume you don't mean the town of Sanctuary?"

"Yes, assume," he said dryly; the tiny town northwest of Fort Worth was definitely not his destination.

"Then where?"

"My sanctuary."

For a moment, she seemed to just absorb that. He wondered if she had any idea, any understanding of why he would even need such a thing. He was a Colton, after all, rich, famous, powerful—what in the world did he need sanctuary from?

It must be awful, to always carry the weight of all those Colton expectations. I think I'd prefer no expectations at all, except bad ones. It's a lot easier to be pleasantly surprised that way.

The words shot through his mind, words she'd spoken years ago, when they'd gone on a ride, leaving baby Emma in the capable hands of Moira Manfred, the head housekeeper who after thirty years was as much a fixture at the ranch as her husband, Aaron, the butler.

Something Moira had said, about being glad to see him take some time for himself, had apparently triggered the observation. He'd often felt exactly that way but had never expected anyone outside the family to ever see or understand it. It hadn't been the first—nor the last—time he'd underestimated her.

And this time was no different. She studied him silently and when at last she spoke, it was quietly.

"A place to get away from the family chaos? I'm glad you have one."

He should have known she would understand.

The question remaining was, after he let her invade that very private space, where would he go to get away from thoughts and memories of her?

Chapter 11

Jolie had lost track of how far they'd come when T.C. slowed the big SUV and pulled off the paved road. She glanced around, puzzled, seeing nothing but more open land, and a faint dirt track with an odd pile of flat rocks stacked waist high beside it. A marker? He started down the track. This was where the four-wheel drive was necessary, she thought; her little sedan would be struggling on this rocky ground.

She wondered if she was thinking of such inane things to avoid second-guessing the choice she'd made. He had every reason to be angry with her, after all. Four years would have cooled it, but seeing her again, especially when she'd had the nerve to approach him asking for help, could easily have fired it right up again.

And yet, once he knew the full story, he hadn't hesitated. And that it was likely for Emma, and in spite of herself, didn't matter. Couldn't matter. Because when it came down to it, Emma was the only thing that did matter.

She stayed silent as they went onward. He was obviously familiar with the area. She remembered Fowler once laughing at his younger half brother, and how after college he'd set out to ride over every part of the ranch. As if, Fowler had said with a derisive sneer, it mattered knowing one gully from another, one winter puddle from another. T.C. had calmly replied the ranch would be his domain, and he didn't feel comfortable making decisions about things he hadn't even seen.

She'd said nothing—she'd only been at the ranch a few days at the time—but she'd remembered. She'd also remembered how Fowler talked in front of her as if she weren't there, or as if she were no more aware than the kitchen counter she stood at, making his expansive breakfast. It had been T.C. who had looked at her behind his brother's back, rolling his eyes and grinning.

She'd started to fall in love with him at that moment.

Not, of course, that she'd ever, ever thought anything would come of it. She'd fully expected to be one of those awful clichés, the lowly employee sighing after a man who was, in essence, her unattainable boss. And she'd done her best to quash those unwanted feelings, been careful not to look at him any more than anyone else when she helped serve meals, or stare when she caught glimpses of him setting out for one of those long, exploratory rides. Although she couldn't deny the way her pulse leaped when she watched his jeans-clad figure swing aboard his big paint. She was a Texas girl through and through, and cowboys were in her blood.

But she allowed herself small things, such as learning how he liked his coffee, his eggs—breakfast was the only meal she was allowed to handle alone—and his toast, and made sure they were done to perfection when he was there. It wasn't something he'd notice—after all, it was expected—but it gave her a small amount of pleasure anyway.

And then one day he'd thanked her for it, and she'd slipped a little further toward that precipice.

She had to stop thinking about it. The past was the past, and she'd blown it all up when she took the money and ran. It was no small miracle that he was helping them at all. She'd be worse than a fool to keep dwelling on things she couldn't change.

Somewhat desperately she searched for a safe subject. But what she came up with was still colored with those memories. "How is Flash?"

He'd told her once he'd named the horse after his brother Fowler kept calling the big paint flashy. "No point in denying the obvious," T.C. had said with a grin.

She'd liked how he'd deflated Fowler's implied insult by adopting it. In the same way, he'd dealt with the disparaging childhood nickname Fowler had given him, The Crawler—he was, he admitted, always crawling into and under things, to see how they were made—turning it into the initials he cheerfully went by to this day. She felt a deep ache as she remembered the day he'd explained that to her. Most thought the T.C. stood for Thomas Colton, only family knew the real origin.

But he'd told her.

He didn't look at her when she asked after his horse, but kept his gaze on the faint, rugged track that could hardly be called a road. They'd left the asphalt ribbon out of sight behind a rise now, and they could just as well be in the middle of nowhere as within a mockingbird's flight of the huge Dallas metroplex.

"He's good. Still goofy, but still the best working horse on the ranch."

The big black-and-white pinto indeed had had a silly personality, once carefully nibbling away half of her straw hat while it was still on her head. Of course, she'd been distracted by his rider when they had dismounted so he could reunite the tiny lost calf they'd come across with its mother, who bawled out a welcome that had made him smile.

And there she was again, she thought in annoyance, thinking about those lost days. Next thing she'd be thinking of the sweltering day he'd pulled off his shirt to dip it in the water tank, and she'd gotten her first look at his bare chest and flat, ridged abdomen. Tall, wide-shouldered and lean-hipped, he was like an illustration of the perfect male form come to life, for her.

Why don't you just torture yourself all the way, and think of when he kissed you the first time, or that morning when you first made love, in a pile of fresh, sweet-smelling hay...

"Emma would love to meet him."

The girl actually had seen the horse before, but she'd been so young Jolie knew she wouldn't remember. Then a flash of the drawing the child had made, of the black-and-white blobs that were almost recognizable as a horse, went through her mind and she wondered.

"That can be arranged. I made her a promise." He didn't look at her when he added, "And I keep my promises."

Unlike some. Jolie thought the words he didn't say. He

didn't have to say them. She knew perfectly well who the promise-breaker was in this car right now.

"Meet who, Mommy?"

Emma's sleepy voice made her turn in her seat; the rougher road must have waked the girl.

"The horse that looks like the one you drew, honey."

The girl was instantly wide-awake. "'s that where we're going? Where he is?"

"No," T.C. said, "but we're going somewhere I can bring him to."

"'Kay."

The girl said it simply, happily, immediately accepting his words. Did the child somehow know this was a man you could trust? Or was it the fact that this was who her mother had turned to for help?

Jolie let out a quiet sigh. She didn't know if the child even realized what was going on. She hoped not, not really. She needed the girl to be careful, but she didn't want her terrified and haunted by what had happened last night. How did you explain to a four-year-old that this stranger was dangerous, but this one trustworthy? She didn't want to raise a child who was perpetually frightened. She wanted Emma to be a bold, confident person with the courage to seize her dreams. But how did she do that and keep her safe? Especially now?

"It's nothing fancy," T.C. said as the track lifted over another slight rise, and she assumed they must be getting close. "You won't be watching a big-screen TV. Or any TV for that matter. Or using your phone, although you might get a couple of bars up on this rise."

She doubted that; she'd already noticed her low-rate, inexpensive phone was getting zero reception out here.

"And no heat other than a fireplace," he went on, "although it's still nearly sixty degrees most nights, so that shouldn't be a problem."

"It's October in Texas," Jolie said dryly. "I'd be more concerned about the eighty degree days."

"No air-conditioning, either," he said.

It struck her suddenly that he wasn't just preparing her, he sounded…not worried, but wary. What did he think, that she'd belittle the place, think it not good enough?

"If it will do what needs doing," she said, with a glance back at her daughter, "it could be a tent with an outhouse."

She saw his mouth quirk. "No outhouse. I drew the line at outdoor plumbing. But the water comes from a slow well, so it won't do to waste it. And the stove is on propane, so same warning."

"No campfire cooking?" She put all she could manage of exaggerated disappointment in her voice.

"Marshmallows!" Emma chirped at the word *campfire*.

"You want toasted marshmallows, little mockingbird, put 'em on a rock."

Jolie's heart nearly stopped as Emma giggled. *Little mockingbird.* He'd called her that when she was just a baby learning to make noise, and had been surprisingly adept at imitating the sounds she heard.

He remembered. And it had slipped out as easily as if they'd never been gone.

"What's a mock…mockbird…what you said?" asked Emma.

"It's the state bird of Texas," T.C. answered.

"Oh. That's good, then."

Jolie saw T.C. smile, as if in spite of himself. "Yes, it is."

"What bird is Mommy?"

Jolie winced. She couldn't even guess at his answer,

and when after a thoughtful moment it came, she wasn't surprised.

"I think she's more of a loggerhead shrike."

"Charming," Jolie muttered as he named the bird more commonly known as the butcher bird for the habit of impaling its meals on thorns or barbed-wire fences. Thankfully the name was too complicated for Emma to even try, but her laugh said she found the sound of it funny.

"But appropriate." T.C. said it without any tone of malice, but the meaning of his choice was hard to miss.

Before she had to react to that, they were coming down the other side of the rise, and Jolie saw a small building amid a cluster of pecan trees. There were also splashes of still green plants here and there, so she knew there must be water underground. The building itself looked old, but it had clearly been repaired much more recently. The roof looked new, and it appeared to have some newer windows. It looked more like a cabin than anything, solid, sturdy. And safe? That was paramount, after all. But the isolation should see to that, she hoped.

They pulled to a halt beneath the branches of one of the big trees that were clinging to leaves despite the hot summer they'd had. Emma squirmed, clearly anxious to get out. T.C. turned in the driver's seat to look at the girl.

"Emma, I need you to listen to me." Something in his voice made the child settle, and she met his gaze. "Be watchful when you're outside. Especially for snakes. It's nearly past their time of year, but there might still be some around, and they prefer to be left alone. If you bother the wrong one, it can hurt you. All right?"

The girl's eyes were wide as she nodded.

"If you see it, leave it," T.C. said. "Can you say that?"

Emma repeated the words carefully.

"Good girl."

He turned back then, and Jolie quickly looked away, her heart aching, her stomach knotted up. She didn't want him to see the moisture welling up in her eyes. Back then, once he'd gotten over the nervousness of dealing with a baby, he'd been wonderful with Emma.

Clearly he hadn't lost the knack.

She realized in this moment more than ever just how much she'd hurt him, not only by betraying him, but by taking away this child he'd come to love.

And yet here he was, helping them.

Helping Emma, she mentally corrected.

It would not do to think this was anything more than a kind, generous man helping an innocent child who needed him.

Chapter 12

"Welcome to the refuge," T.C. said as he opened the door.

She glanced at him. "The refuge?"

"It's an old line shack the crew once used. We built a newer one farther west when we added the acreage out there, so I took over this one." He shrugged. "It's where I hide out when it all gets to be too much."

She knew what he meant. Even when she'd worked there he'd occasionally vanished for a while now and then, usually after some big bit of drama brought on by his mother, or even more often, Fowler's conniving girlfriend, Tiffany Ankler. The flashy blonde never missed a chance to cause chaos. Even then Jolie had known the woman's goal was to get Fowler to propose, but she wasn't quite sure how Tiffany thought the constant upheaval was going to accomplish that. Then again, she'd likely get a better welcome from Whitney Colton than she had.

Or maybe not, maybe they were too alike, and not just in looks.

Jolie yanked her mind out of that morass and looked around. The cabin surprised her on many levels. It was bigger than it seemed from outside, although still just one big room except for the small bathroom T.C. showed them back in one corner. It was, as he'd said, completely modern, and even had a small shower. She fought off a sudden flash of memory, of the time they'd taken the three-hundred-mile drive down to San Antonio for a long weekend, the first time they'd gone off alone together. T.C. was out of context there, and not as immediately recognizable as he was in Dallas, which in turn made her feel so much freer.

Free enough to join him in the shower of the elegant hotel, and the memories of what had happened next made her pulse speed up even now.

She turned away so he couldn't see the color she was afraid had risen in her face, because she was sure he would see. And he'd know, somehow he'd guess what she'd been thinking of; he'd already shown he still read her far too easily.

Her avoidance move didn't work so well, because in the opposite corner was a double bed up against the wood-paneled wall and covered with a Texas Star quilt. She slammed a mental door on the thoughts that engendered; if she went down that road, she'd be jumping him right here and now. And she knew how well that would go over. She made herself continue to look around as if inspecting the place was the only thing that mattered to her.

At the foot of the bed was a storage chest. Another sat outside the bathroom. To the left of the doorway was a small cooking setup—it was too small to be called an actual kitchen—consisting of a two-burner stove and a cabinet whose top served as a counter. On it sat an old-fashioned coffeepot, a saucepan, a cast-iron skillet and a large bowl. Above that was an old-fashioned pump-handle-style faucet that looked so genuine she wondered if you actually had to pump it to get water. The cabinet doors were fastened with a latch held with a small carabiner, she supposed against foraging critters of all sorts.

A couple of feet away was a small table, with a single wooden chair. No company, ever? Jolie wondered. Somehow that made her feel both better and worse.

The bookcase that covered the one free wall didn't surprise her, nor did the fact that it was full; T.C. had always been a reader. She'd seen him reading everything from ranching magazines and copious breeding records to Shakespeare and Homer to the latest bestsellers. A large, comfortable chair sat next to the window on the other side of the front door, with an upended crate beside it that was serving as a table. Obviously, from the stack of a half dozen books there, this served as a reading spot.

No e-reader out here, she thought. And then she realized the only light fixtures there appeared to be were a couple of oil or kerosene lanterns, one of which sat on the crate next to the books. All reasons he'd chosen this place, she guessed. He'd wanted isolation and peace, and he'd apparently gotten it.

"This one fell down," Emma chirped as she picked up a book that was on the uneven wooden floor a yard or so from the chair. Jolie recognized the cover. It was a novel that had been the rage in certain parts of the country this summer.

To Jolie's surprise, T.C. grimaced. "I'm afraid I threw it."

Emma's eyes widened. "Mommy says you should r'spect books."

"And she's right," he said, taking the book from her and putting it on an upper shelf.

"Why'd you throw it?"

"Because I couldn't find anybody I liked in the story," he said. "Sometimes you have to deal with mean or nasty people in real life, so I didn't want to read about them, too."

Jolie's eyes stung at the way he was explaining, in words the child could understand, carrying on a conversation with a four-year-old, as if it were the most important thing in his day.

"I like stories with ponies. And fairies," Emma announced.

"Much better," T.C. agreed, his voice solemn. "Sorry I don't have any here."

"S'okay. Mommy will tell me one."

Jolie half expected a snide comment about her making up stories. But it didn't come, so she looked around the place once more. She noticed some smaller touches this time. A photograph on one of the shelves, and she smiled inwardly to see it was of the five Coltons she'd always mentally labeled "the nice ones." T.C. and his half siblings Zane and Alanna, his adopted sister Piper and his brother Reid. Apparently she wasn't alone in her assessment.

A set of longhorns was mounted over the doorway, with a well-used rope looped whimsically over one horn. She wondered if it was from his calf-roping days. A pair of ornate silver spurs sat on the window sill, the spurs that had been his father's, and his grandfather's before him, and that she knew Eldridge Colton had presented him the day he'd taken over the ranch operations. On a rack near the door was an almost equally ornately engraved rifle, and she guessed it was the one that had been presented to him by the statewide rancher's association last year. That some stories about the Coltons couldn't be avoided no matter how hard she tried was something she'd learned well in the last four years.

And some people would, she knew, be amazed that a Colton would choose to live like this, in this tiny—relative to the expansive mansion they referred to euphemistically as "the ranch house"—shack with no power and minimal convenience. She wasn't. But again noting the lanterns did make her ask, "You could have a power generator out here that runs on the propane, couldn't you?"

"I could. Thought about it. But I decided I liked it this way. It reminds me of what it was like, for the ones who came before." His mouth quirked. "Minus the plumbing, of course. Which I suppose makes me a bit of a hypocrite."

"You're too honest to be a hypocrite."

He looked as if he was about to say something, then glanced at Emma and stopped. Jolie guessed it would have been about her, and not too flattering.

"Thank you," she said.

And then she saw something that made her breath jam up in her throat.

The bracelet. The woven grass bracelet she'd made for him that long ago day, from the grass beneath the tree where they—

She cut off her own thoughts, focusing on the narrow braided band, now dried and probably fragile.

He'd kept that? Why?

Her gaze shot to his face. And as he had before, he

read her easily. "It's a reminder," he said, his voice harsh as he didn't hold back the words this time, "about trusting people I shouldn't. I don't ever want to have to learn that again."

Emma turned away from the window, where she'd been looking at the ornately engraved spurs, clearly reacting to his tone.

"Are you mad?" she asked.

"No more than usual," he muttered, then managed a smile for the child. "And certainly not at you."

Emma looked at Jolie as she tried to decide if that meant he was mad at her. *If you only knew*, she thought, and was immensely grateful T.C. had too much class to air their dirty laundry in front of a little girl.

"I was just thinking about something that happened years ago," T.C. said, his voice gentler now. "Nothing you need to worry about. It's over and done."

"Oh. 'Kay."

That simply, the child took his word for it and continued her explorations. As if he'd just thought of it, he walked over and took a rather large book off one of the higher shelves.

"I do have this, however," he said, holding it out to the girl.

"Horses!" she exclaimed, and took it. It was awkward for her, the book large, but she clambered into the reading chair and settled in happily with what Jolie now saw was a history of the quarter horse, full of pictures of the famous lines of the breed.

T.C. watched her for a moment, and the wistful expression that came over his face stabbed at the raw spot within her that never seemed to heal. He had loved Emma. She had lost him, true, but he had lost both of them. No wonder he was bitter about it. He had every right.

She had to stop thinking about it. She couldn't change the past, and when she looked at him and thought about it she could barely function. And she had to function, for Emma. She had to treat him as if he were just someone who was helping them, as if there were no other connection to him.

Good luck with that, she told herself.

He turned to her then.

"I need to run over to the house. There's not much here in the way of food, probably nothing she would like. Just canned stuff like tuna and soup. Oh, and there's chili."

She started to say he didn't need to do that, that they would get by on what was here and be thankful, but somehow it shifted to teasing. "Canned chili? But it might have beans in it. The horror!"

"That's why it's in a jar, not a can. And homemade."

Her eyes widened much as Emma's had earlier. "Bettina's homemade Texas chili?"

"Three home-canned jars of it."

"Heaven," she said.

"But probably not for a four-year-old."

Jolie was so relieved at this almost amiable exchange that she risked some more teasing. "My daughter is a Texan through and through. She loves chili."

T.C. glanced at the girl, who was cooing over a photograph of a palomino horse.

"Although at her age, she does go for the pretty colors," Jolie explained.

"He's not just pretty, he's Cutter Bill," he said. "He was a fine cutting horse. Hall of Fame level. She's got good taste." He flashed her a grin. "We won't talk about his owners."

She lifted an eyebrow at him.

"Cowboy Mafia," he said.

She blinked at the mention of the infamous marijuana smuggling ring. It was before she was born, but it was legendary in Texas history. And T.C. had talked about it once, ruefully explaining the term was occasionally applied to the Coltons, thanks to Fowler's less than ethical dealings.

"Didn't you once think that your father—"

"Yeah, I wondered if he was involved. Seems right up what was his alley at the time."

Eldridge Colton made no bones about how he'd come up; he'd been a petty thief who'd graduated to bank robber before he'd amassed enough to start building the ranch and go legit. In fact, he was proud of it. And Jolie had often thought those who said Fowler was a chip off the old block weren't far wrong.

She heard a musical tone—"Deep in the Heart of Texas"—and T.C. pulled out his cell phone.

"At least you get a signal here."

He shook his head. "I don't. But we have a ranch-wide system in the vehicles. It'll notify me of calls, or relay voice mails and texts. Excuse me."

He left, apparently to go to the vehicle. A moment later she heard the SUV start. A sudden flash of fear shot through her, the thought that he was abandoning them here looming in her mind.

She recognized the old, familiar pattern and talked herself down, forcing herself to think logically. He was only heading up the rise where he'd said the signal was better, that was all.

She sat on the arm of the chair by Emma, looking at the photos of famous quarter horses with her. They'd gone through several before T.C. was back, phone silent now but still in his hand. And he was staring at her.

"Why didn't you tell me?"

She drew back slightly at his tone. She bent to Emma, who was watching them curiously, and kept her tone quiet and encouraging when she said, "Keep going with the book, honey. Pick me out your favorite."

The child complied happily enough, and she straightened and turned to face T.C. Silently she walked over to where he was standing just inside the door; whatever he was edgy about, she didn't want Emma to hear it.

"What are you talking about? I told you everything I could think of."

"Except one little detail."

Her brow furrowed. "What?"

He stared at her. And when he answered she wasn't sure what the emotion was that echoed in his voice.

"You didn't think I should know the woman who was murdered looked just like you?"

Chapter 13

She was honestly surprised. T.C. couldn't deny that; it was all over her face. That lovely, expressive face.

Did she really think that detail was minor, unimportant?

"I don't know. I didn't think—"

He cut her off. "Well, that's an understatement."

She drew herself up, as if she were preparing to face him down. There had always been a line with Jolie. She would take a lot, and back then she had to because he was in a way her employer, but when it was personal she stood up for herself. She'd told him once it was a lesson hard-learned, and she wasn't about to forget it.

"I did think about it. It bothered me, at first. Gave me a chill. But I decided it had to be a coincidence. Lots of women resemble me. It's not like I'm… I'm Tiffany."

And just like that she disarmed him. For she was right. No one could be further from his flashy, not-too-bright but shrewd would be sister-in-law than Jolie Peters. Tiffany's expensive taste and over-the-top style had all the subtlety of a tank. And somehow he knew even if she'd ever had the means, Jolie would never go for that kind of blatant exhibitionism.

In his view, she'd been a million times more attractive because of it.

And judging by his roiled emotions and the knot in his gut, he still felt that way.

He only realized how long he'd been standing there, staring at her, when she spoke in that uncomfortable tone people got when the silence had gone on for too long.

"That was your police friend?"

"Yes." He glanced at Emma, who seemed engrossed in the AQHA history book, or at least the many photographs. He turned back to Jolie. "He wanted to be sure you were somewhere safe. Apparently someone's been asking about you."

He heard her suck in a breath. "Asking who?"

"Neighbors. If they'd seen you, where you were. So far Manny says most people they talked to said they told her to mind her own business, but there could be someone who didn't."

"Her?"

He nodded.

"Was it…?"

"He can't be sure, but the general description matches."

"You think someone might have told her…what?"

"Maybe nothing. Or maybe she found someone who saw my car." He grimaced inwardly as he acknowledged one of the facts of who he was. "Or recognized me."

Her mouth twisted slightly at one corner.

"Rethinking who you came to?" he asked.

"You told me once the Colton name was both shield and magnet."

In that instant he was transported back to that day, when he'd arrived home late, in a foul mood because he'd been followed to the gates by a reporter of the worst sort, the salacious, social gossipmongering type. He'd been at a fund-raiser and been seen speaking to a woman he didn't know or recognize who had turned out to be some reality show personality. But she had known him, and had zeroed in on him from across the crowded room.

He'd only talked to her as long as he had because he'd been boggled by her sense of self-importance, and that she and his brother's girlfriend apparently shopped at the same places. The woman had explained with great pride that she had a stylist who took care of that, and T.C. had come away thinking rather bemusedly that at least Tiffany's style was her own concoction.

Of course the gossip reporter was determined to turn it into some kind of sordid romance. He had been so uninterested it had been laughable.

But that had been before he'd admitted to himself that the only woman he was interested in was at home, working in the family kitchen. The woman who had, the next morning, set a plate of credible New Orleans–style beignets in front of him, one of his favorite indulgences. The woman everyone else dismissed as a mere kitchen assistant had troubled to ask Bettina what might cheer him up, and then proceeded to do it. The fact that she had gone to all that effort, that she had even noticed his mood and thought to try and brighten his morning, had touched him in a way nothing had in a long time. Thinking back, he realized that was probably the moment he'd begun to truly fall for her.

He could just imagine what the reporter would do with that.

He shook off the reverie and tried to focus, ruefully aware he ran the entire Colton Valley Ranch operation with less effort than that took.

He asked, in his most brusque, businesslike tone, "Are you clear now it was not some coincidence?"

She still looked doubtful. "But—"

"Jolie, you need to realize there's not just—" he glanced again at Emma "—one person in danger here."

He understood her reluctance; it was quite enough to think Emma was a target. And besides that, he guessed it didn't matter as much to her that she could be, as well.

"You may have been the original target all along," he said. "How can I protect you if you don't tell me everything about what we're dealing with?"

"Don't worry about me. It's Emma's safety that's paramount."

Her answer didn't surprise him. He'd always known what kind of mother she was. It was another of the things that had drawn him to her. Probably because his own mother wasn't anything like that, and would be incapable of the kinds of sacrifices Jolie had made for her daughter.

So the path ahead seemed clear. And despite his reluctance, one thing was obvious. They would both keep Emma safe, but apparently keeping Jolie safe fell to him.

So be it. It certainly wouldn't be the first time he'd had to do something he didn't want to do. Not that he didn't want to keep her safe; he'd want that for anyone, especially the mother of a young child.

He just didn't want the forced togetherness that was going to take. In fact, he didn't want to spend another minute in her company now, at least not until he'd regained his equilibrium and banished this silly response to her back into the cage where he'd shoved it four years ago.

"Do you remember how to shoot?" he asked abruptly.

Jolie grimaced. "How, yes." He'd taught her, on both pistols and long guns, and as women often were she'd been a naturally good shot. "If you mean have I done it recently, no."

She didn't say *since I left*, but he heard it anyway. He ignored the jab in his gut.

"There's a Colt .45 in the blue box on the shelf," he said. "But if you have time and room, go for the rifle. You were pretty good with one."

She was staring at him now. "Do you really think… anyone could find me here?"

"They found your home."

She opened her mouth, then closed it without speaking. He hoped it meant she'd realized there was no room for argument here.

"Try not to shoot any of the hands," he said. "As a rule they don't hang around here, but one might come by to water his horse, and they check on the place for me now and then."

Mutely she nodded.

"Anything in particular I should bring back for her?" he asked with a last look at the little girl in his chair; she was about halfway through the book, and showing signs of restlessness, skipping ahead and only stopping to look at certain photos.

"She loves peanut butter and jelly sandwiches," Jolie said. "Would live on them if I let her."

He couldn't help smiling at that. "I think I did, for a while. As long as Bettina would let me, anyway. There's a little PB in the cabinet, but no jelly. I'll bring more."

He left, pondering going back to the road to get to the house; it would be quicker. But he decided it would be better—and less visible—to stay on the ranch and make the rougher trip. As he drove he made a mental list of things he would bring back, and framed his apology to Bettina for raiding her stores. She would probably forgive him if he told her why. She'd always had a soft spot for Emma in particular, and had been one of the few who hadn't outright condemned Jolie, although she'd been staunchly on his side and done her best to comfort him in her own way.

Maybe he'd bring Flash back, he thought. If it wasn't for the supplies, he'd just ride him back. But he could trailer him back, so Emma could meet and maybe ride the horse that looked like the one she'd drawn in that childlike way.

And again he wondered if somehow, some hazy memory had stuck in the child's mind. It didn't seem possible; she'd been so very young, and she could just have easily—and more reasonably—seen pictures of a pinto when she was old enough for it to register. But it did still nudge at him a little, even knowing there was no way to ever be sure.

Flash would be fine in the shed and corral behind the refuge. He knew it well enough, and even though it was smaller than the stalls in the stable, it provided shelter from the heat if needed. He'd have plenty of water and the straw was fresh. The horse would give the girl something to think about and maybe keep her from wondering exactly why she was here and not in her own home. Because he was sure she thought of the apartment as home. Jolie had seen to that, turning into a cozy nest for the two of them.

He wouldn't let himself dwell on that, either. *Just focus on the logistics*, he told himself. *Don't let the emotional sneak in. That's when you get into trouble.* Especially when Jolie Peters was concerned. She—

He stopped short as he came up on where the track divided as it neared the main house. He'd intended to park in the back, but coming in from the side he couldn't miss what was sitting out front. Nor was there any mistaking the too obviously plain vehicle for anything other than what it was.

The sheriff was here.

Chapter 14

T.C. wheeled the SUV around, jammed down on the accelerator, kicking up a cloud as the tires bit into the dirt. Then he was on the curving, paved drive that took him to the front in less than fifteen seconds.

He jumped out, glanced at the parked, unmarked unit, betrayed by the small light bar atop the dash and visible through the windshield. He looked inside as he passed, saw the radio under the dash, the microphone in its hanger.

The old man. Had they found him? Alive, or dead? Were they finally going to get confirmation of what he'd feared and suspected?

He hit the front steps at a run and took them three at a time. He burst in through the front door; the ornate two-story foyer with the flanking curved staircases and the crystal chandelier always made him cringe. *Some ranch house*, was always his thought when he came in this way, and was why he preferred the back door that came in through the much more casual den.

No one was there, so he headed for what his mother grandly called the salon, since that was usually where they took people they wanted to impress, or to remind who they were dealing with.

"Mr. Thomas, you're home. Is everything all right?"

He turned to look at Aaron Manfred, the tall, thin man who had been a fixture at the ranch for T.C.'s entire life. At seventy-five, the mustachioed butler who never left his room without his suit and tie on, never left the house without his perfectly groomed Stetson and who had been with T.C.'s father for thirty years was feeling the situation as personally as any of the Coltons.

Probably more than a couple of them.

"The sheriff," T.C. said shortly, with a jerk of his thumb toward the front.

If he had not grown up with the man, he might have missed the slight shift in expression that told him whatever was going on, Manfred didn't approve.

"Sheriff Watkins is in with Mr. Fowler." He didn't sniff, but it was in his tone.

"Did they find…?"

"Oh!" Manfred's tone became immediately apologetic. "No, no, not that. I'm so sorry, I should have said right away."

T.C. breathed again. "Then what?"

"Your brother called them." As T.C. turned to head toward the salon, the older man added, a gentle note in his voice, "You might not wish to go in there, Mr. Thomas. You might find this…theory personally uncomfortable."

T.C.'s brow furrowed. Then it hit him. Fowler's earlier wild speculation. "He's blaming Jolie."

"I believe so."

"Son of a—" He had his hand on the ornate door handle before he caught himself. Was he really going to go in there and defend her? Fowler would be shocked, after what she'd done, that he would even speak up for her. And Fowler being Fowler, he would begin to wonder why. If he found out Jolie was here, on the ranch, who knew what he might do?

But at least if she was right here on the ranch, and stayed unnoticed, the sheriff wouldn't find her. And in the meantime they could figure out how to clear her. Bursting in there now and defending her to probably the sheriff himself in front of Fowler could end up causing the very thing he wanted to avoid. His other siblings, Piper in particular, would understand that regardless of his feelings about Jolie, Emma was innocent. And she was in real danger, as well as her mother.

Maybe if I just thought of her as Emma's mother, I could stop...remembering.

Because he was remembering. The good times, those blissful days when all had been beautiful between them, when the sunrises were more colorful, the stars sparkled more, his entire world was brightened by her presence in it. The days when he'd bristled at any hint of condescension or amazement that he could be genuinely interested in the kitchen help. The days when Fowler's congratulations, because he assumed T.C. was simply screwing her since she was there and willing, resulted in him decking his half brother with one swing.

He let go of the door handle. He backed away a couple of steps, thinking. He glanced around. Manfred had gone about his duties; he and Moira seemed determined the house would run as if Eldridge Colton were still here, holding the reins.

And for the first time he questioned himself. Did he really believe Jolie had had nothing to do with this? After all, she'd taken money once. How could he be sure she wouldn't do just what Fowler had said, come back for more?

Instead of going into the salon to stop whatever tale Fowler was telling, he headed for the stairs. Moments later he was in his suite, digging through the bottom right drawer of the desk that sat by the window that looked out toward the working ranch. He'd moved from his old rooms to here precisely for that view. He enjoyed looking out in the mornings and evenings, seeing that all was well in his part of the Colton domain.

Well, and to get a bit farther from Fowler and Tiffany, and all that that entailed.

In the back of the drawer, crumpled and ripped almost in half, he found what he'd been looking for. The canceled check his mother had waved in front of him when she triumphantly proclaimed she'd known all along Jolie Peters was a gold digger. He'd grabbed at it in disbelief, hence the tear. But there had been no denying it was Jolie's signature on the back.

But that wasn't what he was looking for now. Now he was looking at the faint printing on the back, from the institution where she had deposited the six-figure check.

He pulled out his phone and called Hannah. She answered before the first ring completed.

"I need some information, as discreetly as possible."

"Of course."

He told her what he wanted. She promised to get back

to him as soon as she had it. He had no doubts she would manage it as efficiently as she did everything else.

He realized he'd been pacing while on the phone. He stopped, in front of the window that looked out to the west. Toward the refuge, that small place that had saved his sanity more than once. He was wondering if, with his impulsive action, he'd destroyed that sanctuary. It had been a place free of memories, of might-have-beens. Not that he was ever truly free of them, not when he carried them around inside him all the time. And more than once he'd spent a long night in that reading chair where Emma had sat, questioning his instincts and judgment, for having been so totally, utterly wrong about Jolie and her feelings for him.

When this was over, when she and Emma could safely go back home again, would that quiet place now forever be haunted with images and sounds of her? Of both of them? Would he ever sit in that chair again without the sight of little Emma poring over that book coming to mind?

Probably not, he admitted. He'd done a lot more than just make a quick, perhaps rash decision; he'd possibly trashed his hard-won equilibrium in the process.

His work had been his salvation, in the days after Jolie had gone. He'd wondered, on occasion, if his father hadn't turned the ranch over to him at the young age of twenty-four to distract him, although it had always been the plan that he would take over the ranch operations. When he was younger he'd never realized that meant he would end up spending more time in his office in the Colton building than here on the ranch. If he had, he wouldn't have been so eager to take over.

He had been trying, again, to talk his father into letting him set up an office here, had even had plans drawn up for an addition to the main barn, so he wouldn't have to take up any space already in use by the ranch hands or the livestock. But the old man had resisted; the downtown Colton building was his nose-thumbing to the world that had looked down on him in the old days, and he didn't like that his own son preferred not to spend his days there.

He'd been working the angle that the ranch was also part of that show-the-world attitude, in fact, the part that had made the rest possible, when the kidnapping happened. And now, three months later with still no word, it occasionally struck him that if his half sister Marceline got her way, and got the old man declared dead, he could do exactly what he wanted. It gave him no pleasure to contemplate. He didn't want to go over or around his father. He wanted his father to agree with him.

It wasn't impossible to achieve, despite Eldridge's reputation for being irascible. He'd agreed to the purchase of the small herd of longhorns, to preserve the huge animals as part of their Texas heritage, and now it was a bustling sideline of the ranch business, between leasing the herd out for filmmakers and schoolkids and tourists wanting to see the living bits of history. The old man had also agreed to starting their own quarter horse breeding program, which was still in the early stages, but its first colt, Colton Destiny, was already making a name in halter classes across the state.

Of course, he'd turned stubborn on Piper's plan. She'd wanted to set up a foster care group home at the ranch, a cause dear to her heart because of her own near escape from that kind of life. Eldridge had turned her down flat, saying he didn't want a bunch of rug rats running around the ranch, and had forbidden T.C. to contravene him. That had brought on one of the biggest fights they'd ever had.

"You'd better decide, am I in charge of the ranch or not?"

Those were the last words, angry and spoken as he turned his back and walked out, that he'd said to his father.

Maybe the last words ever.

He couldn't just wait. And he did have things to do. He left his rooms, went down the back stairs and into the kitchen. It was deserted—today was shopping day— but soon Bettina would be here to begin dinner preparations for those who would be at home. Most of them were considerate enough to stick to the system Piper had started years ago of signing in on the whiteboard by the back door everyone but Fowler used regularly, indicating whether or not they'd be home for the evening meal. As with most things that helped others, Fowler didn't bother.

He tried not to think about the fact that the sign-in system had been Jolie's idea, to help Bettina. She'd been too uncertain of her position to suggest it, but she was friendly enough with Piper to mention it, and his sister had thought it brilliant and run with it.

He began gathering items into a box he found in the utility room, cereal, fruit, a loaf of bread, some cookies he thought Emma might like, then grabbed the cooler he used to bring perishables when he knew he was going to hole up for a while. He emptied the ice maker into it, then added milk, some cold cuts, cheese and anything that looked appetizing. He was going to have to leave an apologetic note to Bettina; she was used to this happening now and then, but not on this scale.

He moved quickly, using the motion to tamp down

unruly emotions. Things had been chaotic enough with his father vanishing, but Jolie's sudden reappearance was the icing on that messy cake.

And Emma.

When he'd thought about what she'd be like, back in the days when he was so confident he would be witnessing every stage of this precious girl's life, he never quite imagined how amazing she would be. Even in this short time he could see she was as smart as her mother, and seeing her look at him with Jolie's big gray eyes was disconcerting. He—

The sound of his phone jolted him out of his reverie. Hannah's name was on the screen. He glanced at the time before he answered, startled to see nearly forty minutes had passed.

As usual, she wasted no time with niceties but got right to what he'd asked for.

"It's all there," she said. "In a trust for the child. Some of the generated income was pulled out in the first couple of years, all in checks made out to a day-care center, but the principal was never touched."

"And the withdrawals stopped?"

"Yes, after the last one over two years ago."

"Thank you, Hannah."

"What I'm here for. Anything else?"

"No. Not now. Except… I'll need my schedule trimmed for the next few days."

"All right."

He heard some clicking, guessed she was pulling up his calendar.

"The only anvil is the auction."

He smiled despite it all; anvil was what she called the immovable objects, the meetings that couldn't be moved or appointments that simply must be kept. It was so appropriate he'd adopted it himself.

"I'll take care of that." He'd send someone with a good eye for horseflesh, he thought. Harlow, maybe. "And I'll keep that appointment with Cyrus Wainwright."

"I'll clear the rest."

"You're a treasure, Hannah."

"Don't you forget it," she said, leaving him feeling rather wistful as they disconnected. As he lugged the box and cooler out front to his SUV, he pondered his indispensable assistant. It was funny how such a razor-sharp, amazingly efficient person was hidden inside that motherly looking woman. And impressive that she was actually both, depending on what was called for. He had no doubts she had been the warm, loving, generous kind of mother, but he also guessed she'd been a fierce protector when necessary.

While his own mother, he thought wryly as he headed across the foyer on his way back to the kitchen to write the note, would simply manipulate someone else to solve the problem. She—

"Mr. Colton!"

He halted at the commanding call. Turned to see Sheriff Troy Watkins, who had the bad luck to be the only one Fowler would talk with regarding their father's disappearance. Deputy and investigator Charlie Kidwell was ostensibly in charge of the investigation, but Fowler was Fowler and only the top law enforcement official in the county was good enough for him to deal with.

"Sheriff Watkins," he said with a respectful nod. T.C. had always liked the man with the steady gaze, and felt badly that he had to play this political game with the likes of Fowler Colton.

"I need to talk to you, if you don't mind."

T.C. was fairly sure whether he minded didn't really play into it. "About?"

"A new suspect in your father's disappearance," Watkins said. "One you'll be able to tell me more about than anyone."

A movement behind the man caught T.C.'s attention. He glanced over Watkins's shoulder and saw his brother. Fowler was standing in the doorway of the salon, looking at him past the cop. Smirking.

He'd really done it. T.C. shifted his gaze back to the detective. He didn't need to ask, and had they been alone he wouldn't have. But that smirk was like a cattle prod, and that was how he reacted.

"So, what crackbrained theory has my brother come up with this time to throw the suspicion off his precious girlfriend?"

In his peripheral vision he saw Fowler jerk upright, knew his jab had hit home. *Yeah, I know what you're all about*, he told him silently.

Watkins looked a bit disconcerted, but when he answered, it was what T.C. had expected.

"Jolie Peters. I need to ask you some questions."

"Then walk with me," he said.

He would text Bettina, he decided. Since she was out anyway, it would be better if she knew right away her stores had been raided. He couldn't stand to be under the same roof as his brother another moment. He gave Fowler a last, disdainful glance, but took some heart in the fact that the smirk had vanished.

"I need some clean air," he added, and turned his back on Fowler Colton.

Chapter 15

Jolie stared down at the picture she held, impossibly moved both by the image and the fact that he'd kept it. She'd found nothing of the few photos there were of her, photos she knew he'd had made into prints for his desk at work and home, but she wouldn't have expected them. In fact, she was sure he'd deleted them in short order after she took off, and probably burned the prints. But this one, this lovely shot she had taken, he'd kept.

The details went blurry as moisture brimmed in her eyes. But it didn't matter; she knew it so well, that picture, because a duplicate of it resided in a upper cupboard in her apartment, still in a frame that matched this one. The image of T.C. holding baby Emma, looking down at her with loving wonder as the tiny girl cooed up at him, was forever etched upon her heart.

The picture was not out for him to see anytime he

was here, but it had been tucked between books on an eye-level—well, for her at least—shelf, and once she'd recognized the frame that matched hers, she hadn't been able to resist the urge. She'd half expected it to be something else, to find he'd replaced the image with something he loved now.

But he hadn't. He'd kept this. Proof that he would never blame an innocent child for the hurt inflicted by her mother.

"What's that?" Emma asked.

She'd been so rapt, so held by this precious image of far happier days, that she hadn't realized Emma had come up beside her.

"Just a picture," she said, sliding the frame back where she'd found it before the child could see the photo. Although it was unlikely she would realize who the baby in the picture was, Jolie didn't want to have to lie to her, and explaining in four-year-old terms was beyond her at the moment. She was searching her mind for a distraction when Emma herself provided it by announcing she was hungry.

"Well, let's see what's here," Jolie said, heading for the kitchen area.

Soon Emma was ensconced in the chair at the small table with some crackers spread with peanut butter.

That single chair, Jolie thought. One chair at the table, one chair to sit in. One coffee mug, one plate, one bowl, and one set of utensils. Double bed, but T.C. was a big guy.

The moment she realized she was taking comfort in the signs that he spent his time here alone, she silently called herself every kind of fool she could think of.

Why don't you go in and see if there's only one tooth-

*brush? Don't you have bigger things to worry about?
Like what if they never find that woman, that killer who
knows where you and Emma live? And what if it really
isn't a coincidence that the poor, murdered woman had
looked like you?*

But who would want to kill her? Even in her worst
years as a reckless kid, she'd never really hurt anyone
but herself. And the one person she'd truly, seriously hurt
was the one helping her now.

She had no answers. Not to any of it. The idea of having to leave the life she'd worked so hard to build, of up-
rooting Emma, of leaving the job she was starting to love,
and brusque Mrs. Amaro, who had trusted her and been
so concerned, telling her not to worry, her job would be
waiting for her when it was safe to come back, was more
than daunting. It was heart-wrenching. But could she risk
Emma by staying?

The only thing she was certain about was that she'd
done the right thing, coming to T.C. For Emma's sake.
He would keep her safe, because that was who he was.
But she was also certain this couldn't go on for long. It
would be beyond unfair to expect him to put up with this
for long, not after what she'd done to him.

With no hope of any immediate solution, she found
herself perusing the shelves of books. On a lower shelf,
toward one end, she found a foot-wide run of books that
surprised her, then warmed her as she realized she should
have known. It was a series of books written about a boy
growing up on a ranch, and each one looked well read and
loved. She pulled one out, and inside the front cover saw
in a bold, boyish hand, a young Tom Colton's signature.
That he'd kept these was a touch of sentimentality that
would surprise anyone who knew him only as a Colton.

But not her. She knew better. And after all, it was that gentleness beneath the tough, decisive, practical exterior that was making him help her now. If she hadn't known it was there, she would never have dared to come to him.

She pulled out the first of the books. Scanned the first few pages. Then she turned to Emma, who had finished her snack and was tidily wiping her fingers on the paper towel Jolie had set out.

"Would you like to hear a story about living on a ranch?"

Emma's eyes brightened. "Like this one?"

"Sort of," Jolie said, guessing there were few ranches that could match the CVR in size and scope, "but in a different state."

"'Kay," the child said.

Moments later they were both comfortably cuddled in T.C.'s big chair, and Jolie began to read aloud. The child listened raptly until the middle of chapter three, when Jolie realized the girl had drifted off to sleep. After last night, another little nap wouldn't hurt, and she gently lifted the child and carried her to the bed. For a moment, in the sleepiness-inducing warmth, she thought of joining her; she'd had even less sleep than Emma. But the thought of lying on a bed where T.C. slept was too much, and she turned and went back to the chair.

As he drove back to the refuge, T.C. mulled over the freakishness of this day, that Jolie was suddenly back in his life, with a vengeance. Coming at him from two sides, his father's situation and hers. What were the odds?

Of course Fowler's accusations were just more of his usual, trying to deflect attention from Tiffany. T.C. wasn't sure the woman was quite clever enough to have thought through a plan to get rid of the old man so as to send Fowler into such turmoil that he would turn to her and finally put a ring on it. But T.C. had heard the rumors, and the investigators had questioned Tiffany more than once, so somebody was taking the idea seriously.

And thus had begun Fowler's campaign to implicate somebody else. Anybody else. T.C. supposed it was a sign that the man really cared about her, deep down. As much as he could care about anyone other than himself, anyway. Although it would be very like Fowler to jettison even his own family to avoid the inconvenience of finding someone who suited him as well as the by turns vacuous and shrewd blonde.

By the time he pulled up outside the refuge, he was no closer to any answers than he had been for three months. And things were only getting more and more complicated. Not to mention that Jolie was messing with his mind, making clear thinking even more difficult.

He'd hoped that if he ever ran into her again he would be cool and uncaring, even dismissive. That had gone up in flames like an oil well fire the moment she walked into his office. Why on earth had he let himself get sucked into this?

And then, the large box in his arms, he awkwardly opened the door. The first thing he saw was Emma, curled up on the bed asleep.

This was why.

His gaze flicked to the chair, where Jolie had apparently been dozing herself. She snapped awake and rose as he set the box down on top of the cabinet.

"She all right?" he asked, nodding toward Emma.

"Yes. It's just been a rough night and day for her."

"And you."

"If it's rough for her, it's rough for me."

He had no doubt that was true.

"You brought a lot." Her voice seemed carefully neutral, and he wasn't sure why. Was she worried she might be stuck here for a while?

"There's milk and cheese and other stuff in a cooler in the car. Want to get that while I bring in the chair?"

She blinked. "Chair?"

He gestured toward the small table. "I figured you'd need another, so I took one from the tack room, where it wouldn't be missed. Oh, and remind me to show you how to use the ranch comm system later, just in case. Your phone won't work on it, but there's a direct intercom from the car to my cell."

"You've...thought of everything."

Except how to get out of this, he thought.

Jolie grabbed the cooler and took it inside while he lifted the wooden chair out of the back of the SUV. He started to take it inside, then stopped. It wouldn't be good for Emma to wake and overhear what had to happen next. So instead he set the chair on the small, covered porch, then went inside and got the other one.

Jolie watched him with a raised brow as he picked it up and headed for the door. He glanced back at Emma, then nodded toward the porch. Whether she thought he simply meant not to disturb the girl, or that they had things to talk about she shouldn't hear, he didn't know. But she followed him, stepping outside. She didn't close the door completely, he presumed so she could hear if Emma called for her.

She was a good mother, in an up-close and personal way. He knew it deep in his bones the same way he knew his own mother hadn't been, had handed off her children to various nannies and tutors, bringing them out occasionally to display as part of what she saw as the complete Colton picture. As a kid he'd envied some of his friends who had warm, loving parents, something he'd kept to himself because he'd learned early on that no one took a Colton envying anyone seriously. Maybe if he'd been born back in the days when the old man was a literal crook...but it was a moot point, given that his mother would never, ever have even considered marrying that incarnation of Eldridge Colton.

Jolie sat down in the chair closest to the door, and he took the other. T.C. swung his feet up to rest on the porch railing. Jolie said nothing, but he could feel her gaze and knew she was watching him, waiting for whatever it was he had to say.

For a moment that irked him; couldn't he just want to sit out here to make sure Emma didn't wake? Why did she assume he had something to say? Why would she think he wanted to talk to her at all?

Except maybe to tell her to go to hell, as his father had often suggested.

You're the one who paid her off.

She's the one who took it and ran.

After about the third exchange like that with his father, he'd never mentioned it—or Jolie—again. He'd kept his pain to himself, outwardly presenting the image he knew his father wanted to see, that of a strong, cool Colton, far above being damaged by a mere love affair gone wrong.

Funny, he'd always treasured Jolie's quietness, how she never felt compelled to fill silences with inane chatter. Yet now he was wishing she was more like his mother, or Tiffany, loath to endure even a moment of silence.

Finally he turned his head to look at her. She met his gaze and still waited, saying nothing.

He let out an audible breath, then, finally, spoke. "You may need to get a lawyer."

Chapter 16

Jolie blinked. Her attention was finally ripped from the sudden heat that had swept her when he swung his feet up to the rail, when she'd had the long, powerful length of his legs right before her eyes. A vivid memory of those legs, muscled, strong and naked as he lay beside her, had taken her breath away.

And then he'd spoken and shattered the vision.

Of all the things she could have imagined him saying, that wouldn't even have been on the list. She was the victim here. She and Emma both were. Why on earth would she need a lawyer?

"You're going to explain that, I hope?" she said when he didn't go on.

His mouth twisted at one corner. Then his feet came down, and his boots hit the planked floor of the porch. He leaned forward to rest his elbows on his knees, still looking at her. "When was the last time you saw my father?"

She drew back, her brow furrowing in puzzlement. "You already asked if I'd seen him. I told you no."

"When?"

"You know perfectly well when I last saw your father."

"The day you took that check."

"Yes."

"You never saw him after that."

She laughed, was a little surprised at how bitter it sounded. She'd thought she'd put that behind her. "Your mother made it quite clear that was a requirement, that I never have contact with a Colton again." She grimaced. "I guess I've blown that."

He didn't react. It hit her then, belatedly.

"Is that what you meant?" she asked, sitting up straighter. "That your mother's going to try and take back Emma's money because I came to you for help?"

He looked startled for an instant, as if that hadn't even occurred to him. That both relieved and unsettled her; if not that, then what?

"My mother has no idea you did, or that you're here," he said, looking away from her. "No one does."

She wondered if that was because he was ashamed he'd done it. She wouldn't blame him for that. There were some—with his own brother Fowler at the top of the list, along with his uncharming sister Marceline—who would likely call him a Texas-sized fool for having anything to do with her. It could, she realized belatedly, even call his judgment into question, which in turn could cause him problems at work; if Fowler found out he had—

"Fowler," he said, startling her since the man had that instant been in her thoughts, "has sicced the investigators on yet another new suspect in my father's disappearance."

"Another?"

"He's been trying to steer them off Tiffany."

Jolie drew back slightly. "Is she really a suspect?"

"She's on the list. Which is silly. I don't think she's smart enough to have pulled this off." He looked back at her then. "But you are."

She got it then. "What? You mean Fowler aimed them at me?"

He nodded. "He told me his new theory Tuesday, after he spotted you in the city."

Fowler had been that close to her, close enough to recognize her? Immediately she started trying to figure out where he could have seen her.

But T.C. gave her no time to dwell on it. "I never thought he'd really do it. But they were at the house when I got there."

She opened her mouth, but the only thing she could think of to ask was if he believed it. She wasn't sure she wanted the answer. But surely he would have brought the law here if he did. Wouldn't he?

Had he?

"Should I be expecting them to come over the hill at any moment?"

"They don't know you're here, either."

"You didn't tell them where I was?"

"No."

She was relieved, but not surprised. Never mind her; he wouldn't do that to Emma, make her witness her mother being handcuffed and led away under arrest for kidnapping and possibly murder.

"Would you have, if not for Emma?"

"No."

"Why?"

"Because I don't believe it."

The rush of emotion that flooded her at that simple declaration didn't just surprise her, it astonished her. It wasn't just relief at not having investigators, or having Fowler and the sheriff himself, bearing down on her with the destruction of her entire life in the offing, or even the simple demonstration of faith in her...

It was that it was coming from him.

"Why?" she repeated, staring at him with no small amount of wonder.

"You're many things, Jolie Peters, a liar and an opportunist among them. But you're not a kidnapper or a killer."

That quickly he stung her back to reality. "I'm not a liar," she said, knowing she couldn't really honestly deny the opportunist tag.

He let out a disgusted-sounding chuckle. "Aren't you? Wasn't the entire time we spent together a lie?"

"No." She sounded sad, miserable even to herself. "None of it was."

"Then why—"

He cut himself off as if he hadn't meant to let even that much out.

"For the same reason you're helping me now. Emma. I told you that."

He was silent, probably regretting he'd let even that tiny bit of emotion show.

"What did your brother tell them?"

"Just his suspicions. That you'd come back to the old man for more money, he'd turned you down and you killed him."

It was so absurd she couldn't get up even a little outrage. In fact, she nearly laughed aloud. "Based on what?"

"I told you, he saw you in town."

"And?"

He shrugged. "That's it."

She blinked. Drew back slightly. "So your brother's accusation that I kidnapped and murdered your father is based solely on the fact that I'm still alive and in Dallas?"

"Pretty much."

"Well, gee," she drawled, "I don't know why you wouldn't believe it, then."

She thought she saw one corner of his mouth twitch. "You've gotten cheeky."

"If you mean I don't let fear run my life, then yes, I guess so. I've lived there, and I'm never going back." She turned in the chair to face him head-on. "I never lied to you, T.C. I meant everything I said and did."

"But you still left."

"I explained why. If my child's well-being isn't enough reason for you, so be it."

"You could have come to me."

"And you would have been trapped between me and your parents. How would that have worked out?"

His jaw tightened. "We'll never know, will we? Since you didn't trust me enough to even give me the chance."

"If it had just been me, I would have. But your mother's threats to Emma changed everything."

He let out a long breath but said nothing. He turned his gaze out over the land she knew he loved more than any material thing in this world. She wondered what was in his mind now, what he wasn't saying. He'd always said she'd read him too well, but right now he could have been a blank book for all she could tell.

After a long, silent moment, she asked, "Did you wonder? If Fowler was right?"

"For maybe a minute."

She appreciated that he didn't deny he had wondered at all, but then, T.C. always was honest. Unlike his scheming brother. "I'm glad you came to the right conclusion."

He gave her a sideways glance. "You told the truth about the money."

So, she thought. He'd pulled some of those vast Colton strings and checked up on her story. She should have known he would. Not that it mattered, since it had been all true.

"Yes."

"You really never touched it."

"It's not mine. In my mind, it never was."

And neither were you. You were my impossible dream. And then reality bit.

"It would have made your life easier."

"I didn't want easier."

He studied her for a moment. She could see him thinking, assessing. And as usual, when he arrived at his conclusion, he was right.

"Self-punishment, Jolie?"

She gave a half shrug. She looked out over the terrain because she couldn't face him just now. "I was doing something I would probably find…shameful, if not despicable, in someone else. I let myself be bullied, when I swore I never would again."

"Because of Emma."

A vision of her sweet, innocent child formed in her mind. She smiled, because she always did when she thought of her sweet girl. "She doesn't deserve to suffer for my poor choices in life."

He straightened. "So that's what I was? A poor choice?"

Jolie's gaze snapped to his face. "I was talking about her father."

His gaze narrowed for an instant, he started to speak, stopped, then said—and rather lamely, for him—"Oh." There was another long silence before he said, "You never talked about him much except to say he wasn't in the picture."

"I don't talk about the time I crashed my foster dad's car when I was twelve, either."

"I'll bet that went over well."

She heard the smile in his voice. Supposed that for a Colton, wrecking a car was no big deal.

"It was a good thing he was a dog lover," she said.

"Let me guess. You swerved to avoid one?"

She shook her head. "I was trying to take one to the vet. He got hit in front of the house, and no one would help."

"Even your foster dad?"

"He was sick by then." Her lips tightened at the memory. "Really sick. He couldn't do anything."

"I'm sorry."

"So was I. He was the best. Living with them was the only time I really felt like I had a home. They wanted to adopt me, but then he got cancer."

He was quiet for a moment before he said, "You've never told me any of this. All you ever said was that being in the system sucked."

"It did."

"And that's why you're so determined Emma will have a better life."

She met his gaze, nodded. "She will never, ever have to live like that."

"So you really did do it for her."

"I would do anything for her."

Something flashed in his eyes, something quick, urgent, and as hot as a Texas summer sky. And suddenly it was all there again, hovering between them, the fire they'd found together, the unexpected bliss that had had her thinking of forever for the first time in her troubled life.

He repeated what he'd said earlier, in the same flat tone. "Would you."

And again it wasn't really a question. But this time the rumbling undertone from deep in his chest set every one of her long-dormant senses reeling. Because that was how he'd said her name when they were locked together, when his body was moving on her and in her, when he'd sent her spiraling toward that explosion of exquisite sensation she'd only ever known with him.

Was he asking if she would sleep with him again, in return for his help? The man she'd loved never would, but after what she'd done to him, maybe he wasn't that man anymore.

And God help her, if he did ask, would she?

The thought of experiencing that joy even just one more time was more tempting than she could have ever imagined. And the pain afterward would be even worse than it had been, she told herself, fighting her own response to the images that flashed through her mind.

She struggled to find something, anything to say. And then he rose abruptly, putting an end to the moment with a harsh reminder of the turn her life had taken. "You'd better think about talking to that lawyer. Fowler's got a lot of pull in this town."

"I don't have a lawyer." She hated how helpless she sounded, but it was the truth. "I'm not sure I even know anyone with a lawyer."

He chuckled, but it was not an amused sound. "You know me. And the Coltons have a cadre of them."

Her mouth twisted wryly. "The kind who'd deal with murder accusations?"

He looked thoughtful at that. "I'll talk to Hugh Barrington, Dad's guy. He'll likely know someone."

"You don't have to—" She stopped herself, realizing if Fowler was determined to throw her to the wolves, she would need the best help she could get. She couldn't afford it of course, but she could afford to go to jail and have Emma go straight into the very system she loathed even less. She would just have to find a way.

"Thank you," she said instead.

He looked at her for a long moment, a touch of wonder in his eyes that she didn't understand.

"You really would do anything for her sake, wouldn't you?"

She got it then, that look. Because she couldn't imagine Whitney Colton disturbing her spoiled life for anyone, not even—or perhaps especially—her own children.

And in that moment she wasn't sure if, despite the Colton wealth, he'd had it all that much better than she had.

Chapter 17

T.C. got up from the family table when his phone rang, glad of the excuse. He hated being there, thinking of Jolie and Emma alone at the refuge. They would be safe there, but they should have been safe at home, too. He should look into Colton Incorporated putting a bit more investment into the neighborhood. Maybe he would when he got back to the office. It wasn't his bailiwick, but he had some input. And he'd always felt pride in the neighborhood was the key to revitalization.

He waited until he was outside on the rear patio to pull the phone out. His pulse gave a kick when he saw the screen.

"Manny," he said.

"Hey, buddy. Only got a minute, we've got a situation brewing Uptown, but what's up with your girl?"

Uh-oh, he thought. And ignored the spike of…something that shot through him when Manny called Jolie his girl. "Meaning?"

"I ran into Charlie Kidwell at the shooting range. He was bitching about your bro calling his boss the sheriff, and sending them off on another chase. After your old girlfriend."

At least it doesn't sound like either Watkins or Kidwell was taking it that *seriously.* "So I heard."

"You didn't mention you and she had history."

T.C. felt a twinge of guilt. "Years ago. And I had no idea Fowler was going to pull this out of his Stetson. It's crazy."

"What's this about an extortion, years ago?"

"It's a long story. And it wasn't extortion, it was…like I said, long story. But she has nothing to do with it now."

"You're sure?"

"I am."

"She's got an alibi? For the time your father went missing?"

Well, that *should have been higher on the priority list,* T.C. thought. And felt a bit foolish that it hadn't even occurred to him to ask where she'd been at the time. "We're working on that. It has been three months," he told Manny.

"All right, buddy. As long as you're thinking with the right head, y'know?"

That moment on the porch flashed through his mind. His body's response was instant and fierce.

"She's a fine-looking woman," Manny said at his silence.

"Yes. And she also dumped me, so yeah, I'm thinking straight."

"Whoa. Sorry, man." Manny hastened to leave the

subject behind. "Anyway, I didn't tell him you had her, but I don't feel right about it."

"Thanks, my friend. I'm going to get her a lawyer. Then we'll talk to him. Tell him, if you need to. I don't want you caught in the middle of this."

"I will, when I see him again. Which I can avoid for a while," Manny said, and T.C. could almost see him grinning. "He's not a bad guy. He thinks your brother's a bit of a jerk, though."

"Then he's smart, as well," T.C. said.

"He is. So don't keep him waiting too long."

Well, T.C. thought as he ended the call, that was one very big one he owed his old friend. Cowboys tickets maybe, since it looked like they were headed for the play-offs this year. Manny'd love that, as would his son.

He didn't go back to the table. He'd eaten enough, and had enough of the family. His mother had found a new psychic to consult, and apparently after initially reject-ing her silly vision of the old man happily chomping on a pastrami sandwich, she had decided the woman was right and gone back for more. Who knew how much she'd pad the charlatan's bank account before she gave up and switched to the next one? He felt for his mother, and told himself this was a strong indication she'd had nothing to do with this and genuinely cared for his father, but he still didn't want to hear any more of that.

Besides, it was only a matter of time before Fowler started in on his new theory, and the very last thing T.C. wanted was to listen to opinions of Jolie flying around the Colton table.

He fought the urge to jump in the truck and head for the refuge. Somebody would surely notice, and it might lead them to Jolie and Emma. And that would bring on questions he didn't want to answer.

Questions he wasn't sure he had answers for.

He retreated to his rooms, not liking the word even as he thought it. Retreat wasn't in his nature, but when he was confronting his family, it sometimes seemed the only course to take. He hadn't wanted to be here for dinner at all, but he'd signed in this morning and he didn't want anyone wondering what had come up at the last minute. He didn't want anyone wondering anything, at the moment.

He was soon pacing again, but he didn't fight it this time; it helped him think. He had an appointment with Hugh Barrington tomorrow afternoon, at his office near the Colton building. If the sheriff took Fowler's accusations seriously, which he would, since Fowler was a Colton—and according to Manny, Kidwell would follow all leads anyway—Jolie was going to need someone to stand for her.

He was thankful she'd been talking with the staff worker at the day care when the woman in the alley was murdered, or she might be in even more trouble. Being a suspect in two murders was not a pleasant prospect. If Fowler ever realized there was a chance of that, who knew what he might do? He'd certainly crossed ethical and moral boundaries before. And he'd already demonstrated he was desperate to throw suspicion off Tiffany.

T.C. was honest enough with himself to admit that while keeping Jolie and Emma safe was the goal, thwarting Fowler would be the icing on the cake. He'd long ago given up trying to get along with his half brother. They were just too different, had nothing in common except their father and a name. He had no choice about butting heads with him at work, Fowler did outrank him by a step and never hesitated to use that, but T.C. could avoid him at home, and did his best to accomplish that.

Thóughts still swirling, he finally tugged off his boots and stretched out on his bed, even though he knew he was far from being able to sleep. It was still early anyway, barely nine.

He heard a light tap on his door. Piper, he guessed, since Alanna had been out with Jake tonight, and his brothers wouldn't have been so gentle about it. Since she was the only sibling he thought he could face tonight, he got up. Halfway to the door, it occurred to him it could be Bettina, asking about his raiding of the stores. He wondered what the woman would say if he told her it had been for her erstwhile assistant. She had always liked Jolie, and had adored having baby Emma in the house. It had been Bettina who overcame his mother's objections to hiring Jolie in the first place, and Eldridge had sided with the cook. "The kitchen's her domain. Let her run it," he'd said.

T.C. hadn't been surprised. Eldridge liked things the way he liked them, and after all these years Bettina knew his preferences inside out and made sure things were done to his satisfaction. His father might cater to his wife's wishes, but only when it didn't inconvenience him too much.

He pulled open the door and saw his first guess had been right: Piper.

"You all right?" she said.

"Yeah."

"You kind of vanished. I thought maybe that phone call was bad news."

"Just complications," he said. Then, with the best

smile he could muster for this woman who had been the only one to reach out to Jolie when she worked here, perhaps as an orphan herself feeling more akin to her than her adopted siblings, he added, "Thanks for worrying, Pipe."

She grinned at him. "We good Coltons have to stick together."

He grinned back. "We outnumber them," he reminded her.

"Five to two," she said, right on cue.

"Five to four if you count the parents."

They both laughed at the old exchange, but there was a lot of truth in it. So often he, Piper, Alanna, Reid and Zane felt like allies against their own half siblings Fowler and Marceline, and their machinations. Those two had learned too well from their respective parents, and made life generally miserable for those around them.

After she'd gone, T.C. walked over to the window by his desk. The moon was full now. Hunter's moon, he thought. And although the silver light was very different, casting everything into stark contrast, it was so bright he could see almost as well as in daylight. It was the kind of night he'd waited for as a kid—and even now, truth be told—often sneaking out for a midnight ride across the ranch.

He was suddenly seized with the urge to do just that. He scoffed at himself; he was long past the point where a belting race in the moonlight would solve his problems. But then, it had never been about solving the problems, but only about getting his thoughts about them straight in his head. And nothing did that better than being out alone on a horse in the moonlight when the night was still and the heat of the day fading.

No one would think it odd, although his nighttime rides had become rarer as his work life took up so much more time. And Fowler certainly wasn't about to follow him or send anyone to follow him if he went on horseback; the man didn't get any closer to a horse or cow than necessary to maintain the Colton image.

He wavered for a moment. Then it struck him that it would solve three of his problems instantly. The need to do something, anything. The urge to go to the refuge. And his promise to Emma that she would meet the horse so like the one she'd drawn.

The scales tipped. Decided now, he swiftly changed clothes, into his favorite jeans and the worn boots with the stirrup marks up the inside instep. Just pulling them on made him feel better, and he knew he'd made the right decision. For Emma, he told himself. Although she would be asleep when he arrived, Flash would be there in the morning.

He stopped dead in the act of zipping his jeans.

In the morning.

Was he planning on spending the night? On some level, had he made that decision without even consciously thinking about it? What the hell *was* he thinking? Was he going to push Jolie to see if she really would have sex with him if that was his price for helping them?

Heat blasted through him. Finishing zipping his jeans suddenly became problematic.

You really are a Texas-sized fool, Colton.

What else could explain why, of all the women in the world he could have, only this one got to him like this? Why was it only this one sent his senses spinning and his body out of control at the mere thought of having her naked in his arms again?

He hadn't been celibate since she was gone. At least, his body hadn't been. Right at this moment he wasn't so sure about his mind, and he'd given up trying to keep his heart in line.

"I would do anything..."

Would she? Really?

He forced the zipper up the rest of the way with a grimace. He took his dark gray Stetson off the peg on the wall rack, more out of habit than need. He grabbed a few things and stuffed them into the hand-tooled saddlebags that hung from the next peg. He slung them over his shoulder and headed out, down the back stairs and off to the stables.

Flash welcomed him with a soft nicker; the amiable horse was always up for an adventure, and seemed to relish these moonlight rides as much as T.C. did. It was as if he knew work was work, but this was play, and reacted accordingly. T.C. had even sometimes wondered if the horse knew his black-and-white markings made him blend into his surroundings in the silver moonlight, and maybe he felt safer.

He put the saddlebags over the bottom half of the stall door, and gave the dark-eyed animal an affectionate rub under the jaw. The horse bobbed his head in appreciation.

He walked to the tack room to get his saddle. No fancy, silver-trimmed parade saddle for him; Flash was gaudy enough already. He lifted his worn but well-cared-for stock saddle from the rack. He'd forgo the flank cinch, he thought; no heavy roping this ride. He stuck a brush under his arm and a currycomb in his back pocket, then grabbed the thick black saddle pad and turned to head back to Flash's stall.

He stopped midstride when he thought he heard a rustling from the end stall next to the tack room. His brow furrowed. It should be empty; they'd moved Marceline's Queenie to a smaller stall after she turned up lame and the vet suggested it to keep her from moving too much until she healed.

But he heard nothing more and decided he must have heard an echo of one of the other horses moving around. He went back to Flash's stall and began to run the curry-comb over the paint's dramatically colored coat. He noticed some straw clinging to the animal's flowing white tail, and realized it was time to trim the thing. It looked great in a show ring, but it was a nuisance for ranch work, and that was their life now. He'd brush it out for now and leave it; Emma would probably like the flowing tail that was so like her beloved toy ponies.

Emma.

The odd tightness returned to his chest. He hadn't realized quite how big a hole the little girl had left in him. She—

The rustling came again, and this time from where he stood he was certain it had come from the empty stall.

He put down the brush he'd picked up and started toward the sound. Then he hesitated for a moment. After all, his father had been grabbed from the house; who was to say the perpetrator hadn't come back? It wasn't like he was carrying, although he'd thought about it more than once since that night. He knew Fowler was always armed now, terrified he'd be next. Or at least saying so, but that could be to throw suspicion off himself. But the only thing T.C. had with him was the folding knife he always carried, in his mind an essential on the ranch.

Then again, the sound could be a possum, or a stray armadillo or something. Hopefully not a skunk, he thought with an inward grimace. That was one black-and-white creature he preferred to leave alone whenever possible.

"Whoever or whatever you are, get out of there," he said, easing the knife out of the sheath and into his hand, ready to flip the four-inch blade open in an instant.

"Oh! T.C.!"

He blinked, startled to hear Marceline's voice coming from the darkness of the stall. And curious about how relieved she sounded; they didn't get along well enough for her to be glad to see him.

She emerged from the stall looking uncharacteristically flustered. Her silk blouse was half-untucked, her usually perfect hair mussed. And, he noticed, festooned with straw.

"What are you doing out here at this hour?" he asked, slipping the knife back into the sheath on his belt.

"I could ask you the same thing," she retorted, trying futilely to tidy herself. And, he realized, looking very, very guilty.

"I'm going for a ride," he said, jerking a thumb toward Flash's stall with the saddle in plain sight.

"You and your midnight rides. You'd think you were Paul Revere or something."

"I don't think he ever rode a horse like Flash," he said, wondering why she was dodging his question. "You know until we know what happened to Dad you shouldn't be out alone."

"I'm not—" She cut herself off, and he could have sworn her gaze darted to the side, back toward the stall she'd emerged from. Had she not been alone? But who the hell—

"You're here alone," she pointed out, clearly back on track, and on the offensive.

"That's different and you know it."

"Because you're a big, strong man?" Her tone dripped acid, but it seemed a little forced.

"Fact of life."

"Just forget it. Go on your ride."

"When you tell me who else is in there," he said with a gesture toward the stall.

"No one, not that it's any of your business." Her nose came up. "I just came down to check on Queenie. I'm worried about her."

That stopped him. If Marceline had one saving grace, it was that she did genuinely care about that horse. More than most people, he suspected. But it was the only reason he tolerated her at all. "Dr. Daniels says she'll be fine."

"I still wanted to check on her."

"But she's not in that stall anymore."

"I forgot," she snapped. "Honestly, T.C., just go on your ride and quit butting into my business."

She turned on her heel in the imperious, dismissive way only Marceline could do, and stalked away.

T.C. puzzled over her odd presence and actions as he tacked up Flash and brought the horse out into the stable aisle. He made a quick check of the horse's hooves, then led him outside into the moonlight. The animal was alert, ready, knowing what was coming, a good, free run through the night.

He swung aboard and settled into the seat, the saddle feeling familiar and comfortable; if this thing was a car it would have a hundred thousand miles on it and be ready for that many more. Best money he'd ever spent, having it custom-made down in San Angelo. He and Flash could put in a sixteen-hour day and there wouldn't be a sign of a rub or tender spot on the horse when they were done.

He barely had to lift the reins before the horse eagerly started out of the stable yard. And when T.C. pulled him back suddenly, he let out a startled snort of protest. But a movement at the edge of his vision had turned him around in the saddle. Just in time to see a man darting from the stable into the darkness, heading quickly back toward the main barns and the bunkhouse.

T.C. blinked.

Dylan Harlow? He had been the one in the stall with Marceline?

He frowned. That made no sense. If it was anyone but his snotty, snobby half sister he would have guessed at a secretive, romantic tryst—God knows he and Jolie had indulged in an empty stall more than once, and the memories had the power to tighten his gut and other body parts—but Marceline was the last person on earth to ever get involved with a mere ranch hand. Which left her being up to something else, one of her schemes. It would explain why she dodged his questions.

On the other hand, he'd always thought Harlow a straight-up guy, loyal and not prone to deviousness, so what on earth would he be doing plotting with Marceline?

What the hell was she up to?

Chapter 18

"Mommy, Mommy, wake up, he's here!"

Jolie opened her eyes to the excited exclamation of her daughter. She couldn't help smiling, albeit sleepily, at the expression of exuberant joy on her face.

And then memory flooded back and she jolted upright. The refuge. T.C.'s place.

His bed, where Emma had slept peacefully and Jolie had at last surrendered to exhaustion and curled herself protectively around her little girl. She glanced around the room, expecting to see him despite the fact that she knew she would have sensed it if he was there. T. C. Colton wasn't the domineering, attention-demanding Colton Fowler was, but to her he was much more of a presence, quietly taking up a good bit of the air in any room he was in.

Or maybe it was simply that she had trouble breathing around him.

On that rueful thought Jolie swung her feet to the floor while Emma waited with clear impatience. The child was up and dressed in jeans and a T-shirt, although she was still barefoot.

"Hurry, Mommy, I wanna go see him!"

This seemed a new sort of enthusiasm. Caution spiked through her. "See who?"

"The horse, of course." As if she'd just heard the sound of what she'd said, the girl giggled.

"The horse…?"

"The man brought him." The child gestured toward the door. Only then did Jolie notice the blanket on the floor, and a second rolled up into a makeshift pillow at one end.

"He's back," she murmured. He'd slept there, so close, and she hadn't awakened? It seemed impossible.

"He was there when I waked up," Emma explained, practically wiggling in her eagerness to get outside. "Hurry, Mommy," she urged again.

"I'm surprised you're not already out there," Jolie said wryly, realizing the shower she'd been pondering was going to have to wait.

"He told me wait. Till you waked up. 'Cuz you'd be scared."

The simple thoughtfulness nearly put her on her knees. Because he knew had she waked to find Emma gone, she would have been more than scared; she would have been terrified. And likely would have panicked.

It just proved what she'd already known: T. C. Colton was, at heart, a kind man. He might be tough as nails in business dealings, smart enough to outmaneuver even Fowler on occasion and strong enough to work as hard and long as any ranch hand, but at the core he was still the kind, decent man she'd fallen in love with. That she'd destroyed his love for her hadn't changed that, and she was glad to know it. Especially since that was what was making him help her. Well, that and the possibility that he had never stopped loving Emma.

"You'd better get your shoes on, then."

"My boots!"

The girl ran to where her backpack leaned against the wall. Jolie smiled; the inexpensive but adorable pair of tiny red cowboy boots were hardly designed to stand up to an actual horse, but they were Emma's favorite footwear, and she would wear them daily if allowed.

The child plopped on the floor to pull them on. Jolie noticed she was starting with the wrong boot for her left foot, but she waited, saying nothing. And a few seconds later Emma frowned, pulled the boot off and then back onto her other foot, having realized her mistake.

Jolie felt a spurt of both pride and regret, pride at how bright and quick her girl was, and a regret that she was growing and learning so quickly it seemed each precious stage lasted only moments. One minute Jolie was carefully dressing her, the next the girl was doing it herself in a rush. And doing it well, the occasional mismatched sock or inside-out T-shirt not withstanding.

She tugged her own shoes back on, glad she'd had on her one pair of sturdy leather slip-ons when chaos erupted last night. Once it was clear Jolie was up and moving, Emma raced to the door. She glanced back, clearly impatient. But in this new, strange place, Jolie didn't want the girl outside without her, at least for now. She gave up on any other effort at making herself presentable, settling for running her fingers through her hair until it felt a bit less sleep-tangled, and being thankful she'd at least washed her face last night so she shouldn't have raccoon eyes this morning.

Not, she told herself with a wry, inward grimace, that it mattered. It wasn't like she had to look nice for T.C. She could be the hottest female on the planet, and it would make no difference to him, after what she'd done. He just wasn't that kind of guy.

Unless he decided he really did want that payback.

She shivered despite the morning warmth at the cold-bloodedness of that idea. Perhaps she should rethink that. Maybe he really was that angry still. But if he was, he wouldn't have helped them, would he?

No, he would have helped Emma. She knew that.

But it didn't mean he wouldn't exact a price from Emma's mother.

Then so be it.

She steeled her spine and followed the girl, who had finally broken and pulled the door open. She stepped out onto the porch. Stopped. And found herself smiling widely.

He was so familiar, this well-named paint horse who was saddled and ground-tied beside the porch. And to her shock, he lifted his head and looked at her, then nickered softly, as if he remembered her. That was impossible, surely? Then again, dogs remembered people after years away, so why not horses?

Emma was looking at the horse, clearly awestruck.

"He really is my horsie I drew," she said, reverting to the childish term she'd left behind a few months ago when Jolie explained the difference between horses and ponies.

T.C. swept off his gray Stetson and bowed to Emma with a flourish. "Miss Emma Peters, may I present CVR Moonlit Shadow. But since that's a bit much for an ol' ranch horse, we just call him Flash."

Emma giggled. "'Cuz he's pretty?"

"Because he's the quickest darned cow horse I've ever ridden." He leaned toward her and added in a conspiratorial whisper, "He's also the biggest clown."

Emma giggled again. She was clearly charmed, probably as much by the man as the horse. Who wouldn't be? T.C. was charming. And if you just happened to meet him, with no knowledge of his background, you would never guess he came from one of the most powerful families not just in Dallas, but all of Texas. It was the thing that had drawn her to him in the beginning, that utter lack of pretension.

She sighed. Painfully. She wondered if there was a drug to treat chronic nostalgia.

He glanced at her then. His expression narrowed, and she felt color flood her cheeks. She could only imagine what her face had looked like as her heart had filled with longing and need for those days when he had loved her. And in that moment she thought that if he did demand that payment for his help, she would give it gladly, grateful for the chance to hold him once more, to feel the wonder they'd found together.

And then reality rushed back in. Although she doubted T.C. was capable of intentional cruelty, she also doubted it would be the tender, loving thing it once had been. She'd hurt him too badly, and while he was an incredible man, he was also human. How could he not have changed toward her? And did she really want to risk the sweetness of those memories, to perhaps have them replaced with something colder, harsher?

The answer to that was simple.

Withstanding the urge was not.

T.C. busied himself snugging up the cinch. He stared at the latigo for a long moment after he'd properly looped and tucked it, as if he'd never seen the strip of leather before. But he wasn't really seeing it at all. The image of that look on Jolie's face was taking up every inch of his mind.

This is the woman who took a payoff to dump you.

The stark reminder was one he'd used whenever she popped into his mind when his guard was down. Which meant he'd used it often over the years. It had always worked.

But now, with her standing a bare yard away, it seemed to have lost its effectiveness. Not to mention that her version of the story, including the threats to Emma, cast the entire episode in a different light. Normally he had little patience for fools who justified disastrous results with their motivation, but he had to admit that when it came to protecting your child, all bets were off.

His gaze shifted to Emma, who was gazing up at Flash in rapt wonder. He was going to have to have a long talk with his mother about her actions that day. He hadn't yet because of the situation with his father, and he hadn't wanted her wondering why he was suddenly asking about Jolie. Not with Fowler tossing out stupid accusations.

Then again, perhaps now, when she might be too distracted and consumed with the old man's disappearance to fudge about something from years ago, would be the best time to corner her and demand some straight answers. He could tell her Fowler's idiocy had brought it all back.

As if it had ever really left him.

He gave a sharp shake of his head and smiled at the little girl. "What do you think, Emma? Would you like to go for a ride?"

The girl seemed struck speechless, but she nodded

rapidly. T.C. glanced at Jolie, who apparently had her emotions in check now. Or perhaps he'd misread them moments ago; perhaps he'd only imagined that she'd looked at him as she once had, with all the longing of a woman in love.

Or perhaps she was merely remembering how it had been. That didn't mean she was yearning to return to that. Nor did it mean her feelings had been real back then. Maybe it just seemed that way to her in retrospect.

He realized suddenly he was thinking of it all analytically, and wondered if this dispassionate assessment was merely a way to keep his own emotions in check. Wondered why the compartmentalization that always worked for him didn't seem to be working now.

He gave himself an inward shake. *Focus*, he ordered silently.

He looked back at Jolie and merely lifted an eyebrow. "With me, I think, at first?" She had ridden the amiable horse before, but she'd as much as said she hadn't been aboard a horse since.

After a bare instant, she nodded. "I'm way too rusty to risk it. And I was never at your level anyway."

He didn't answer that, just turned and swung up into the saddle. Then he leaned far down and held his hand out to the child.

"I'll pull you up," he told her. "You just hang on and let me do it."

She nodded with an utter faith that sent another jolt of sweet memory through him. He'd so often thought of future times like this, of days of showing this precious child the things that he loved, of guiding her and teaching her. And he'd been more than a little surprised at how much he regretted that loss, after Jolie had taken her and run.

The feel of her little hand in his, so trusting, the way his big hand wrapped around the delicateness of her arm as he grasped it to pull her up into the saddle, made him want to be all the more gentle with her, although he doubted the girl was as fragile as his heart was saying she was.

He swung her up and settled her in the saddle in front of him in one smooth motion. The girl gave a delighted shriek, which settled into happy giggling once she was astride the big paint. A lesser animal than Flash might have shied away from the high-pitched sounds, but the big gelding remained unruffled.

"Look, Mommy! I'm up so high!"

Jolie gave her daughter a smile that nearly made T.C.'s stomach knot up all over again.

"Yes, you are. He's a big sweetie, Flash is."

Emma giggled again.

"All right," T.C. said, still having to work to focus on the matter at hand. "Now pay attention to how he moves, Emma. And how it feels. You'll get so you can move with him, and it will start to feel natural."

"Are we gonna run?" She sounded both excited and fearful.

"Gallop, and not yet. Slow first."

"'Kay."

He lifted the reins gently. Flash seemed to realize this was different, or else he'd taken the edge off in that moonlight run last night. The big horse set out sedately, once more taking Emma's delighted squeal in stride.

This was how it would have been, T.C. thought, if Jolie hadn't given in to his parents.

But she had. They hadn't been worth fighting for to

her. She hadn't come to him for help, hadn't trusted him enough to stand against his parents.

"And you would have been trapped between me and your parents."

Jolie's words came back to him then, and he knew there was truth in them, that it was part of her reason at least. How many times had she told him, when he would complain about his father's authoritarianism or his mother's smug snobbery, to lighten up? That at least he had his parents, and he should treasure that.

Emma looked up at him, with that kind of untainted delight and happiness only a child seemed able to muster.

"I couldn't take that risk. Not with Emma."

No, she couldn't. She wouldn't. He knew that now. Because neither could he.

He smiled back at the girl. The smile became a grin; he couldn't help it. For this sweet moment, none of the rest mattered.

Chapter 19

"Where were you the night of July seventh?"

Jolie's brow furrowed. He'd spoken quietly without looking at her; all his attention was on Emma, who was standing atop a crate and busily brushing Flash. The horse was utterly trustworthy, he'd told her, but that didn't preclude something startling the animal into a reflexive action, so he was watching them both like one of the red-tailed hawks she'd often seen overhead.

"I don't…that was three months ago, and July was crazy with banquets and summer stuff, plus Emma. I'd have to—" She stopped suddenly, realizing why he'd asked. "That was the night…your father?"

He nodded, with a glance at her. "And you need… something that can be verified."

He was being careful for Emma's sake, but she knew what he meant. An alibi. Something she'd never, ever expected to need, especially for something as horrible as kidnapping and possibly murder.

"I think I know," she said. "But to be sure, I'd have to look it up in my planner. And it's at home. I didn't think to grab it."

"No reason to," he said equably, focused again on Emma, who was lovingly brushing the black-and-white mane now. Flash himself appeared to be dozing, as if the child's ministrations were lulling him to sleep. "It's not on your phone?" he asked.

She gave him a sideways look. "A smartphone isn't in my budget."

It stung to say, but it was what it was, and something that would never occur to a Colton. And his expression did change, but to her confusion it was to something that almost looked like admiration.

"I'll pick it up when I go in to see the attorney this afternoon." He flicked a glance at her again. "If you trust me with the key."

She nearly laughed. "I've trusted you with my daughter's safety. My house key is way down on that list."

Something changed in his voice then, and suddenly it was as if these last four years had never intervened; he was using that tone that told her he was deadly serious about what he was saying.

"You can trust me with her, Jolie. I would never, ever let anything happen to her. Not by my mother's hand or anyone else's."

"How about the system she'd end up in if Fowler manages to convince them I did it?" she said, all the worries she'd been fighting off suddenly flooding out.

"He won't."

"Sorry, I've seen too many of your brother's schemes

succeed." She sounded bleak even to herself. "And Emma has no one but me."

And then T.C. reached out and took her hand. He kept his eyes on Emma and the big horse, but he clasped her fingers gently, warmly in his long, strong ones. That he never looked away from Emma warmed her as much as the unexpected touch.

"She has me, Jolie. And she will never go into that system you hate, even if the worst happens. If I have to use every ounce of power and money the Colton name can wield, she never will. I promise you that."

Shaken, Jolie stared at him. At the familiar and loved profile, dark hair, well-proportioned nose, the full, dark sweep of his lashes, the strong jaw, the mouth that could drive her insane. And she knew he meant every word. He would take care of Emma, if the worst were to happen.

"And you keep your promises," she whispered, her throat so tight she couldn't have said it any louder anyway.

He looked at her then, and all the memories, bliss and pain, fairly crackled between them.

"Yes," he said simply.

It seemed strange to be so close to the office and not go in, but T.C. drove past with barely a glance. He was intent on his destination a few blocks over. Hugh Barrington had a large office in a glass-sided building almost within sight of Colton, a place furnished with an opulence and blatancy he didn't care for. But Barrington made no excuses for it; in fact, often spoke of how he'd hired one of the most expensive interior designers in the city and told her to "Make it look like I'm the most successful attorney in Dallas, because I intend to be."

While he appreciated the philosophy and approach, T.C. also knew that a large part of the reason that gamble had paid off was that the newly minted lawyer had taken another risk early on: agreeing to work for onetime criminal Eldridge Colton. Barrington had been right there as Eldridge parlayed his first wife's wealth into building up the ranch, then struck oil, and they had both ridden it to the top. Despite the twenty-year gap in their ages, the partnership had lasted decades now, and Barrington was T.C.'s father's oldest and closest friend.

Probably because they operated on about the same ethical level, T.C. thought dryly as he opened the heavy, solid wooden door deeply etched with just Barrington's name—T.C. had always figured that was his way of saying if you didn't know who he was already you had no business being there—in gold in an elegant script. No removable door plate for him; if he went, the very expensive door went with him.

Barrington didn't keep him waiting, T.C. was a Colton and the man knew where his bread was buttered. In fact, he came out of his inner office—which was even more ostentatious than the reception area—himself to greet him.

The fifty-two-year old Barrington was about Eldridge's height, which made him noticeably shorter than T.C. His hair was determinedly dark, but still thick, and his silver-framed glasses masked slightly the flat, pale blue of his eyes. His handshake was just a bit on the too-strong side, and T.C. guessed the man couldn't help himself. He wondered what it must be like to be at Barrington's level and still feel like you had something to prove.

In fact, T.C. had never cared for the guy, and wondered

at his father's continued trust. He'd finally decided each man knew where the other's bodies were buried, and so could they trust each other in ways they could no one else. But, he reminded himself as he followed him into the office and took a seat on the end of the long, grand leather couch, he wasn't here for the man's honesty, or lack thereof. He was here for a referral.

"It's good to see you," Barrington said as he took a seat in the chair at right angles to T.C. "I can't imagine how you must be feeling, all this time with no word. It's awful, just horrible. I have nightmares about him, wondering where he is, if he's hurt…or worse. I can't believe the sheriff hasn't found anything. How can that be? Are they that incompetent? I thought Reid's case was an anomaly here in Texas, but now I'm wondering. They should have found Eldridge long ago."

T.C. bristled at the reference to his brother, but he tamped it down. Rather easily, since he was astonished by Barrington's string of unbroken words. The man was chattering. As if he was nervous. T.C. didn't spend a lot of time with the man. He had other attorneys he preferred to work with, but they were corporate types, with little to none of the kind of experience needed now.

Plus, he hadn't wanted to put them in the awkward position of feeling compelled to call the police—something Barrington would have no compunctions about, he was sure—because thanks to Fowler, Jolie was now a person of interest in a major investigation.

Not to mention that his faith in the system had been shaken by Reid's situation, so he wasn't certain of anything at the moment.

"Are you in trouble?" Barrington asked when T.C. explained what he wanted.

"No. But a friend might be, if my brother pushes the cops hard enough."

Barrington looked thoughtful. "I presume you mean Fowler?"

"Who else?" T.C. said, his mouth twisting into a wry grimace.

"Is this something to do with your father's case?"

"He's going to try and make it that way." He held the man's gaze. "It's not true, but that never stops Fowler."

"And this friend, you're certain they're innocent?"

"Absolutely."

"I could—"

"No." T.C. realized he'd cut him off rather abruptly and quickly added, "You're too close to this. I just need a couple of names, just in case."

Barrington seemed relieved. "Thank you. Yes, I am. It's so awful. Your father is my oldest and dearest friend, and I've been such a wreck, not knowing, and I just can't...."

His voice fading away, he gave a vague wave of his hand before putting it over his eyes, squeezing his temples between thumb and forefinger. He was, T.C. realized with a little shock, genuinely upset. In fact, he sounded near tears. T.C. felt a stab of guilt; apparently the man was truly grieving the fate of his old friend. He himself had been almost numbed by days upon end of no news, but the sight of all this emotion was bringing it all back for him.

By the time T.C. left, with a couple of suggested names, he was almost convinced the man felt as badly as the family did. He would have been completely convinced if it hadn't been for the split second when he thought he'd seen Barrington peek at him through the fingers in front of his eyes, as if to see how T.C. was taking his demonstration of grief.

Maybe he was reading too much into that, he thought as he returned to his car. Maybe it had been merely a shift of position. Maybe he'd just been embarrassed, the cool, tough lawyer, displaying such emotion.

He shifted his focus, heading back to Jolie's apartment. Oddly he was more on edge about that than he had been about the meeting with Barrington. And once inside—after having to explain to a neighbor who he was and what he was doing—he had to admit he was tempted to snoop, not because he expected to find anything startling, but because of the urge to learn whatever he could about her and her life now. The moment he realized that was what he was feeling, he swore aloud at himself.

"Damned idiot. Get it and get the hell out of here," he muttered under his breath. First he checked Emma's alcove, saw that the window was still boarded up. He'd make a call or two, make sure that was fixed soon; he didn't want Emma coming back to that reminder. He noticed a couple of picture books carefully placed within reach, and on impulse picked them up.

He walked quickly toward the small desk in one corner of the living room, opened the drawer she'd described and saw the edge of the compact, snap-secured book with some loose papers protruding slightly in various places. Jolie had always been a bit of a traditionalist anyway, so perhaps she would have stuck with this even if a smartphone had been in the budget. The budget that was probably tighter than she'd admit to, which made him uncomfortable. But she'd made a good home here for herself and Emma, and he admired her for that. But then she'd always been—

It hit him the instant he picked up the dark blue, leather-bound planner.

He recognized it. He recognized it because he'd given it to her, for the first—and only—birthday of hers they'd spent together. Until then she'd been using a large manila envelope to keep paperwork in, and loose calendar pages with appointments for her and Emma noted.

He remembered the awe with which she handled the gift, and the way she'd investigated every part of it, calendar pages, note pages, pockets, with delight. You would have thought it was an expensive piece of jewelry, the way she reacted.

But then, Jolie never had been impressed with sparkle. She was a practical sort of girl. She'd had to be, he thought.

And she'd kept this. And cared for it well. It was softer, broken in now, but just as clean and unscarred as the day it had come out of the box.

He couldn't stop the questions from forming in his mind. Had she kept it because he'd given it to her? Or simply because she couldn't afford to replace it? Had she thought of him, when she used it, as she obviously did on a daily basis? Or had she completely divorced the giver from the object, as she had so completely removed herself and Emma from his life?

Irritated with himself now, he turned on his heel and headed back for the door. He locked it carefully; there was no sign of any further trouble, and he wanted to keep it that way. And once back in the SUV he forced himself to think of something else. Anything else. And settled on that moment when Barrington had given him that odd glance.

It was just embarrassment, he told himself again. Or,

he thought, rather cynically he admitted, perhaps even an exaggeration, to show his devotion to the Coltons to one of the next generation.

The generation that might well be now in charge, T.C. thought grimly, the by now old worry about his father kicked in.

Nevertheless, that instant of time niggled at him as he headed back toward the ranch.

Chapter 20

Jolie hadn't wanted him to do it.

There was no way she could afford the kind of lawyer that ran in Colton circles. She'd be reduced to a public defender if it came to that. Some idealist straight out of law school with no idea how the world really worked. And she didn't want to be the case that became the object lesson.

But how could she stop it? This time it wouldn't be just the rich and powerful Coltons; it would be the entire system turned against her. And she had too much experience with that grinding machinery to take it lightly.

And Emma. Emma would end up where she'd been, lost, in foster care, shuttled from place to place, some okay, too many more indifferent and some hideous. No real home, no one to love her the way Jolie's sweet girl deserved to be loved.

Panic shot through her. She tamped it down with a great effort. Even if T.C.'s words had only been talk, as so much in her life had always been, it wouldn't happen. Not to Emma. She wouldn't let it happen, she said to herself. She wasn't sure how she would or could stop it, but she wouldn't let it happen. She would never abandon her girl to the anonymity and callousness of the system she'd been trapped in. Even if she had to take Emma and run, she wouldn't let it happen. People had done it, vanished for years, hadn't they? Maybe they were found out in the end, but by then Emma would be grown and able to look out for herself.

And what will she have learned? How to run from her problems?

She veered away from that thought. She shifted in her seat atop the corral rail so she could keep Emma in plain sight as she sat atop Flash. T.C. had assured her it would be fine, and the horse did seem to pretty much ignore the small person clinging in delight to his broad back. He simply went about the business of slowly eating the flake of hay T.C. had tossed him before leaving, leaving the child to coo in delight and excitement as she stroked his mane and traced tiny fingers along the edges of the white patch that ran jaggedly along his neck in stark contrast to the glossy black.

The child was as happy as Jolie had ever seen her. Which was amazing, all things considered. Which in turn was thanks to T.C. He'd done this, somehow turned a trauma that could haunt a child for life into an enchanting adventure for her. She would owe him forever for that.

But could even he stop this? She couldn't believe it was happening. Wasn't it enough that a woman had been murdered, and her precious baby was in danger? Was Fowler Colton really so malevolent as to accuse an innocent woman just to throw the heat off his girlfriend?

Don't be stupid. He's Fowler Colton. You know what he's capable of.

Still, she hadn't wanted T.C. to go see the Colton attorney for her. She was afraid that would simply bring the law down on her, but T.C. had rather sourly explained that was why he was going to this lawyer, who was as ethics-challenged as Fowler himself. Besides, he had no intention of telling Barrington he knew where she was. Which, he'd added, was why he was going alone, that and the fact that she might be seen and recognized.

The horse's head came up, his attention obviously caught by something to the west. She turned, and saw the small haze of dust rising in the air. Too big for a horse, she reasoned, so not one of the hands stopping by. A vehicle, then. Her nerves, already jangled, tightened up another notch. It was a long moment of tension before she could make out that it was T.C.'s vehicle. Since he was leaving Flash here, he'd had a ranch hand drive it out here this morning, then had dropped the man off back at the bunkhouse on his way into town. The pressure eased, and she could breathe again.

Emma looked from the approaching car to her. "Mommy?"

"What, sweetie?"

"Do we get to stay here?"

Get to, not have to, Jolie noticed. Flash was obviously working some equine magic.

"For a while," she answered. "I don't know how long." *Or if it was a huge mistake...*

The blue SUV slowed as it got closer, and the small cloud of dust it kicked up faded away. T.C. brought it carefully to a halt beneath the tree. Fowler would have careened in and skidded to a stop, gleeful at spraying dust, dirt and rocks over everything and everyone in the vicinity. She'd seen him do it often enough. And no one dared call him on it.

Except T.C.

It came back to her in a rush, that day when Fowler's reckless driving had sent up a spray of debris that had spooked a young horse T.C. had been working with. Fowler hadn't even had a chance to get out of his expensive imported car before his brother was there and hauling him out of the vehicle by the lapels of his custom-designed suit.

She'd been in the kitchen, only able to see the action, not hear what was being said, but obviously Fowler's re-action to his brother's anger hadn't been satisfactory, be-cause T.C. put him on the ground with a fierce punch to the jaw. And then he'd grabbed a handful of gravel and pelted him with it. By the time Fowler scrambled to his feet, red-faced and screaming at T.C., she'd been grin-ning. Something she'd had to stop when Fowler stormed in demanding an ice pack and thoroughly cursing out his crazy little half brother. With a lot of emphasis on the "half."

And later, when T.C. came in for lunch, she'd made sure it was his favorite roast beef sandwich with some of the fries he usually told them not to bother with. And she had carefully placed a small pebble on the rim of his sandwich plate. The instant he saw it his gaze shot to her face. She'd smiled. He'd smiled back. And winked.

And so it had begun…

She shook off the memories. She hadn't allowed her-self to think about that day for four years now. It hurt too much. And now, for the first time, she was wonder-ing about her decision. Not that she'd had to do what she did, for Emma's sake—she was rock-solid on that—but about what might have happened had she done as T.C. had said, trusted him enough to stand and fight.

She drew in a deep breath. She knew what would have happened. His parents would never have backed down—Eldridge Colton hadn't built an empire on changing his mind—and T.C. would have been right where she'd known he would end up, caught in an unbearable position. Oh, he would have fought them, she knew that. But the cost would have been horrendous, and probably would have doomed them anyway.

He would have become bitter, and ended up questioning if it had all been worth it, and she couldn't have borne that. Nor could she have subjected Emma to it. He would have done his best to hide it from the girl, but Emma was smart and perceptive, and eventually she would have figured it out. Someday she would have realized what he had lost, and that it was because of them.

He got out of the SUV and headed toward them. Emma called out a happy "look at me!" greeting just as Flash whinnied a welcome, as well.

"I am looking at you," he said as he got to the corral fence. "And you look great up there."

"I slipped once," the girl confessed.

T.C. handed Jolie the planner without even looking at her. She wondered if he even remembered giving it to her, the birthday that seemed an eon ago.

"What did you do?" T.C. asked the child.

"I grabbed his mane." She looked concerned. "Does that hurt him?"

"Did he jump? Or snort?"

She shook her head. "He jus' looked at me."

"Then I'd say it didn't hurt too much."

"I won't do it again," she promised solemnly.

"How about only in emergencies," T.C. suggested.

"'Kay," Emma agreed happily, throwing her arms around the horse's neck in a hug, at least as far as she could reach.

He would have been a great father for Emma, Jolie thought, moisture stinging her eyes. She had to look away or she was afraid she would lose the battle not to weep at their loss.

She focused on the planner, asking without looking at him, "Did you check the date?"

"Of course not."

She realized he meant he would consider that prying where he didn't belong. She felt a pang of longing for the time when it wouldn't have been prying, when everything she had and thought had been open to him, and when he had let her in the same way. He had answered any question, told her about things that happened in ways that made her laugh or shake her head at the so different world he lived in.

She had only later realized what a risk that was, for a Colton. How so many tried to get inside so they could use the Colton name or wealth for their own ends. She couldn't imagine living like that, never knowing for sure if someone had an ulterior motive. How had he ever believed in her, a mere kitchen worker? How had he ever decided she wasn't one of them, the hangers-on, the climbers of various sorts?

"What?" he asked, looking at her quizzically.

"Just wondering," she said softly, "why you ever trusted me. Not to be one of the multitude who just wanted what they could get from a Colton."

His expression changed, tightened, as if he were questioning that himself. "So, tell me," he said after a moment, "how is what you did different from what one of them would do?"

She didn't answer. They'd been here before. She just looked at Emma, who was now busily trying to tie strands of Flash's mane into a bow.

She heard T.C. let out a breath. "Maybe it was just rebellion," he muttered offhandedly. "I knew what my parents thought, so of course I had to think the opposite."

Jolie's own breath stopped in her throat. For some reason this had never occurred to her, that this might be the reason behind…them. She knew he had truly cared for her, she couldn't doubt that, but had he chosen her out of some kind of youthful mutiny?

"Thanks," she said, her voice unbearably tight. "For shattering the memories." Even as she said it she told herself it was no more than she deserved. But that didn't ease the pain.

"I think you did that."

He was right, but that didn't lessen this particular sting. "I may have had to make a horrible choice that destroyed us, but I never doubted that we'd been real. That's what made it horrible."

"Mommy?"

Emma was looking at them with concern, and she realized the child had picked up on the emotional current that had rippled to life between them.

"It's okay, sweetie. It's just one of those grown-up things you don't have to worry about."

The girl looked from her to T.C., then back. "Don't wanna grow up," she said decisively.

"Amen," T.C. muttered.

Emma seemed to accept that and go back to cooing

over her newly beloved Flash, but Jolie stayed unsettled for the rest of the afternoon. The only bright spot in the gloom came when she'd checked her datebook and found that, as she'd thought, the seventh had been the date of the governor's fund-raiser at the hotel. She'd worked the banquet room kitchen that night, seven hours straight, with any number of witnesses who could swear she'd been there doing cleanup with them at the time Eldridge Colton went missing.

"Good," T.C. said when she'd told him. "Make a list for the sheriff, and that should be that."

He said it like it was any other business or ranch chore that needed to be done. At this point she wasn't sure why he was staying. They weren't speaking much, and what he'd said before hovered between them.

At least, in her mind it did. She wasn't sure what he was thinking about. Early on, it had been a joke between them that every time she thought he'd gone quiet because he was having second thoughts about their relationship, he'd really been pondering when to have the blacksmith come out, since it took a good week to get through all the Colton horses that needed to be shod.

Emma resisted going to sleep that night. She fretted, fussed, even whined, which she rarely did. Thinking perhaps the child was sensing her own mood, she tucked her into the bed and stepped out onto the porch. With an effort, she did it without glancing at T.C., who was in the reading chair, making notes about something.

She stared out into the twilight, rubbing up and down her arms as if it were chilly, when in fact she doubted it had dropped below seventy degrees yet. The cold, she knew, was still coming from inside her, and had nothing to do with actual temperature and everything to do with pain and loss and broken memories.

She didn't know how long she'd been out here when she heard it. But her chest tightened almost unbearably as the sound of a rich baritone voice reached her, singing a quiet, sweet folk lullaby. A Texas song, one she'd heard so often, but never more sweetly than in his unexpectedly beautiful voice. The words washed over her, bringing back the times she'd heard him sing it to Emma when she was just a babe in his arms.

"...when you wake, you shall have, all the pretty little horses, blacks and bays, dapple and gray..."

She remembered the times she'd told him he'd missed his calling, that he could have been a singer. He'd laughed, saying he had neither the urge nor the drive to make it in that particular world.

She couldn't help herself, she got up and looked inside. He was seated on the edge of the bed, rubbing Emma's back as he sang to her. She knew the scene wouldn't be believed by those who only knew him by reputation. And she also knew this proved he'd spoken the truth before, that no matter the situation between them, he would ever and always care for Emma.

The relief of that was almost overwhelming. All the time and pain seemed to vanish in that instant, vanquished by a man singing to a child. She sagged against the doorjamb as she listened and watched, storing every second of this precious vision away against the inevitable time when they would be without him again.

He stopped, and she stifled an instinctive protest. Only then did she realize Emma had gone to sleep, just as she always had when he did this for her.

He stood up, turned and saw her in the doorway.

Something flashed across his face, in his eyes, something intense, almost fierce. And hot.

She knew what it was. Knew she wasn't the only one who remembered the times he had sung Emma soundly to sleep so they could steal away for some very private time.

And there it was, alive and crackling between them.

He crossed the room in three long strides, grasped her arms. He took another step, propelling them back out onto the porch, never taking his eyes off her. Heat blasted through her, making the earlier chill a silly phantom.

And then his mouth was on hers, fierce, demanding, and her heart leaped with the joy of sweet recognition. This man, only this man, had been able to do this to her with merely a kiss, wake her entire being to prepare for the soaring flight she had only ever taken with him. And if there were murky, less than sweet motivations behind it, if the pure, scorching response was tainted by what she had done, by what had happened now, by what he had just said, then so be it.

He was a bottom-line kind of guy, and she'd known that all along. She'd expected that her payment would come due. And in that moment, with him looking down at her with such heat and need in his eyes, with the memories of how it had been between them sending an echoing need along every nerve in her body, the only thing she could think was that she would pay it.

Gladly.

Chapter 21

How had he survived these years without her? How had he convinced himself this had been less than it was?

The instant his lips touched hers, it was as if the four years since he'd done it last had vanished. Fire erupted, his body slammed to attention and his breath jammed up in his throat.

He pulled her against him, hard. Deepened the kiss, probing, aching even more when she gave him access and he ran his tongue over the even ridge of her teeth. She tasted him in turn, the barest brush, and he felt it down to his toes.

Back then he'd never really tried to understand why it was this woman, and only this woman, who could rev him up so much and so fast; he'd just been happy he'd found her.

Now he was face-to-face—and body-to-body—with

the reality that nothing had changed, that she still had that power. And the long absence had only intensified it.

He could feel every inch of her against him, and was unable to resist the need to slide his hands over her even as he still kissed her. He found his favorite spot, that indentation of waist above her hip that seemed made for his hands. Then he slipped his hands farther, cupping her and pressing her against his fiercely aroused body.

At last he broke the kiss, but only to say on a gasp, "Jolie." It was all he could get out.

"Yes."

It was a breathy, low-pitched reply, and it sent another burst of heat through him, along nerves already brought to roaring life by that kiss. Under normal circumstances he knew exactly how he'd interpret that yes. But things were far from normal right now. And he wanted no mistakes or misunderstandings, not now, not between them. "Yes to what?"

"I knew this time would come."

He wasn't sure he liked that. "That sure of yourself?"

She shook her head. "That sure of our…chemistry. Even if…"

"Even if what?"

She let out a tiny sigh. "Even if the rest was never real."

He drew back, frowning. "Never real? How can you say that?"

She blinked. "I didn't. You did."

"I never said that." He was genuinely puzzled, and more than a little stung that she would say he had.

"You said the entire time we spent together was a lie."

"I meant you were lying," he said, just managing to stop himself from the humiliating admission that everything he had felt then had been 100 percent real.

"Then how about, 'Maybe it was just rebellion. I knew what my parents thought, so of course I had to think the opposite'?" she quoted back to him.

It was his turn to blink. Because he had said that—damn, how did she remember things word for word like that?—but he hadn't meant it like she was saying it. "But that was just about my parents."

"That you took up with me just to rebel against your parents is only about them?"

"No, I—" He broke off, shoved a hand through his hair in exasperation, took a deep breath and tried again. "I won't deny it might have spurred me in your direction."

Her mouth—that luscious, beautiful mouth—quirked up at one corner. "Thanks for not lying about it."

He grimaced. "Once I got to know you, it didn't matter anymore."

This was insane, he thought, wondering why he was defending a casual comment that had been nothing more than idle musing. And to her, the woman who had walked out. She was the one who'd left, so why the hell did it matter to her if it had been real in the first place?

But he found it mattered to him that she could even doubt it. Which was also insane, because it wasn't like they were going to pick up where they'd left off. He was doing this for Emma, that was all.

Of course, none of that explained why he'd gone into overdrive the moment he touched her.

Chemistry, she'd said. Well, they certainly had that. And then some. Together they'd been hotter than a Texas summer. And his gut—and body parts somewhat lower—were telling him they still were.

"Look, it was a throwaway, Jolie. I was focused on your alibi, and how to present it to the cops so you could get out from under Fowler's crazy. Emma didn't need to lose her mother after all she's been through."

She smiled at him then. It was a soft, loving expression, and even though he knew it was at just the mention of the daughter she clearly loved more than herself, he couldn't help remembering the days when she had looked the same way at him.

"I know you did it—are doing it—for Emma. And I will always thank you for that."

Something dark and nasty stabbed at him then. "Wait. Did you say yes just now because of that?"

"I owe you—"

"You owe me nothing," he snapped, stung more than he would have thought possible that she would consent because she thought she owed it to him. Stung more than he *should* be, he realized. After all, she didn't matter to him anymore, did she? But if that was true, why was he so ticked off?

"But I—"

She stopped when he abruptly let go of her. "So," he said, pulling back and crossing his arms over his chest as he stared down at her, "you've resorted to that, have you? Paying debts with your body?"

She gave a shocked little gasp. Her eyes widened as she stared at him, and the hurt he saw there almost made him regret his words. But the idea that she would have sex with him as payback—

His own thought hit him as if he'd been head-butted by a longhorn. Followed by his own words echoing in his head.

Maybe I do want that payback...

"Damn," he muttered. This whole thing had gone south damned fast.

She stepped back from him. He saw her draw herself up straighter. She met his gaze levelly. "I swore I would never again live on charity," she said, her voice as steely as her spine. "And it's not like I have any other way to pay you back for your help."

"Jolie—"

"But that has nothing to do with why I said yes, and there are no words for how much it hurts for you to think it did," she said, ignoring his attempt to speak. "I said yes because, much to my dismay, I still—" her voice lost a little of its steeliness "—wanted you."

She ended it on a whisper that made his gut knot up all over again. And then she turned and walked back into the cabin, leaving him there in the darkness. And in that moment, it was more than just a figure of speech. The past tense of her last words echoed in his mind.

He stood there on the porch for a while, reeling internally. He hadn't felt like this since after she left, four years ago. A half dozen different emotions were battling for dominance in his head, and he hated the sensation. He remembered Piper telling him back then that women felt like that a lot of the time when dealing with men, and he'd grimaced and muttered, "Not worth it."

Maybe he'd been righter than he'd known.

It built up inside him until he had to move, do something. He spun on his heel and left the porch, forgoing the steps in a jump. He strode across to the corral, where Flash was standing peacefully. The horse nickered at him; here he was welcomed at least.

That decided it. He took the bridle that was looped over a fence post and pulled it over the horse's head. The big paint took the bit eagerly; he'd had a quiet day and likely had some energy to burn. He didn't bother with the saddle but grabbed the same hunk of mane Emma had been trying to braid and swung himself up on the horse's back.

The well-trained horse sidled up to the gate with the ease of long practice, and T.C. slid the latch free and it swung open. Flash sensed T.C.'s mood, and when he lifted the reins the horse took off like his name, hitting full stride in seconds.

He hadn't skipped the saddle in a while, but he'd wanted to now, wanting the extra effort and concentration it took to stay in tune with the horse, anticipating any quick moves or dodging of rocks or brush. He made a mental note to do it more often, for the closeness of horse and rider. He'd almost forgotten the power of that moment when the connection clicked and you were truly with your mount, savoring the power beneath you, and marveling at the willingness of a half ton of powerful animal to let you control him.

Yes, riding bareback definitely needed to happen more often.

And he swore at himself as other connotations of that phrase shot through his mind, catapulting him back into the morass of tangled thoughts he was trying to escape.

He hoped Flash had a lot of that energy to burn.

Chapter 22

Jolie watched him ride off into the moonlight, aching inside even as she admired his seat, needing no saddle to keep him solidly aboard the big pinto horse.

Her heart was still racing from the feel of his mouth, of his hands on her. She'd been sent straight back to four years ago and that wondrous sense of discovery, that sex could be more than just pleasurable, it could be incredible. With the right person. That having a partner that loved you, that was there for your pleasure, not just his own, made all the difference.

And yet she had abandoned it, and him.

No choice.

It had been her mantra for every day of those four years. She'd been like a small creature caught in a steel-jawed trap, twisting, fighting, panicking. And in the end the only way to freedom was to gnaw off a part of herself. Him.

She went to lie down beside Emma, but sleep eluded her. She knew it would, knew she would not rest until he was safely back. Not that she thought anything would happen to him; he was a Colton riding over his own domain. But as good as Flash was, there was always the chance of a snake or a gopher hole causing a problem.

She cuddled Emma, who slipped even more deeply into sleep, and Jolie was glad she'd heard nothing of their discussion. She couldn't call it an argument; there had been no shouting. T.C. had snapped once, but the rest had come in forcedly hushed tones, both of them aware of Emma sleeping just inside. She'd appreciated his caution even as she'd been hurt by his words.

Did he really believe she'd said yes because she owed him?

Then again, hadn't she told herself—and him—that she'd pay any price to keep Emma safe?

Finally she sat up, unable to stay still. Without waking the child she got up and walked back out to the porch. Her arms were wrapped around herself, but not because of any chill. She felt as if she needed to hold on, because her thoughts and emotions were whirling so fast she thought she might spin apart if it didn't stop soon.

Her adult life had been of her own making. Once free of the foster system, she'd gone at life a little recklessly, she knew that. Once she'd been cut loose, she spent the first four years of freedom careening around as if nothing else mattered. And then everything had changed with the appearance of a plus sign on a plastic stick.

Emma had changed everything. Her father—Bio Dad, Jolie called him, since he'd had no interest at all in becoming an actual dad—had vanished practically before the plus sign had fully shown up on the pregnancy test.

She hadn't been surprised; she'd known Kevin wasn't much for responsibility. But neither had she been at the time, and they'd gotten along well in their brief, carefree relationship, Jolie thinking she was making up for all she'd missed while in the system.

She'd pondered her options, but the thought of having someone she would forever be connected to, someone who would ever and always be her child, was a lure she could not resist. And for the first time she looked more seriously at her freedom from the system, and finally realized freedom meant little if you didn't do anything with it.

She'd reveled in knowing it was now up to her, that she would make it or not based on her own efforts, intelligence and drive. She would build a life for herself and her child, alone if she had to. And it would be a better life than she had had after the day her parents were killed. And, in an unexpected aspect, she'd realized this also meant she had to take better care of herself, not for her own sake but for Emma's. Not for anything would she have her baby girl end up in the same situation.

So she'd cleaned up her attitude and her life; she'd found something she enjoyed and was good at, went to school to learn it, had accepted help until she didn't need it anymore, then stood on her own. She was proud of what she'd accomplished, but by no means did she think she was through. She had plans, to move up to a job on Mrs. Amaro's level one day, then maybe higher still. She didn't just cook. She had a knack for organization and presentation as well, and she wanted to parlay that into something bigger. And she would, once Emma started school and she had more time to plan out the next stage.

She'd been so certain of that. Had felt in charge of her

life at last. Until those moments outside the day care, when everything had careened out of control. The moments that had driven her to the only refuge she'd been able to think of in those panicked hours after she'd truly realized what had happened, that someone was trying to kill her baby girl.

She wouldn't second-guess that anymore, she told herself as she paced the small wooden porch, staring out into the moonlit night. It was done. They were here and safe, which meant she'd made a good choice, didn't it? And if she had to pay for that with some uncomfortable conversations and memories—and a lot of heated, shockingly arousing feelings—then so be it.

She wouldn't have said she was waiting for him to return until the moment she saw Flash in the distance, and realized she'd been doing exactly that. At first she'd thought an unfelt breeze had rippled the brush, making the shadows shift, but then she realized it was indeed the black-and-white horse she was seeing, stark in the silver light. Just as she was certain the animal slowed from an easy canter to a walk, and she guessed he needed to cool out. Which meant they'd had a good long run. Which meant T.C. had needed it. It was what he'd always done, when he'd needed to work something out.

She wondered, with some trepidation, what conclusion he'd reached.

He was going to need to take care of the horse when he got here, she realized. And it was already late. She left the porch and walked to the corral and shed. The as-yet-unused stall—Flash hadn't had any need or desire for shelter yet—held the box on one wall where she'd seen T.C. get the brush he'd given Emma to use. She went to it and got out a currycomb, brush and hoof pick.

She also saw the water trough was low, and walked over to it. There was a classic old pump handle beside it. She wasn't sure it even still worked. Perhaps he filled it with a bucket from inside. But she tried it anyway, and was rewarded with a light but steady stream of clear water. She filled it to where she could see the waterline usually was. Wondered idly if other creatures visited this man-made water hole when T.C. wasn't here. Or perhaps even when he was; as long as they didn't bother his horses, T.C. was pretty much a live-and-let-live kind of guy when it came to other animals.

It hit her then that she could add Emma to that. If anything ever threatened her, she knew on a gut-deep level that live and let live would go out the window.

And then he was there, sliding down from Flash's back and landing with a lightness that belied his size. He might be an inch over six feet, but T.C. had always been light on his feet. Graceful, although he'd scoff at the term.

She saw him look at the tools she'd gathered, then at the water. And then at her.

"Thank you," he said. And she couldn't tell a thing from his level tone, except that he was calmer than when he'd left.

He went about caring for the animal, first the curry-comb, then leaning hard into the brushing, which told her the horse had indeed worked up a sweat, which had dried on the long, slow walk back. Less than he would have under saddle, but still, it needed some attention.

"Can I help?" she asked quietly.

He looked across Flash's withers at her. It was a moment before he said, "Remember how to use that hoof pick?"

"Of course," she said, picking up the small metal hook.

Flash was as docile about this as he was about the rest, and let her pick up all four feet in turn. She found a small stone in one. Too small to have caused a problem right away, and likely would have fallen out on its own soon, but she levered it out anyway.

"He's so calm," she said, patting him when she was done.

"Hard to believe how explosive he is when you point him at a calf," T.C. said.

She remembered the change that came over the animal when he went into real action. "He knows when it's business."

"Yes."

"And he's quite the ambassador for your horses."

"He's built our rep," T.C. agreed as he finished, slipped off the bridle, gave the horse an affectionate slap on the rump and sent him off into the corral. Flash went to a spot in the far corner, then looked back at T.C., who laughed. "Go ahead, y'old mule. I know you're going to do it anyway."

On cue, the big horse lowered himself to the ground and rolled in the dirt, making all the effort seem pointless. Except Jolie knew it wasn't; it would have been a much bigger job in the morning if he'd rolled while still sweaty. And it still made her laugh to watch. It always had.

T.C. looked at her. Tentatively she smiled at him. He smiled back.

"I'm sorry," they chorused, and both stopped.

T.C.'s mouth quirked, and he let out a short chuckle. That was one of the things she'd most loved about him; Colton or not, he wasn't above apologizing, unlike a few other members of his family.

"I shouldn't have made such a big deal out of a passing comment," she said.

"And I shouldn't havc accused you of…what I did."

She nodded, accepting the sincerity she heard in his voice. "I guess the past isn't so far behind that it can't jump up and bite."

For a long, silent moment T.C. watched the horse, who was back on his feet now, and shaking in that twitching way horses had to get rid of the dust he'd picked up in his rolling.

Then, without looking at her, he asked quietly, "Did you mean it? About…wanting me?"

Honesty was the very least of the things she owed him. "I've never, ever stopped wanting you."

His eyes closed. The silvery light made his lashes stand out as a dark, thick sweep above his cheeks. He turned then. Looked at her straight-on. "You'd better get inside, Jolie. Or we're going to start this dance again."

She saw it all in his face, in his eyes, the old heat, the need, the promise of that incredible pleasure, the union she had found nowhere else in her life.

She wasn't sure why he would still want her, after what she'd done. Perhaps it was to prove to himself that he was over her. Or that it hadn't been as incredible as he might remember. She wasn't sure why she was even thinking about this. But she wasn't sure thinking was the right word, either, since she had the feeling some part of her had already decided, from the moment he'd kissed her.

"Then let the music begin," she whispered.

And this time, she kissed him.

Chapter 23

"Flash won't mind," T.C. said, his voice sounding low and thick over the rustle of the straw beneath their feet. It sent a shiver down Jolie's spine, a delightful shudder of anticipation. Now that her mind had allowed it, her body seemed to have slipped the leash and was running free, already halfway to the peak they were about to climb.

"It won't be the first time we've used the nearest stall."

The moment she said it she regretted the words; she didn't want to think about before, because she didn't want to think about how it had ended. More important, she didn't want him thinking about how it had ended. So she did the only thing she could think of to keep his mind from veering in that direction. She kissed him again.

He responded fiercely, as if he was as hungry as she was after all this time. His hands were on her, caressing, searching, and hers on him, seeking all the places that thrilled her, the strong cord of his neck, the broad expanse of his chest, the flat, ridged belly, the lean hips.

And then one of his hands was on hers, urging her downward to the swell of his erection, pressing her palm against him. She stroked him through the denim of his jeans, heard him make that low sound in his throat that had haunted her dreams ever since that awful night when she realized that, for Emma's sake, she had to leave.

She didn't realize she'd gone still until he did in turn.

"Second thoughts?" he asked gruffly.

She shook her head. "Emma. If she wakes up," she began, even knowing it was unlikely; after her busy day, the child was soundly asleep.

"She'll call out for you."

Of course she would, she thought.

"Besides," he added, his voice only slightly rueful, "this is going to be quick, I'm afraid."

She looked up at him, and even in the moonlight she could see the need and urgency in his face. She suspected it echoed her own.

She let out a harsh breath. "Oh, I hope so."

He groaned then, grabbed her and pulled them both down to the fresh straw he'd spread just last night. She wondered if he'd thought of this when he did it, if he'd remembered all the times when they had done this before, at the stable or at the big barn, when things were new and joyous and they couldn't keep their hands off each other.

She knew she was letting herself in for more painful memories, knew she would likely regret this decision.

But she would regret not doing this more. Just once more, to remind her what it could be like, should be like, for those times when she thought she might settle. For she had had chances, over the years, men who had seemed genuinely interested. She had always declined, citing her total focus on Emma, which was true. But there had been another reason, as well; she knew nothing could compare to what she'd had with this man, and anyone else would be lacking in comparison. So she didn't even begin.

And this was why, she thought as his strong hands cupped her breasts, because no one else had ever made her feel like this. And then he moved his fingers to her nipples, catching them, plucking them, and even through her shirt and bra the fire sparked. She arched to him, silently pleading for more. If she'd still been standing her knees would have gone weak.

She tugged his shirt free, needing the feel of his skin more than her next breath. He was still lean, strong and solid, and her hands traced the lines of his body as if they had never forgotten. She fumbled with the button and then the zipper of his jeans. Realized he was doing the same to hers. The urgency built with every movement, every contact between them, until they were merely shoving the inconvenient clothing out of the way.

He touched her, traced every curve, probed every bend, until she was shaking with need and ready to beg him to finish it.

And then he paused, holding her hands still, looking down at her. "Jolie," he began.

"You promised quick," she said breathlessly, thinking she was going to scream if she didn't have him in the next instant. "Hurry."

"I don't have a condom," he bit out between clenched teeth.

"Don't need it," she said. "I'm on something."

She had been ever since Emma, just in case. Even though she had no intention of getting involved with anyone, she lived in a big city and anything could happen. But right now she was in no mood to explain; she wanted only one thing and she wanted it now. She wanted him now.

She said it, in a voice she barely recognized as her own. He made a low sound that was practically a growl. And then he rolled, taking her with him, until his back was to the straw and she was atop him.

"Then take me," he answered, his voice as tautly strung as her own.

She hadn't expected it, but some still barely functioning part of her brain told her she should have. He would want to be very sure, would want no regrets. What better way than to give her the lead?

And then even that part of her brain shut down as she reached for him and guided him inside her. The blunt probe of his flesh, so familiar and yet so long missed, sent a new wave of shudders through her. She sank down on him, gasping anew as he filled her, inch by inch. It had been a very long time—four years, to be exact—for her, and it felt new all over again.

She lost herself in the wonder of it, the sweetness of it, and the glory of feeling whole again at last as her body recognized him and responded with a searing heat. When he was in her to the hilt, she heard him swear, but it was a worshipful sound that had nothing to do with the word but everything to do with the sensations that were building. He reached up and grabbed her hips, locking her to him. A cry escaped her, of pleasure, relief and joy.

"Yes," he hissed out.

And then they were moving, together, flesh stroking flesh, until she was nearly screaming with the building pressure. She rocked on him, savoring the fullness, the stretching. Yet still it wasn't enough. She wanted his weight, wanted to be pressed to him head to toe, wanted him driving into her, and she shifted, rolled, urging him on top of her.

As if the four years between them had never been, they were together in movement, in touch, in finding each other's most sensitive places. And at last, when she cried out to him, he drove in hard and deep stroke after pounding stroke. She had a split second of realizing it was beginning, but the explosion hit her so fast and so strongly she couldn't breathe but could only ride it up and over. She heard him say her name in a low, harsh growl in the instant before felt the pulse of him inside her, saw the same explosion of pleasure reflected in his face.

And she knew, as he collapsed atop her, his breath coming in rapid pants, that no matter what, she could never regret this, even if this was all she was ever to have of him again.

"Not exactly the Ritz," T.C. murmured, plucking a piece of straw from her hair.

"But it's us," Jolie answered.

His mouth tightened slightly. "It should have been a better place, but I never planned this."

How could he have? He'd never expected she would have an even more powerful effect on him now than she had four years ago. He'd never expected her to have an effect on him at all.

And instead she had fired his senses to an unbearable peak, until his body demanded her in a way he'd not felt in…ever. Even more than the sweetness they'd found back then. No, this was different, this was fiercer, more insistent—and, if he was honest, more needy—than it had ever been.

"It was exactly what it should have been."

His gaze narrowed. What was that supposed to mean? That this had only been a literal quick roll in the hay? And then he wondered why that bothered him. After all, he wasn't looking for more. He hadn't even been looking for this. In fact, if he'd had any sense, he would have run like hell the first instant the thought of getting tangled up with this woman again began to form.

"It's where we made love the first time, after all."

"Is that what this was?"

He said it wryly, almost ruefully, and for an instant pain flashed in her eyes. But she recovered quickly.

"A quick roll in the hay, then?"

His expression froze as she used the exact words he'd just thought. "I didn't say that."

She sighed, and it sounded almost sad. "I understand, really. From where you stand, I'm sure you're having second thoughts."

"Standing was the hard part. You put me on my knees. You always did."

The admission widened her eyes. The sadness vanished. "It's only ever been you."

His brow furrowed. "Are you saying you haven't... been with anyone since you left?"

Her mouth quirked. "Couldn't you tell?"

The memory of how slowly she'd taken him in, how tight she'd been around him, accomplished nothing but hardening him all over again. He fought the urge to begin again, slower this time, driving her mad by increments until he took her again. And then again, and again, until the sun began to rise in the east.

"Why?" he asked. "I know there can't be any shortage of men panting over you."

"You flatter me. But there are many reasons. Two main ones."

"Emma."

She nodded, smiling that loving smile that made him feel oddly wistful. "I didn't want her confused by having guys around I wasn't serious about. It wouldn't be fair to her. Or to them, in fact."

"Fair to them?"

"Reason two." She met his gaze levelly. "Because none of them could measure up to you. Ever."

As a declaration, it was pretty powerful. His gut reaction was still instantaneous, a pained *then why did you leave?* But he knew her reasons now. And if she was telling the truth, he even understood them. How could he not, looking at sweet, innocent Emma, and picturing the child at the mercy of his mother's untender ministrations? He'd seen his mother tear apart more than one person with her cold, calculating tactics over the years, and while he didn't like to think she'd turn her malevolence on a child, he wasn't sure he'd put it past her, either. And if she had, Marceline would have followed. And Fowler, of course, but that was always a given.

"I need to check on Emma," she said, and rose on one elbow.

"She's fine."

"But—"

"It can wait a minute."

He looked at her bare breasts, savoring the way her nipples tightened under his gaze, as if she were thinking about him touching them, suckling them. In that moment, doing just that became the most important thing in his universe. He tugged her back, just far enough that he could lift his head and flick his tongue over one taut peak. She sucked in an audible breath, and he saw a quiver go through her, saw her stomach muscles tighten as if the deeper muscles were clenching. As they had around his erection, driving him nearly out of his mind.

She moaned his name, low and husky in that way that never failed to slam him into full arousal.

"No one," he muttered. "No one ever measured up to you, either."

She closed her eyes as she shifted slightly, offering him the neglected other nipple.

It wasn't nearly as quick this time, but it was just as fierce, and hot enough to burn away much of the pain and regret. And for the first time, he let himself wonder if there might be a chance, a genuine chance, to begin anew.

Chapter 24

It was afternoon before he asked her, "Got that list?"

Jolie nodded. She walked to the table and picked up the page she'd been working on while Emma and T.C. were out with Flash this afternoon; the girl's squeals of delight had been a wonderful accompaniment to the task that would hopefully free her from this particular shadow over her head.

Just as her own cries of delight last night had shattered another cloud, one of regret and pain. She felt herself flush, and marveled at how merely thinking of last night could have her aching for him all over again. He'd always been able to do that to her, but she thought she'd successfully quashed that response in the years since. Obviously she'd been wrong. Very wrong.

She watched him as he looked at the list of names. She'd started with those she'd worked most closely with that night, and their job titles, then included the two supervisors who had been there; she'd had contact with them both throughout the night. She'd read it over, thought for a moment, then added one last name.

She glanced now at Emma, who was sitting at the table eating the peanut butter and jelly sandwich T.C. had fixed for her while Jolie was in the shower. A shower that had been hurried, because she started remembering again all the times they'd showered together and ended up sliding weak-kneed to the shower floor after some of the hottest sex she'd ever imagined. Actually she had never imagined it, because she hadn't known it was even possible, until him.

Lucky this shower is too small. And that Emma's here.

The child was humming as she approached the task in her usual unique way, tearing off a section of the sandwich and nibbling the edges off until it was a nearly perfect circle before she popped it in her mouth.

"Mike Cortez?"

She looked up at his surprised tone. "Yes. I wasn't sure I should add him, but I had a conversation with him toward the end of the evening. You said that was the time it was most crucial to account for."

He was staring at her. "You had a conversation with the governor's chief of staff?"

He was saying it as if he thought she didn't realize who the man was. "Yes. He was very nice."

"He is nice."

Of course, she realized. "You know him," she said, feeling foolish. He was T. C. Colton; of course he knew the man.

"Yes. Alanna went to school with him. Explain. Please."

He sounded rather odd, but it was a reasonable question, she thought. "It was a fund-raiser for the governor, so of course he was there. And he came back to thank the staff on the governor's behalf. Like I said, nice."

"Don't you think maybe he should be at the top of the list?"

Her brow furrowed. "I wasn't sure he should be there at all, since we only had the one contact. But it was at the right time, so…"

Her voice trailed off as something in his expression changed. He smiled, a small, wondering smile. "It didn't occur to you that his name might carry enough weight to stop this whole thing in its tracks?"

"I…no." She felt silly now.

"Because you just don't think that way, do you? People are people, nice or not, good or bad, not to be assessed for what they might be able to do for you."

Her mouth quirked. "That's Fowler territory."

"Yes, it is." He chuckled. "Next thing you'll be saying you chatted with the governor." Her eyes widened. His chuckle became a full laugh. "You did, didn't you?"

"Briefly," she said. "He came through the kitchen. He was charming."

"He is that. Why isn't he on the list?"

"He wouldn't remember me," she said.

"He is a devoted husband, would never stray, but he's a man to the core. Trust me, he'd remember."

She flushed, pleased at the implied compliment.

"I'll ask Mike to give the sheriff a call. That ought to put paid to this whole thing."

She stared at him. Realized he could do just that, pick up a phone and call the chief of staff for the governor. And have him not only answer, but in turn call the highest law officer in the neighboring county, who of course would immediately answer and take action.

"What?" he asked.

"Sometimes I forget just how thin the air is in your world," she said wryly.

"You're the one who sucks all the air out of my world." His voice was soft, suggestive, and sent a ripple of that heat through her again. "I have to remember to breathe when you're around."

"Funny," she said. "You have the opposite effect on me. I breathe faster. A lot faster."

He smiled then, a smile of acknowledgment, appreciation, satisfaction. And in that moment it was as if it all had never happened, as if they were back in that sweet, halcyon time when they'd been so completely in love and were planning their future as a family. She had never forgotten what she had loved about him, but she was learning that, at the core, none of it had changed. T.C. was still the man he'd been. The man she'd fallen for.

The man she'd never really stopped loving.

Jolie finished washing and drying the bowls they had used for Bettina's delicious chili. As she washed the single spoon, she smiled; as with many things, Emma had her own way of eating this. Scooping it up with crackers was her favored approach, and Jolie was happy enough to indulge it, since she enjoyed it so.

"Sweetie, I'm going to go dump this water. I'll be right back."

"'Kay."

The girl barely looked up; she was busy drawing another in the seemingly endless pictures of Flash. Jolie looked over at the one tacked up above the table, the one with a tall man with a gray cowboy hat astride the pinto that was looking more like T.C. with every effort. He had put it there, with a smile that Jolie thought had meant he was pleased Emma had included him. And Emma had clapped her hands in glee as her artwork was placed where he could "see it all the time."

He really was so good with her, she thought as she carefully carried the bowl of dishwater outside. He'd told her he always dumped it at the foot of the big tree; even used water was not to be wasted out here. She'd noticed the soap he used was specifically formulated for such use, and the tree certainly didn't seem to mind; it was tall and broad and healthy-looking.

"Is he coming back?"

Emma's question sounded almost as if she feared he wouldn't. That quickly T.C. had fascinated her. Just as when she was six months old and he'd been able to make her smile and laugh and had put an end to any tears. Jolie had laughingly said he should rent himself out and called him the baby whisperer, thinking he'd probably groan. But instead he'd laughed and said, "This is the only baby I'm worried about. It only works because I love her."

For the first time, one of those sweet memories didn't bring a wave of pain and anguish. Instead she felt a rush of hope. And no amount of telling herself it was foolish, that one passionate interlude didn't mean they were on the road back, that T.C. could truly understand and forgive.

The only thing she was certain it meant was that it would be just as hard to go on without him this time as it had been before.

"Mommy?"

"Sorry, sweetie, I was distracted. He just went to make

a call. He had to take the truck to get to a place where
his cell phone will work."

And catch the governor in his office? Jolic wondered.

Sometimes she truly did forget what his life was really like, what merely his name gave him access to. But
in a way, that was the highest compliment she could give
him, in her view, because he never lorded it over anyone,
never wielded the Colton name and power in the way his
half brother did.

As she finished drying the bowl that served as a sink
and was setting it back in place, she heard something that
sounded like a vehicle outside. She smiled automatically;
that hadn't taken as long as she'd expected. But the sound
stopped some distance away. She waited, listening, but
it didn't start again. Curious now, she glanced at Emma,
who was happily paging through one of the books T.C.
had also brought, her favorite story about a mouse, a
cat and a dog. Jolie had read it to her often enough that
she knew it by heart, and was telling it to herself as she
stopped at each familiar drawing.

Jolie stepped outside to look around. The shadows
were growing longer as the sun dropped in the sky, but
it was still warm and still. She looked out toward the
trees that provided some very welcome shade to the little cabin. She walked to the end of the porch slowly, in
no rush, pondering all the reasons T.C. had chosen this
place for his refuge.

She reached the far end. Put her hands on the porch
railing. Leaned out.

And froze as she saw a figure in dark clothing darting away, vanishing over the low rise behind the cabin.

Chapter 25

Well, that should take care of that.

T.C. smiled with satisfaction as he neared the refuge. A call from the governor's office, not to put on pressure but as personal corroboration of Jolie's alibi, ought to clear that up nicely. One fewer thing to worry about.

He pulled up under the big tree and stopped. Jolie was out on the porch, rising from one of the chairs she'd apparently brought out, and he felt a jolt of pleasure at the sight of her waiting for him. Even if that wasn't really why she was out here, he liked the idea enough to hang on to it.

"It's handled," he told her as he took the two steps as one. "Your name should be crossed off the suspect list by now."

"Thank you," she said, but she sounded…odd.

"Emma?" he asked quickly.

"I think it's all catching up with her. And it got warm, so she got sleepy. She's napping."

"Is she?"

It came out huskily as his mind instantly jumped to all the ways they could utilize this time while the little girl was asleep. And then a chill slammed through him as he noticed the chair she'd been sitting on.

His rifle was lying on the seat.

"What happened?" he demanded, his pulse kicking upwards.

"I...somebody was here."

"Who?"

"I don't know. I heard a car, but it stopped over there, out of sight," she said, gesturing toward the back of the cabin. "I listened, but it didn't start again. So I came outside. Walked over there, just in time to see somebody running back over the rise. I would have followed, but..."

He shook his head instantly. "Like hell. You couldn't leave Emma."

"Yes." She smiled, as if relieved he understood. How could she doubt that, of all things?

"Man or woman?"

"I couldn't be sure. I only caught a glimpse before they got out of sight. Dark clothes."

"Never saw the car?" She shook her head. He let out a breath. "Must have been a curious ranch hand. I haven't used the place much for a while, he was probably surprised to see somebody here."

"But why didn't he come on in?"

"He probably saw Flash in the corral. Thought it was me in residence, so he knew better," T.C. said.

She blinked. "That bad?"

"I come here to get away from everything. They know

that. It would have to be an emergency for one of them to intrude."

After a moment she nodded. She glanced at the weapon. "Now I feel silly."

He reached out, brushed the back of his fingers over her cheek. "Don't. When it comes to protecting Emma, you use what you have."

Something shifted in her expression, and when she said, "Yes, I do," it was a bit more fervently than the situation merited. And he knew she wasn't talking just about now, but four years ago.

He'd spent four years alternating between hating this woman and missing her as if she were an amputated limb, always conscious of the loss, adjusting his every action and thought around her absence. Not going to this place because they had gone there, picking that place because they hadn't.

And now she was here, and he felt helpless against this fierce, driving need for her. And helpless was not a feeling he was used to.

Except with her.

And now, for the first time, he was thinking, really thinking, what it must have been like for her then.

"How did you feel?" he asked. "What were you thinking, back then, when you decided you had to go?"

He couldn't believe he'd said it. He wasn't the kind of guy who pried into people's feelings. He barely acknowledged his own.

Except with her.

She met his gaze steadily. "That I had no choice. That I had to protect Emma." She drew in a slow, deep breath. "And I wasn't surprised."

He drew back slightly. "What do you mean?"

"I wasn't surprised that I was going to lose it all. It had been too good to be true anyway."

Pain stabbed at him, setting up a tight knot in his gut. A flash of the first time he'd seen her went through his mind, a quiet girl in the corner of the kitchen, not even looking at him as he came in. She'd looked up as Bettina introduced them, and in that moment before she'd lowered her gaze he'd seen the doubt, the fear. He'd thought then it was just wariness on a new job, and who he was related to that, but now he realized it had been more. It had been fear, and anticipation, of exactly the kind of thing that had eventually happened. A young mother, finally on a straight path after an ugly childhood and adolescence when she'd probably expected the worst every day, and then having it all yanked out from under her again.

"You asked," she said. "I'm sorry if you don't like the answer."

He realized that his expression must have become rather grim. "What I don't like is other people messing in my life. I'm going to be having a little talk with my mother, sooner rather than later."

Jolie sighed. "And what makes you think that will change anything?"

He smiled at her then. "Maybe because you're right, you won't be so easy to bully this time." She blinked, then stared at him. "And," he added, "this time I know what she did, and I'll call her on it."

"This time?" Her voice was tiny, almost shaky.

"I didn't know then, Jolie. I swear to you I didn't."

For a moment longer she just looked up at him. Looking nothing like the fierce protector who had been ready to shoot to protect her child.

He wanted to protect her. And Emma. He wanted them

both safe and able to grow and blossom as he knew they would. He'd never felt the urge this strongly in his life.

Except with her.

He couldn't stop himself; he reached for her. She came into his arms easily, and he realized with a little jolt she was trembling.

"Jolie?"

"I'm scared," she whispered.

"They're gone, whoever it was," he assured her.

She leaned back again to look at him, gave a tiny shake of her head. "Not that. You."

He went still. "You're scared of me?"

Again the small gesture of denial. "Of how I feel about you. How you make me feel."

Making her feel was exactly what he wanted to do right now. He wanted to make her feel everything he'd felt, he wanted to make her move in that urgent way, wanted to hear the tiny sounds she made when he touched her in all those places, wanted to hear her cry out when she shattered in his arms.

On some vague level he knew she was talking of deeper things, but that reasoning part of his brain was shutting down as need blasted along every nerve in his body.

"I think we should check on Flash," he breathed against her ear.

He felt a shiver go through her, hoped it was for the same reason he was practically shaking in his boots.

"You think he might be getting in trouble out there?" she whispered.

"I think I already am in trouble."

"No fun getting in trouble alone," she whispered, and reached up to cup his face with her hand. He turned his head, pressed his lips against her palm. And read the longed-for answer in her eyes.

He grabbed a blanket from the storage chest at the foot of the bed; last time he'd been picking straw out of uncomfortable places. He supposed she had, too, but she'd never complained.

But then Jolie didn't complain. She assessed, formulated and acted on her best plan. It struck him then that she was exactly the kind of person he preferred to deal with in business. No manipulation, no backroom maneuvering, just honest decisions made with the best information she had at the time.

Like she had made four years ago?

He was still going to confront his mother, armed with this new knowledge of what she had done, threatened. But the more time he spent with Jolie again, the more he remembered who she really was. And he already knew his mother would do almost anything to get her way. And that she was shrewd enough to realize Jolie's weak spot would ever and always be Emma.

And she'd homed in on it like a heat-seeking missile, he thought sourly.

Flash whinnied at them from the corral, and the memory of Emma's delight with the big animal made him smile. Which only stoked the inner anger that was building; his mother had a great deal to answer for. Even the old man wouldn't stoop so low as to threaten a child.

He opened the gate and they slipped through. Jolie seemed to hesitate. She was looking at Flash. He couldn't tell what she was thinking. Maybe the same thing he'd been moments ago, how happy Emma had been sitting atop the big paint. Or maybe the couple of times she'd ridden him herself; she wasn't practiced, but she did well enough.

Something ticked in his brain, a realization that he'd never really worried much about what any other woman he wasn't related to was thinking. But he'd always wanted to know where Jolie's mind was, what mattered to her, how she looked at things, what her opinion was on something. Everything.

Apparently that hadn't changed, either.

He pulled her to him and kissed her, long and deep, fearing she would change her mind. Not fair, perhaps, but his aching body didn't care about that. It only cared about slaking this incredible need that had apparently been banked, hiding, while she was gone from his life. Not that it wasn't her call in the end. He knew that, but he didn't have to encourage second thoughts.

Moments later they were in the stall, the blanket providing a bit more comfort than before. To his surprise he was in as much of a hurry as he'd been last time, and it took all of his restraint to go slowly. But he wanted her as hot for this as he was. And he wanted to revisit every beautiful, long-missed inch of her with his hands and then his mouth.

He followed that plan, although rational thinking about it fled the moment they'd shed their clothes and her luscious curves and long, lithe legs were bare to him. Every bit of evidence that she wanted this as much as he did was fuel to the fire that was soon out of control. The way she touched him, the look of wonder in her eyes, the way she whispered his name.

By the time he sank into her, and her legs wrapped around him to draw him deeper, he was on the edge of crazy out of his mind. And when she made it clear she wanted him hard and fast, he lost the last semblance of sanity and went wild in a way he never had done before. And when he heard her cry out, when he felt it begin for her, her slick, hot flesh clenching around him, he let go completely, wanting her to remember this instant forever. Wanting to be imprinted on her and in her forever.

And in those moments he didn't even think about the time with her when he'd once before thought of forever.

Jolie checked Emma, wondering if she should wake the child so she would be better able to sleep tonight. She decided against it; after the last four days her baby needed all she could get.

She straightened, and flushed as newly tender parts of her brought back the memory of the sweet interludes spent in a hospitable horse's stall. It was as if it were new all over again, which in a way it was, since there had been no one since T.C. anyway. Sometimes it was as if she could still feel him inside her, driving her to that peak, her every nerve firing, her body awaiting only his harsh cry of her name to leap into that inferno they created together.

Perhaps—no, probably—it was beyond foolish to have done this. Twice now. She was likely setting herself up for another heartbreak.

And she, who always tried to be honest at least with herself, refused to admit how much she was clinging to that tiny margin between probability and certainty. And almost regretted that the shower T.C. was occupying just now wasn't big enough for both of them.

She picked up the hairbrush she'd left on the table and ran it through hair almost dry from her own shower. It wasn't going to look its best after just air drying, but it would have to do. Emma wouldn't care, and T.C. didn't seem to. Especially not when he had his hands in it as he tilted her head back for a deeper kiss.

She felt that inner heat building again, and made herself stop thinking about it. Because thinking about it made her hope, and hadn't she learned hope was a kid's game? She—

A flicker of motion at the window over the makeshift sink caught the edge of her vision. She spun around, and for an instant found herself staring at an all-too-familiar face.

Whitney Colton.

The woman dodged away the instant she realized Jolie had seen her. Jolie was too stunned to move, and simply stood there, hairbrush in hand, staring at the now empty square of glass.

T.C.'s mother. The woman who had shattered her life. The woman who had treated her as less than dirt on her designer boots.

The woman with blond hair and from whom T.C. had gotten his green eyes.

Green eyes.

"The mean lady, Mommy."

"Her eyes were like Liddy's."

The green eyes of a killer?

She sank down on the hard, wooden chair, shaking.

Chapter 26

The fact that Whitney Colton had been here, spying, bothered Jolie the least. In fact, she felt a spurt of relief that she hadn't been here earlier, when she and T.C. were in the shed.

But the realization that she resembled the murderer...

This was crazy.

As nasty as the woman was, Jolie simply could not picture her committing murder. At least not herself, up close and personal.

Besides, why would the woman murder someone with no apparent connection to the Coltons?

But she could easily have been there. They hadn't been too far from the headquarters of the family business.

But why would she have been in an alley, blocks away, following a stranger?

Unless she didn't think it was a stranger.

T.C.'s words came back to her in a rush. *"The woman who was murdered looked just like you."*

Could Whitney have thought she was killing her? Fowler could certainly have told her he'd seen her, just as he'd told T.C.

But the thought of Whitney Colton hunting her down was ridiculous. She'd never even attempted to contact T.C. again, just as ordered, so Whitney would have no reason. Besides, Whitney knew perfectly well what she looked like. She wouldn't mistake a total stranger for her. She hadn't changed that much in four years.

Then again, Whitney wasn't the type to pay much mind to those she considered beneath her.

Or perhaps all this with her husband had unhinged her completely?

Her mind made a giant leap to wondering if the woman in the alley hadn't been her first. Maybe she'd killed T.C.'s father and gotten away with it, and that made it easier for her to go for it a second time?

She heard the bathroom door open, realized T.C. was done with his shower and was coming out. She reined in her careening brain fiercely. And welcomed the sight of him wearing only jeans slung low on his lean hips, baring his chest and taut abdomen to her gaze. An echo of the heat they created together skittered along her nerves. Even now, she thought, this man had a hold on her unlike anyone in her life except the child who was likely going to be waking up at any moment.

"Jolie?"

She realized what her expression must be as she looked at him.

She wondered if she could discover if Whitney had been in the city the day of the murder without betraying why she needed to know. She discarded that idea quickly; T.C. was too smart to be fooled by whatever convoluted way she might try to find out.

She saw him glance toward Emma, realized that had been his first thought, to make sure she was all right. And in that instant she realized with a little shock that she trusted him to do the right thing, even if his mother was somehow involved. Because that was who he was.

At that moment Emma stirred, then sat up, rubbing at her eyes after her long nap. It would likely be a late night, Jolie thought, but guaranteed sound sleep was a good trade off. She immediately wanted to go see Flash, and Jolie had to remind her to put her boots on first. Jolie saw T.C. check the area outside for anything that might spook the usually calm horse before he lifted the girl up onto his back, where she crowed with delight. His care made her even more certain he would do the right thing, no matter what. Even though she had destroyed his love for her—she wasn't foolish enough to mistake his need for her for love, at least she hoped not—nothing could change his feelings for Emma.

So when he walked back to the fence where she was sitting and joined her on the top rail, she told him what she'd seen.

"My mother?" T.C.'s brow furrowed in puzzlement. "She never comes out here. She thinks I'm crazy to spend time without all the mod cons."

"It was her. Do you think I've forgotten what she looks like?" She knew she sounded a bit combative, but her mind was in complete turmoil as it wrestled with the possibilities.

"I never said I doubted you, only that I have no idea why she'd be out here."

She drew in a deep breath, steadied herself. "Your mother has green eyes."

He blinked his own eyes of the same color. "Yes."

"She's blond."

"With help, yes."

It sounded hesitant, puzzled, as if she'd only stated the obvious. She waited. He got there much quicker than she would have expected.

"You think it was her? The killer?"

He didn't sound nearly as shocked as she would have expected, either.

"I'm only saying she fits the description. And Emma's day care isn't too far from the Colton building."

He let out an audible breath. Shifted on the top fence rail. She watched him intently.

"Worse," he muttered. "The place she gets her hair done is on the same street."

Jolie stifled a gasp, not just at the admission but at the miracle that she hadn't encountered his mother at some point before. But then she belatedly realized something else. "You're not surprised."

"No."

"Did this already occur to you?"

"Not exactly."

She waited. Silently.

His mouth tightened; then he turned to face her head-on. "I've been wondering for two and a half months, starting as soon as the shock wore off, if she had something to do with my father's disappearance."

Her own eyes widened. Despite everything she knew of Whitney, this hadn't occurred to her. "Do you think she did?"

He let out a disgusted sounding sigh. "I don't know. I've suspected by turns her, Fowler and Marceline."

"That's...understandable," she said carefully. She knew what he thought of those particular siblings, and for that matter his mother, but going from unpleasantness and conniving to this was a huge jump.

"I've been tracking them." His mouth twisted upward at one corner. "Spying a bit. But all I've learned is that Fowler spends all his spare time with Tiffany, Marceline has uncharacteristically taken to spending hers with her horse—or one of the hands, which is even harder to believe—and my mother has developed a weakness for phony psychics."

Jolie processed this. While the idea of Marceline hanging out with a ranch hand was preposterous, so was the thought of determinedly sophisticated, social-climbing Whitney Colton consulting psychics.

She hesitated, then said, "Maybe that's a sign she's really concerned about your father."

"I've thought that," he agreed. "But it could be a cover, too. Her idea of what a grieving spouse would do."

"Did they have a prenup?" He gave her a sideways look. She shrugged. "She was a lot younger. And your father always struck me as a very...experienced man."

A brief but potent grin flashed across his face. "If that's your way of saying he suspects everyone of ulterior motives because he usually has them himself, you're right."

She smiled back. He was still, she noted, referring to his father in present tense. So he had not given him up for dead, at least not yet. And she suddenly realized what hell it must be, to suspect your own family. But it could be worse; at least he wasn't suspicious of any of the "good Coltons," as Piper had called them.

"They did have a prenup agreement," he said, but he didn't sound as if it helped much. "I don't know how much he settled on her. It was incremental, I think, starting at five years."

His expression changed, all traces of lightness vanishing.

"But?"

"It had a thirty-year expiration. Which they just passed."

Jolie's breath stopped in her throat. He'd just admitted his mother had a very powerful motive to have done away with his father.

Chapter 27

At family dinners, T.C. often wished himself anywhere else. But tonight his wish was much more specific; he wanted to be at the refuge with Jolie and Emma. They only gathered like this because the old man had demanded it. T.C. suspected he liked to exercise his power over the family. And stopping now would be tantamount to admitting he was dead, which he at least wasn't willing to do.

But it didn't stop him from wondering if there was one of them sitting at this table who knew perfectly well Eldridge Colton was dead, and was only here to hide that fact. Only his mother was absent tonight, and he wondered if she was off consulting another psychic.

Or if she wasn't here because she was the one who knew he was dead.

Fowler had been on a tear all through his usual predinner drink, ranting about his usual favorite subjects. Marceline, who had arrived only just before they sat down, didn't even listen before starting to nod in agreement. It was, as Jolie had said, an odd coalition. Now he surreptitiously studied his half sister, wondering yet again if her urging to have his father declared dead lay in something more than simply wanting the inheritance that had also been in the prenup. He'd forgotten to tell Jolie about that part, that Marceline also had a powerful motive, although her take would be considerably less than their mother's.

She had straw in her hair.

T.C. blinked, leaned slightly to confirm what he'd seen. But there was no doubting the piece of dried hay clinging to Marceline's hair in the back.

If he hadn't been indulging of late himself, he never would have thought of it. But the memory of picking straw out of his own hair and various other places was too fresh—and too hot—in his mind to ignore. He fought down the instant response of his body to the memory of those precious times with Jolie, and looked away before Marceline caught him staring. And probably gaping.

He'd heard a vehicle on the gravel just before she came in. Marceline, coming up from the barns—and the bunk-house?

Was it true? Had his snooty, imperious and usually immaculate stepsister unbent enough for a tumble in the hay with ranch hand Dylan Harlow? And what the hell was Dylan thinking? He'd been here long enough to see what she was, what he was risking. All it would take was one wrong thing said to set her off, and—

"—see that little bitch tossed in prison for the rest of her life. T.C. can go visit her. It'll be a nice payback for what she did to him."

T.C.'s attention snapped back to his half brother. "What?"

"I said you can go visit that tramp in prison. You'd like that, wouldn't you, after she dumped you for all that cash that was as cold and hard as she is?"

T.C. fought down the fierce denial that rose to his lips. He couldn't let his brother see, or even suspect, where Jolie was. It didn't matter now as far as their father was concerned, but Fowler couldn't and wouldn't keep his mouth shut and anything he said could get back to the killer.

Especially if the killer was their mother.

His stomach churned as he tried to think.

So Fowler didn't know yet that Jolie had been cleared in his father's disappearance. And whoever the hand was who'd been at the refuge hadn't seen anything or said anything. Unless it had been his mother that time, too. But she would hardly hold back, would she? She would have been bursting with the news that Jolie was here and unable to stop herself from blurting it out, no doubt in over the top outrage, the moment the family was gathered. In fact, she would have waited until he was here to do it, for maximum effect, and—

Waited until he was here.

He leaped to his feet, shoving his chair back heedlessly. God, he was an idiot. He should have realized instantly why his mother wasn't here. That vehicle he'd heard minutes ago wasn't Marceline arriving; it was his mother leaving. She'd waited until she knew he wouldn't be at the refuge.

He left the room without a word, hit the back door at a run and was in the SUV in seconds. He didn't care about kicking up gravel and dust as he roared off. He covered the distance to the refuge at twice his usual pace, even once leaving the big loop of the track and cutting across a small rise and down the other side so fast the wheels lost traction for an instant as he went over the top before grabbing again.

He spotted the Jeep, the silver one with the CVR logo on the door his mother drove on the rare occasions she went anywhere on the ranch, just coming to a halt about fifteen feet from the cabin. He floored it; he wanted to stop this before it started. Not for anything did he want Jolie to have to deal with this right now. Nor, he thought, his stomach seeming to turn over, did he want Emma to see it.

He skidded to a halt between his mother and the cabin. He was out before she had finished shrieking at him for spraying dust all over her. He figured he'd start with the biggest gun. Maybe he'd catch her off guard.

"Why did you kill that woman?"

His mother's brow furrowed. "What?"

"You heard me. You were seen, described."

There was no mistaking her utterly blank expression. He knew his mother well enough to know she had no idea what he was talking about, not even enough to formulate a denial.

She wasn't the killer Emma had seen.

He should feel relieved, he supposed. But he didn't. "What are you doing here?"

"Checking on you. I'm worried. Everyone is talking about you. You left work, just vanished, for days now. They think you killed Eldridge and are hiding! And to find you with her, that scheming little money grubber—"

"Get out." He cut her off sharply. "This place is off-limits to you."

Her nose went up immediately. "Don't talk to me like that. I'm your mother."

"Much to my dismay."

"How dare you!"

"How dare I?" He was barely able to keep his rage on a leash now that she was here. Something about her intruding here, spying, skulking about, brought it all to the surface. "I dare because I finally know the truth."

"The truth? Whatever that little tramp has been telling you—"

"Stop. I've had enough of your manipulations."

"That gold digger in there likely killed your father! As if what we paid her to stop ruining your life wasn't enough, she came back for more and when Eldridge wouldn't cave she killed him!"

"Cork it, Mother. Jolie has an unassailable alibi. Not that I needed it."

"My God, you've fallen for her lies again, haven't you? Just like you did four years ago."

The leash snapped.

"Oh, yes," he said, his voice going low, lethal. "Let's talk about four years ago. Let's talk about you bullying an innocent woman whose only crime was falling in love with me. Let's talk about you threatening to make her life a living hell if she didn't leave. Let's especially talk about you threatening a helpless baby!"

She backed up a half step. "I never—"

He told her in crude terms what she could do with her denial.

"Thomas Eldridge Colton, you mind your manners."

He knew he'd gotten to her. She only dragged out his full name when she was out of other ammo.

"I'll take no crap about manners from a woman who

has less class than Jolie has in her little finger. What you did was unforgivable. A tiny baby, and you used her as a weapon. You're disgusting."

His mother went pale. "Thomas—"

"Shut up. I love Jolie. I always have. So get used to her being around. If I ever hear you've been anything less than kind to her, then I will make *your* life a living hell. And so help me, if you ever threaten Emma again, you will pay a higher price than you can afford. I'll see you out on the street before I'll let that happen."

She was staring at him, appearing dumbstruck. Then her gaze shifted slightly, to look past him.

"It won't matter." Jolie's quiet, steady voice came from behind him. He kept his eyes on his mother. Saw her nose wrinkle with distaste.

"That's exactly what I mean," he said to his mother. "If I see so much as a sneer on your manufactured face, I will come at you with both barrels until nothing's left. Do you understand?"

She was looking shaken now. This was his mother. He supposed he should feel some twinge about that, but he thought again of the baby he'd once held in his arms and there was no room for feeling sorry for the woman who had sworn to terrorize her.

"You won't have to," Jolie said as she came down the porch steps, still in that same steady voice. "If she dares to try she'll find I'm not the frightened pushover I once was. I will defend myself, and my child."

She came to a halt beside him. A glance told him her head was up, her gaze as level as her voice as she faced the woman who had ruined her life, threatened her child. Pride filled him. She was one hell of a woman, Jolie Peters.

He reached out and put his arm around her, pulling

her close. Then he looked back at his mother, who for the first time he could remember looked at a loss. There was no bluster, no haughtiness in her now. T.C. had never seen her like this. He didn't relish it, but welcomed it nevertheless. She needed to know he meant every word.

"It's up to Jolie to decide if there will ever be a relationship between you and me. As long as she doesn't feel safe, as long as Emma isn't safe around you, you're out of our lives. Forever, if need be."

Whitney Colton was apparently speechless, which was an accomplishment not to be taken lightly. Her gaze flicked to Jolie, then back to him. And in the moment before she turned on her heel and got back in the Jeep, he thought he saw fear in her eyes. Of what, he wasn't sure, but perhaps she'd finally realized she might have lost this son forever.

And then she was gone. He hugged Jolie, smiled at her. "You did good. Faced her down good and proper."

"I had all the strength in the world," Jolie said quietly, "after hearing what you said to her."

He'd been hoping she'd heard. Most of what he'd said had been for her as much as his mother. "I meant it. All of it."

"I know. I don't know why, how you could forgive what I did—"

"Knowing what she did makes all the difference."

"You didn't have to believe me. She is your mother."

"Again, to my dismay," he said wryly. Then he looked at her, considering. "Now the only question is, can you forgive me?"

"Forgive you? For what?"

"For believing her side. For letting you and Emma go without a real fight."

"Maybe we were both too young then."

She was letting him off easy, he thought. But then, Jolie always did. Giving in to the urge that was nearly undeniable anyway, he kissed her. Long, and slow and deep, until only lack of air made him break it off.

He stared down at her as a sudden realization hit him. "Look... I made a big assumption tonight."

She blinked, looking as if she, too, was a bit dazed by how quickly the heat flared between them. "What?"

"That you...feel the same way."

She smiled, in a way he hadn't seen in four years. "Not an assumption. Fact."

Relief blasted through him, telling him just how worried he'd been that he might have jumped the gun. He kissed her again, gently this time, sweetly.

"Are you gonna keep doing that? I'm hungry." Emma's chipper voice came from the doorway.

T.C. could see she held a small, inexpensive music player with a set of earphones attached. He guessed that was how Jolie had kept her from hearing the confrontation that was occurring just outside the door. He admired her presence of mind. As he admired so many other things.

"You know," he said, walking up the steps and sweeping the child up in his arms, "so am I."

"There's one last jar of chili," Jolie said.

"Sounds perfect."

And a few minutes later he sat down to a meal that wasn't nearly as fancy as the one he'd left, consisting of one course of chili with crackers, but it tasted better than anything he'd ever eaten.

Chapter 28

"She'll talk, won't she?" Jolie asked. "Back at the house?"

T.C. finished rinsing his chili bowl before speaking. "She will."

"So they'll know we're here."

"Yes." He looked at her. "You want to leave? Go somewhere else?"

Jolie felt her stomach lurch. She felt safe here. After all, it had been his mother, not the killer—at least, not the killer she was most worried about—who had found them. And she was sure of that now; Whitney Colton wasn't a good enough actress to have faked that blank look.

"Should we?"

"You could get lost easier in the city, but it would also be easier to sneak up on you amid the crowds. We could go to the house. You'd both be safe there—"

"But under the same roof as the person who accused me."

"Even Fowler will shut up now."

"And the one who still thinks I'm a money-grubbing gold digger?"

"I think they call that projection."

She had to look away from him for fear she'd smile. T.C. really did have few illusions left about his charming mother. But she wasn't sure that was enough to make being in the same house tolerable.

"That first person I saw out here," she began.

"I know. We can't be positive it was a hand, but it makes sense that it was, that he mentioned in passing that he'd seen Flash here, and that got back to my mother."

She nodded; it did make sense. But she'd long ago learned that what made sense wasn't always what happened. In the end, she gave him her truthful answer. "I like it here."

For a moment T.C. just smiled at her. "You do?"

"Yes."

"With no refrigerator, TV, cell phone, not even a radio and having to pump water and dump it outside?"

"A roof, peace, quiet, books, a place to sit and sleep, a working bathroom," she countered.

He shook his head, as if in wonder. "You've hung on to it, haven't you? That knack for looking at the bright side."

"If I lost it, I'd have given up long ago."

He reached out and took her hand. She saw him glance at Emma, who seemed remarkably unperturbed by the new closeness between them.

"You're an amazing woman."

Only this man had ever made her believe that. She'd always thought of herself as scrambling from one crisis to the next her entire life. She'd bounced from one foster home to another, her grief over the death of her parents coming out in unpleasant ways. When she'd finally landed in an understanding place, that, too, was yanked out from under her with her foster father's death. Once out of the system, she'd dug herself into a gradually deeper hole, going from one scrape to another. Then she'd fallen for a smooth-talking pretty boy who'd turned out to be a petty criminal who'd not only vanished the moment he'd learned she was pregnant, but landed himself in jail, so there was never any question of him being there for her.

T.C. knew he'd never been in the picture; she'd told him long ago.

That you're here now, that you've turned your life around, is proof you're amazing.

His words had been salve to her battered soul, and she'd clung to them, allowing herself for a brief moment to believe. To believe in herself, and in this man, and the future unfolding before them.

And two months later it was all over, and she was skulking away in the middle of the night with her meager belongings in a worn suitcase and her most precious thing wrapped in the worn blanket she'd come to the Colton Valley Ranch with. She'd left behind the things T.C. had given her, with some idea of Eldridge or Whitney accusing her of theft. He'd had a habit of picking up things he said made him think of her: a scarf the exact color of her eyes, a colorful mobile for Emma's crib, with brightly painted horses dancing. It had hurt to leave that more than her own things.

The only thing she'd taken was the leather planner he'd given her, because that had been before they were actually together, and she'd already put it into full use anyway.

And now it had helped save her from Fowler's viciousness.

Well, it and the governor, she thought with an inward smile.

"C'n I go see Flash?" Emma asked from where she'd been sitting on the bed with one of the books T.C. had brought from the apartment. A small thing, perhaps, but it was typical of him to think of it.

"It's kind of late, sweetie," Jolie said.

"I know. I wanna say g'night."

"He'd like that," T.C. said with a glance at Jolie.

"Well, in that case," Jolie said with a smile at her daughter. "But then it's time to get ready for bed."

Emma didn't protest that but happily slid off the bed and trotted toward the door.

Jolie and T.C. followed, rather leisurely. He hung on to her hand, and just that simple thing warmed her to the core. This felt like they once had, the three of them, like a family, a unit, with a future they would face together.

Emma waited, as T.C. had taught her, until he checked the area for anything that might spook the horse. The moon was beginning to wane, but there was still plenty of the stark light that made the piebald horse seem a part of the night. He nickered a welcome as they got to the fence, which made Emma in turn giggle happily. T.C. lifted her up to the top rail of the fence. Flash stepped up to the girl, who proceeded to pat his nose, and then rub the spot under his jaw that T.C. had shown her.

After a moment T.C. said quietly, "I'm going to the car for a minute. The message light's flashing."

She nodded, giving him a smile before she turned back to watching Emma. The girl's simple delight never failed to fill her heart near to bursting. And now, with

T.C. back in their lives, she wasn't sure she could hold in her happiness. It threatened to bubble over until she was giggling like her little girl. It was a good feeling, a very good feeling.

It must have been a short message, because in moments T.C. was walking back to them. And he was smiling, a very satisfied smile.

"You're clear," he said as he reached the fence. "The voice mail was Sheriff Watkins. Seems he got a call from the governor."

She drew back, her eyes widening. "The governor himself?"

"Yep. Told you he'd remember you."

She shook her head in wonder. "But he called…himself?"

"Not sure he actually made the call, but he talked to him. Told him he could vouch for exactly where you were when the old man went missing." T.C. grinned. "And the sheriff said he was about to call Fowler and tell him the same thing. He sounded a bit pleased to be able to drop the governor on my charming brother's head."

Jolie couldn't help herself, she laughed. "What will Fowler do now?"

"Oh, he'll think of someone else to accuse." His expression changed to a more thoughtful one. "Although I think his main partner in crime might be a little too preoccupied to help much."

"Marceline?"

He nodded. "I saw her at dinner, before I realized where my mother was headed." He glanced at Emma, who was busy now stroking Flash's mane, then back to Jolie before saying pointedly, "She had straw in her hair."

She got the connection immediately, that Marceline had been up to…well, what they'd been up to. "Really?"

"I think it's a hand, Dylan Harlow. A good, decent guy."

"That sounds…" She let her voice trail off, because nothing she could think of to say was anything less than insulting.

"Yes," T.C. said, apparently agreeing with what she hadn't said. "I just hope she doesn't hurt him too badly."

Jolie winced inwardly. "Like I hurt you?"

He looked at her. "Or Emma's father hurt you."

She hadn't expected that. Her face must have shown it, because he added softly, "I can't imagine how it felt to live like that, Jolie. Always expecting to lose everything, because, well, you always did."

"Except Emma."

"And you will never lose her," he promised, his voice solemn. "No matter what happens."

Jolie was amazed at the slow, burgeoning peace that filled her heart. She had a promise from T. C. Colton, and you could, as her father had been wont to say, take that to the bank.

It seemed appropriate that she think of her father now. Because for the first time since his death she was starting to feel safe again. As if the rough seas might truly be over, and she and her little girl could start to live the kind of lives she'd always wanted. The police would catch the killer of that woman, and she and T.C. could go home and begin to rebuild what had been stolen from them. Just the thought of having him back in her life, solid, unshakable and forever, made her heart soar.

But somewhere in the back of her mind, that hard-earned warning bell was going off. *It's too perfect. Some-*

*thing will go wrong. Something always goes wrong. You'll
lose everything again.*

She quashed it. Not now. Not this time.

This time they would win.

Chapter 29

He'd underestimated his mother's ability to spread gossip quickly, T.C. thought with a sigh. It had been barely a day and a half and even the ranch hands were in conversations that suspiciously stopped when he walked in. Well, except for one of the newer guys, who was bragging about the hot blonde who'd been flirting with him at some trendy honky-tonk last night, and making bets on how long it would take him to get her into bed.

T.C. much preferred his own quiet Saturday, spent teaching Emma to ride and watching the sunset with Jolie. He liked it so much he was going to see that it happened often, and to that end had packed a duffle bag with some items to take back to the refuge. Even sleeping on the floor with them close by was better than his comfortable bed here, alone, and he planned on staying for the duration.

After that…

Shaking off the stab of doubt—not about his own feelings, but Jolie's—he picked up the bag and headed downstairs. He went to the dining room, where coffee was always at the ready. He poured himself a cup, and stood sipping it while looking out to where Flash was hitched to the deck railing. He'd ridden the big paint back to the house, taking a long way around since he was starting to get restless. The horse was used to working, and T.C. needed to make sure he stayed calm enough for Emma, which would be hard if he was brimming with pent-up energy. Besides, he hadn't wanted to leave them without any way to contact him, so he'd left his SUV with the ranch-wide system there.

He pondered whether to take a second horse back with him, for Jolie to ride. He could round up a pony for Emma, too, except she was so enamored of Flash he suspected it would be a disappointment for her. He'd had to wait until she was deeply occupied in one of her storybooks to saddle up and head to the ranch house, because Jolie had told him the child wouldn't want him to take the horse away.

He'd felt a pang as he heard that echo of Jolie's own fears of losing everything that mattered, and he'd silently repeated his promise to the little girl that she would never have to deal with what her mother had dealt with.

But maybe later on the pony, he thought as he finished his coffee. She wouldn't be ready to actually ride alone for a while yet anyway.

"Called in your buddy the governor, did you?"

T.C. didn't even turn to look. "Haven't talked to him in a month," he answered honestly, with enough cheer to provoke his brother. Fowler never paid attention to those below the top. T.C. doubted he even knew Mike Cortez's name.

Fowler walked past him, turned, looked at the duffle bag on the floor at T.C.'s feet. Odd, T.C. thought. He felt armored in a way he never had before, facing his insufferable brother. Strange how that worked, the feeling that nothing could really get to you when you had someone like Jolie backing you up.

"And now you're literally shacking up with that little gold digger of yours. At least that run-down hovel is suitable for the likes of her."

"I suggest you go back to formulating wild theories," T.C. said, his tone becoming ominous, "unless you want to go to that board meeting of yours looking like you've been hit by a train."

Fowler backed up a step, warily. And rightfully so, T.C. thought. He had twice before put his bloated brother on his ass and left him looking the worse for it. For that matter, so had most of his other siblings. Including, if his guess from that incident years ago was right, Alanna. That thought made him grin inwardly.

"More physical threats?"

"Promises," T.C. corrected, knowing his reputation for keeping his promises would make his point.

"If you think you can force that woman on this family—"

"This family is already in free fall," T.C. said. "Or hadn't you noticed?"

"That will end soon," Fowler said confidently. "Now that I know who really did it."

T.C. groaned inwardly. He hadn't really meant it when he told Fowler to go back to formulating his wild theories. He'd just meant to warn him to lay off Jolie or he'd be dealing with him. Not to mention that he'd be finding out Jolie could and would probably put him on the floor also. "Now who's the lucky one?"

"The one they should have looked at first," Fowler declared. "The one Dad turned down when she came begging for money for that ridiculous foster care home she wanted to build. Here, on Colton Valley Ranch!" The indignation fairly crackled in his voice. "Besides, everybody knows she's not a real Colton anyway."

T.C. stared at his brother incredulously. "Piper? You're seriously accusing *Piper*?"

"It's obvious, isn't it? I heard her and our father arguing about it not a month before he vanished. He told her he didn't want rug rats running around the place, and he certainly didn't want ones who would likely be thieves or worse. And that made her very, very angry."

"It makes me very angry," T.C. snapped. He thought of Piper, and how she could well have ended up in the same system that had chewed Jolie up so badly. And Jolie herself, and how hard she'd had to work to stay a straight, decent human being in the face of a by-nature impersonal structure. "And if you start this ball rolling," he warned Fowler, "you'll regret it."

For an instant T.C. thought he saw something akin to desperation flash in his brother's eyes.

"It's already rolling. I told the sheriff when he called."

T.C. could only imagine how Troy Watkins had taken that. But that look he'd seen made him frown slightly. And then, moved by something he didn't quite understand, he asked something he'd never asked before. "Why don't you just marry Tiffany? It's obvious you care about her."

Fowler frowned, clearly puzzled by the apparent non sequitur. "What's that got to do with this?"

"You think we don't all know this shotgunning of yours is really about protecting her?"

For once T.C.'s brother had no snarky comeback. He simply stared, as if he really believed no one had realized the truth behind this particular set of machinations.

T.C. gave up, turned on his heel and headed off to track down his little sister and warn her she was the next in the crosshairs. The idea of gentle, kind Piper being a suspect at all was absurd; the thought that she'd done it, beyond ridiculous. They'd get her through this, he thought. And at least the heat was off Jolie.

Now if they would just find the killer of that poor woman, he could finally relax. And he and Jolie and Emma could begin again, building the new life they should have had four years ago. He knew she was still wary, and they had a lot to work out. Things had changed. So had she, and he had, too.

But what hadn't changed was the core of who and what they were together. And that was as right as it had ever been. He just had to convince her of that. He understood her doubts—after the life she'd had, she couldn't help not trusting anything good to last—but he would convince her.

No matter what it took.

He couldn't find Piper, so he texted her a warning message. He headed back to where Flash was standing, docilely now that he'd had a good run. He slung his bag over the saddle horn by the loop on one end. It was awkward, but it would do for the trip back to the refuge. Flash was used to much stranger things; after he'd carried injured calves, a soaking wet, squirmy dog and the carcass of the biggest rattlesnake ever found in the entire county, an inanimate duffel bag was nothing.

He was about a mile out when his phone activated with the buzzer indicating a signal from the ranch system. Piper must have gotten his text, he thought as he slowed Flash and pulled the phone out.

It wasn't Piper. It was a signal from his SUV.

He hit the icon instantly. "Jolie? I'm almost there—"

"Hurry." The sound of her voice was like a blow to his gut. She sounded terrified."

"What is it?"

"Emma's gone."

Chapter 30

T.C.'s urgency transmitted to Flash, and the big horse responded with reckless speed. A good quarter horse could cover a half mile in less than forty-five seconds. Flash was one of the best. T.C. slowed only to answer when the phone signaled again.

"There's a gold car heading west. I'm trying to catch up."

"I see the dust. Still no Emma?"

"No. God, I think she took her!"

He didn't have to ask who. Emma might only have minutes before the killer thought she was far enough away to simply kill the child—the only witness—and dump her body.

T.C. flicked a swift glance at the second cloud of dust rising, calculated. He was closer. And he had Flash, who could take shortcuts the big SUV would never make.

He leaned over and urged the big horse on. "I need it

all, boy," he told him. "Our little girl needs us as fast as you can get there."

Again the big horse responded. He stretched out, his powerful hindquarters delivering every ounce of speed. They topped the rise, and T.C. took in what he saw with swift calculation. The gold car, almost blending into the surroundings, was nearly to the turn the dusty track made to head to the main road. Behind it—too far—was his own SUV. It bucked as Jolie tried to keep it on the track at speed. But she wouldn't make it. Not before the car reached the road and could pick up speed.

But he could.

Possibilities slammed through his mind. Too many involved the gold car crashing and Emma possibly getting hurt, or worse.

Use what you have...

What he had was a knowledge of the terrain and the best cow horse in the state, still driving hard under him. T.C. made his decision in a split second. They had to beat the car to the turn. Flash seemed to realize the car was the goal, and poured it on even more. T.C. knew he was relying on equine instinct, but it was all he had. All Emma had. He had to trust that Jolie could take care of herself. Knew she'd want him to focus on rescuing Emma. He pushed everything else out of his mind.

He could see her now. Through the back window. Saw her tangled blond hair. She was in the backseat. Crammed into the farthest corner from the driver. And then she looked around, rather wildly.

And spotted them.

Her small, frightened face changed in an instant. Joy filled it. T.C. thought he'd never felt like more of a man than in that split second of time.

He tightened the right rein the tiniest bit. Flash responded instantly, shifting his track the perfect fraction. They pulled up alongside the car. For a horse capable of bursts of forty-five miles an hour, keeping up with a car barely doing fifteen on a dirt trail was nothing. And this was where T.C. had to hope Flash understood that, as with cattle, sometimes staying even with them was as important as catching up with them in the first place.

And that Emma understood what he needed her to do. The driver hadn't even looked back yet, and had all the windows closed against the dust. For once he was thankful there hadn't been enough rain to tamp that down yet. He made a gesture at the back window, praying silently that while the woman had no doubt locked the doors, she hadn't thought or didn't have the capacity to lock the windows in the up position.

It took the child a moment, but she was as smart as her mother, and the window began to slide down. T.C. knew the killer would realize almost immediately and do... something. He had his guess, and did what he could to signal the horse to be ready. He was counting on Flash's incredible instincts and ability to react to unexpected moves to save all three of them.

The window vanished down into the door. He leaned down, reaching for Emma. She took his hand unhesitatingly. The driver yelled. And hit the gas.

Simultaneously he dug his heels into the paint's ribs and pulled Emma. Hard and fast. The big horse stayed even with the accelerating car. Gave him the two seconds he needed. And then Emma was clear. He had her in his arms. He shifted his weight back in the saddle, gave a slight tug back on the reins and Flash slowed.

"That's it, boy," he said. "You did it." Emma was clinging to him. "And so did you, sweetheart."

Those huge eyes so like her mother's were looking up at him, and he sensed that she wasn't sure how she should feel.

"You were as good as any rodeo trick rider," he said with a grin.

Emma giggled, tipping over into happiness, to T.C.'s relief.

"And Flash," she said.

"Yes, him, too," he agreed, giving the horse's neck a good, solid pat. Heedless of the horse's sweatiness, Emma leaned down and gave him a huge hug, cooing happily. Only then did T.C. look around, figuring the gold car would have made it to the road and be long gone by now.

Except it hadn't.

They'd rounded the turn now. His SUV was stopped across the dirt track.

The gold car was nose down in the gully beside the rough track. Jolie had maneuvered the SUV so that the only escape was a path that led right into it. The killer obviously hadn't realized until too late that her city car wouldn't make it.

"Mommy!"

Emma's delighted cry brought Jolie running. T.C. brought Flash to a halt and slid off, the girl in his arms. He found to his surprise he didn't want to put her down, and hung on until Jolie was there and he could put her safely in her mother's arms.

"Did you see, Mommy? I was a trick rider!"

Jolie was hugging the girl fiercely, but her gaze was on T.C. "I saw," she said. "Oh, I saw. Both of you—" she glanced at Flash "—no, all three of you were perfect."

"You did all right yourself," T.C. drawled, nodding toward the wrecked car. "Is she...?"

"Just dazed, I think. She's pretty much pinned in there, though. Don't really care."

"Me, either. Recognize her?"

She shook her head.

"She's the mean lady," Emma said helpfully, giving a wary glance over her shoulder at the gold car.

"Emma, honey, did she say anything to you?" Jolie asked, smoothing back her tangled hair.

"She yelled a lot. Like mean people do."

Jolie hugged her tighter. T.C. reached out and cupped the girl's cheek and said firmly. "And now she's going to go away where she can't be mean to you ever again."

The child considered that for a moment, then nodded and snuggled up to her mother.

T.C. walked over to the car then, where the woman appeared to be coming out of it. Jolie was right, she was trapped by the compressed car door, and although she was aware enough to look at him fearfully, he doubted she was up to trying to climb back to get out through the open window. He'd keep an eye on her, and if she did try, he'd make sure she got exactly nowhere.

He went back to Jolie and Emma and, thinking it might help, gave the child the task of walking Flash around to cool him down after the crazed run. She was delighted at the task, and cooed lovingly at the horse as they walked the short path he'd sketched out for her from the road to a big rock, back and forth.

T.C. made the call to the police. Then they waited.

"I'm sorry about your car," Jolie said after a moment.

He shook his head. "You did what you had to do, used what you had. Worth more than a car to put her away."

"How did she find us?" Jolie said it in a musing tone, as if not expecting an answer.

"I have a clue," he said.

She gave him a startled look. "What?"

"One of our newer hands was talking about a woman who started flirting with him at a bar, after she found out he worked here. Description matches."

He heard a siren start up in the distance, and guessed a patrol car was on the way to take control of the scene. By then he told Emma Flash was cooled out enough and she could stop.

That was when the girl looked toward the car in the ditch and said, sounding only puzzled, "She knows my daddy."

Jolie froze. T.C. felt her shock as if it were a physical thing.

"She said that?" T.C. asked gently, when Jolie was clearly unable to speak.

Emma nodded. "She said she was making sure."

"Of what?"

"That he wouldn't ever see me."

Jolie shuddered visibly. "Oh, Emma," she whispered.

"Don't care. Don't want him." She looked at T.C. "Want you."

Later, he would swear his heart stopped. It stopped, and when it started again it was a bigger, fuller heart, all because of two small words from a little girl.

Chapter 31

"One of those prison pen-pal romances," Detective John Eckhart said. "Never understood it myself, but there's a kind of woman who goes for it."

Jolie sat silently, the shock of all that had happened in the last twelve hours making the uncomfortable chair barely noticeable. Of all the things she might have expected, learning that the woman was Kevin's girlfriend was probably the last. She looked at T.C. Her mind was reeling, careening in so many directions at once she felt helpless to even know where to begin to ask any questions.

"When was the last time you saw Oberman?" Eckhart asked.

"The night he walked out," she said. "The night he found out about Emma."

Eckhart's mouth tightened at one corner. "Big man, that one."

T.C. uttered a term that made Jolie glad Emma was with Officer Wilcox, the patrol officer who had been so kind the day of the shooting. Not that she didn't think T.C. was absolutely right, but Emma didn't need to hear it. So she was glad Eckhart had called the woman in when Jolie told him Emma had been okay with her before. Emma had remembered her and gone willingly when she had suggested an ice cream in the department lunchroom.

But Jolie was still bewildered. "But why would Kevin's girlfriend come after Emma? Kevin never wanted her."

"She didn't come after Emma," T.C. said quietly. "She came after the only witness."

Jolie's breath caught. For a moment, so caught up in her panic and focused on what had nearly happened to her precious little girl that she had forgotten exactly what began all this. But now the ramifications tumbled into her mind in rapid succession.

"It was no coincidence that woman looked like you," T.C. said, his voice so cold it took her a moment to realize he was angry. Very angry.

"She thought...it was me."

"Yes," Detective Eckhart said. "Apparently Oberman had started talking about wanting a relationship with his daughter, which obviously would mean being in contact with you."

"A little late," Jolie muttered.

"Too late," T.C. said, in that same icy voice. She had a moment to marvel that such a cold tone could warm her so, but then all she could think about was the awfulness of what had happened.

"That poor woman." Regret flooded her. "She died for no reason except she looked like me."

"It's not your fault, Jolie." T.C.'s voice was urgent now as he sat beside her and slipped an arm around her shoulders.

Before she could slip any further down that rabbit hole of guilt, Detective Eckhart continued in a very brisk, businesslike manner that seemed to help. She supposed he knew that; he'd clearly been at this awhile, and she could hardly be the first thoroughly shaken person he'd had to deal with.

"We'll match her DNA to what we got from the ski mask you grabbed, but there's no real doubt. She had all the gear in the trunk of the car. Garbage bag, duct tape, a shovel. Probably wanted it to look like the girl just got lost. Lots of premeditation there."

Jolie shuddered as the words made clear just how close Emma had come to death. If not for T.C., and Flash, she might have died. Even if she'd managed to stop the car as she had, Emma could have been badly hurt in the crash; she'd had no seat belt on. His dramatic, utterly cowboy rescue seemed even more heroic now. And the fact that he had made Emma feel like she'd done something magnificent herself, making it seem almost an exciting game to the child, meant more to her than she could even find words to express.

"Plus," Eckhart added, "she had an hour's drive from where she and Oberman were living to the day care. Lots of time to reconsider. She's in a whole lot of very deep trouble."

"So all this was to…what?" Jolie asked, feeling sluggish, like she couldn't quite grasp it all at the moment.

"Keep him to herself. You and your daughter were competition in her eyes."

"For Kevin? I've not even spoken to him since that

night. I only knew he was locked up because I saw it in the news. That's crazy."

"She went looking for a romance with a convicted felon while he was still in prison," T.C. pointed out. "That's not exactly high on the normal scale."

"And apparently she started a correspondence with several inmates. Oberman was just the one who got out first."

Jolie's breath caught. "He's out?"

Eckhart nodded. "Six months ago." He gave her a steady look. "He swears he didn't know about any of this. And so far, his alibi checks out for the times everything has happened."

"You've talked to him," Jolie said, starting to feel a little numb.

"He came in voluntarily, once we contacted him. If he did know, he sure threw her under the bus in a hurry. Said it was all crazy, that she was crazy. And he was about to break it off. Which may be what set her off."

"Do you believe him?" T.C. asked.

"I went at him pretty hard. He never wavered. And his parole officer says he's been toeing the line since he got out. Working hard at a pretty drudge job, long hours. I don't usually cut cons much slack, but we both think that on this he's telling the truth. And he's scared. She had a gun, he's a convicted felon. He could be in big trouble if we could prove he knew about it."

He started to say something more, then stopped himself.

"What?" Jolie asked.

"Nothing factual. Just a feeling, after twenty years of being a cop."

"What?" T.C. repeated her question.

"I got the feeling, from talking to him, that he's determined to stay straight. Some talk the game, but my gut tells me he means it."

"So Emma's father, the guy with the prison record, is innocent, but his girlfriend, with no record, is guilty?" T.C. asked.

Detective Eckhart's mouth quirked upward. "Unexpected, but it does happen."

"He's not her father," Jolie said firmly. "He's never done a thing beyond making a biological contribution."

"I'm guessing you don't want to see him, then?"

Jolie blinked. "He's here? Now?"

T.C. leaped to his feet. "No." He looked at her. "You don't have to see him."

Jolie stood more slowly. "Did he ask for this?"

Eckhart nodded. "He has something he wants to say. But it's up to you. And he knows that. He said to tell you if you never want to speak with him, he understands."

Jolie was feeling stunned, her head almost spinning. She wanted more than anything to just grab Emma and run home, now that it was safe.

"Let me talk to him," T.C. said. Jolie lifted her gaze to his face. His jaw was set in that way she knew so well. "I'll make things clear to him. That he has no claim on Emma, or you."

Panic clutched at her throat. She hadn't thought of that. She looked at Eckhart. "Could he? Come after Emma?"

"Legally he has a claim. I don't think that's where his mind is, though."

"It better not be. If he tries to make a move, he'll come up against every lawyer Colton's got. And he won't find a decent lawyer in the entire city who will touch him. And if that doesn't stop him, I will. Personally. Unless and until Jolie changes her mind, he gets nowhere near Emma."

She couldn't doubt he meant it. Resolve echoed in every word. And she knew in that moment that T. C. Colton was exactly who she'd always thought he was, a man who would do anything for the ones he loved.

Loved.

This at last, out of everything that had happened, both took her breath away and restored her shivering heart to warmth. And that was what gave her the courage to face Kevin.

She stopped dead when she stepped into the small interview room Eckhart led her to. It shocked her. He looked worn, thin, and the thick blond hair he'd been so proud of was getting sparse on top. She did a quick calculation, realized he was only thirty-eight. He looked a decade older. And he looked wary; T.C. had indeed talked to him first without her, and whatever he'd said had clearly been taken to heart.

"I was young and stupid and irresponsible," he told her. "I had no right to do what I did to you. I'm more sorry than you could ever believe. But I swear, Jolie, I had no idea Lena would do anything like this."

She came away believing him, as Detective Eckhart had. This was a mere shell of the cocky, pretty boy she'd fallen for, and she didn't think he had enough energy or drive left in him to do this. She almost felt sorry for him.

Not, however, quite sorry enough to give him access to Emma. Not yet, anyway. And thanks to T.C., if it came to that, she wouldn't be alone and helpless to fight the system.

"Don't want him. Want you."

Emma's mumbled words echoed in her mind. *Like mother, like daughter*, she thought.

"Is Art Reagan still around?" she asked Eckhart after Kevin had gone.

Eckhart looked startled. "He's brass now, a deputy chief over in patrol. Why?"

"He saved me from that," she said, gesturing toward the doorway Kevin had left through. "Just thinking I owe him more than I ever realized. I'd like to thank him."

Eckhart smiled. "He'd like that. Sometimes I think he'd rather still be in the trenches than up top."

"Often the case," T.C. said with a grin.

"I'll get your little girl for you," Eckhart said.

And then they were alone, in an institutional-style room with uncomfortable furniture and carpet tiles designed to last a millennia. But Jolie didn't care about her surroundings, only the person in them, the one man who had always come through for her, even when she didn't deserve it.

"You're quite something, Jolie Peters," T.C. said. "That's a nice thing to do, reaching out to that deputy chief."

"There weren't that many who helped along the way. I remember the ones who did very well."

He seemed to hesitate before saying, "And where do I fall on that scale?"

"You aren't on it."

For a moment he looked stung, drew back slightly.

"Because," she said softly, "the numbers don't go high enough."

Only when he let out a long, audible breath did she realize he'd been holding it.

It was her turn to hesitate to speak. The rest of her life could be determined by the next few words, and she suddenly didn't want to say them. But he'd done everything so far, he'd helped them despite what she'd done, he'd understood why she'd done it as she had always hoped he would if he knew the truth. And he'd saved Emma, in dramatic, effective, Texas-cowboy style. He'd done it all, surely she could do this?

In the end, it came out simply, because there really wasn't anything else to say.

"I love you. I always have."

It was up to him now. If he told her it was too late, they couldn't go back, that this interlude had been just that, brought on only by circumstance, that he hadn't really meant what he'd said, she didn't know what she would do. She'd not fought for him once, but there had been other forces at play, making that nearly impossible. This time it would be his decision, and his alone. She held her breath until he finally spoke.

"I've spent four years telling myself you were just one woman, you weren't worth it, millions of fish in the sea, there isn't just one right person, and all that other crap. And I never believed a damned word of it."

"I never meant to hurt—"

He waved a hand and she stopped. "I know that. I blame myself for never realizing there was something else going on I didn't know about."

"No one would want to believe that about their mother."

He grimaced. "She's going to find things are different this time."

Jolie's heart gave a flutter in her chest. "This time?"

The last time she asked that, they'd ended up in a pile of fresh straw, making love madly, hotly. This time there was much more at stake, and she saw by his expression he knew it.

And then he smiled, that crooked T.C. smile that never failed to make her pulse speed up.

"This time," he said, "she won't be dealing with a scared employee with a child to use as a lever. She'll be dealing with my wife, and my daughter. If you'll have me."

Her breath caught, and moisture pooled in her eyes. For a moment she didn't have the air to speak.

"I'd like to formally adopt Emma. I don't ever want there to be a question."

She opened her mouth, but stopped her own words when he waved a hand, and let him finish.

"I love you, Jolie. I never stopped loving you. Both of you. Through it all. Say yes."

"Yes." It was all she could manage, but it was all she needed.

But she barely had time to process what had happened before the door to the room opened. She turned, expecting to see Emma, already thinking about how they would explain to her that they would now be a family, the three of them. She didn't think it would be hard. The child already adored him. And maybe someday they would add T.C.'s child. Just the thought gave her a little thrill deep inside.

And then her mind froze, stopping her little dream scenario in place. Because it wasn't Emma coming in.

It was Whitney Colton.

Chapter 32

"What are you doing here?"

T.C. said it sharply, with no preamble or even an acknowledgment of who she was. He hadn't expected to have to face her down again so soon, but he was bolstered by Jolie's acceptance, and he sure as hell wasn't going to let this woman mess them up this time.

"I...heard what happened, so I rushed over here."

She sounded oddly uncertain, but he ignored it. "If you think you're going to pull another stunt like you did four years ago, you can forget it."

"I—"

"If I have to leave the ranch, and even Colton Incorporated, to be free of your twisted scheming, then I will. I won't have Jolie or Emma subjected to that. Jolie and I are getting married, and there's nothing you can do to stop it. Don't even try to interfere this time."

"Congratulations."

It sounded utterly sincere. He stared at his mother. Of all the things he might have expected, this wasn't it. And then she startled him even more by turning to Jolie.

"I want to…apologize. To both of you."

T.C. wondered if he looked as stunned as he felt. Jolie looked nearly as shocked as his mother turned back to him and went on.

"You see, I never understood before. I had no idea what it felt like, to lose the love of your life, and not know what happened to him. If I had, I would never have done that to you."

T.C. stared at her. If he hadn't had too much experience with her manipulative nature, he would believe she truly loved the old man. Was it even possible?

"I'm so sorry. And sorry it took maybe losing your father to make me see. And seeing how you felt, how you defended her that day at the line shack."

He had never seen his mother so humbled. Was it real? It certainly appeared to be, but he'd learned early and hard that what appeared to be with his mother wasn't always what was.

But if it was, did he dare turn away this overture, this chance to give them a life without having to deal with her scorn and disrespect? If it was just him, he might accept. With reservations, as always with her. The frog and the scorpion, after all.

But it wasn't just him.

"Even if I believe this sudden change of heart, not to mention soul and very nature," he finally said, "it's not up to me. It's up to Jolie. Your future daughter-in-law, no matter what you do."

He smothered the smile that wanted to break through

at just saying the words, and kept his expression stern as he watched his mother turn back to Jolie.

"He's right. What I did was unforgivable. Especially to your little girl. I know I don't deserve it, but I hope someday you can find it in your heart to forgive me."

For a long moment Jolie said nothing. She simply studied the woman before her, T.C. guessed recalling that ugly day.

"Perhaps we can start by simply being civil to each other," Jolie said at last, "and proceed from there."

His mother nodded, looking grateful. "Thank you."

"You're his mother," Jolie said quietly. "And I love him."

"You're lucky," he said to his mother. "She doesn't have it in her to be as cruel as you were."

"Few do," Whitney said wryly, startling him with the sudden self-awareness. Maybe she really had had an awakening. Or maybe this was just a new, cleverer scheme.

He just wished he could believe her fully, and be sure she really hadn't had anything to do with his father's disappearance.

She glanced at T.C. He'd been on the phone when she came back from seeing Kevin, and it had sounded like he'd been making plans to meet someone. She supposed he had a lot of work piled up, since he'd in essence ignored it for days now to help them. Something she would never, ever forget. But he hadn't seemed in a hurry, and they'd walked back to his SUV at a pace Emma could easily manage, something else that endeared him to her even more.

She hoped nothing too awful had happened at his work

in the interim. Then had the thought that she could just ask him. After all, she'd agreed to marry him, hadn't she? The amazing speed with which it had all happened had left her a bit breathless, but the joy was bubbling up inside her and she was certain it would soon overflow, as soon as she allowed herself to really, truly believe it.

"Is the mean lady really gone?"

"Yes, Emma, she is," T.C. told her, crouching down to look her in the eye. "And she'll be gone for a very long time."

Emma nodded, clearly accepting what he told her. She trusted him so much already, Jolie thought. There would be rough patches, of course, but they already had a good start. Emma would have a father, and she would have the only man she'd ever really loved. And as T.C. carefully secured Emma in the borrowed car seat, commenting he was going to have to buy one so they could give this one back, she felt the urge to wrap her arms around herself to keep from flying apart under the pressure of pure joy.

"Are we going home now?"

Emma's words as they left the city caught Jolie off guard. She hadn't thought beyond getting through the next moment for days now, and the simple question seemed much more complicated than it should be.

"I..."

She looked at T.C. He seemed to understand. "I thought we'd go back to the refuge and pick up your things. Then you can decide what's next."

That made sense, she thought. But when they got to the little cabin, she found herself oddly reluctant to leave. Never had a place been so aptly named, she thought. Refuge was indeed what she'd found here, despite the ugly intrusion of a killer. But then she realized the refuge wasn't the place; it was the man. And she knew he always would be.

"What about Flash?" Emma asked with obvious concern after she had all her things gathered.

"Come on," T.C. said, "I'll show you."

He went out to the car, activated the system, pulled out his phone and voiced a text message. So Emma could hear it, no doubt. He never failed to take the girl's feelings into account.

"Dylan. I'm sending Flash home. If he hasn't shown up at the barn in twenty minutes, let me know."

Then they walked over to the corral, where the horse came to the fence and nickered softly in greeting. T.C. lifted Emma to the top rail so she could reach out and rub the horse's velvety nose while he buckled a leather halter over the big paint's head.

"I don't want him t'go!" Emma exclaimed, clearly distressed at the thought of losing her beloved companion.

"You'll see him again," Jolie assured her.

"What if he gets lost?"

"He won't. He knows his way. He's done it on his own lots of times."

"But what if he does?"

"He knows the way like you know the way to the park," T.C. explained.

"But there's snakes. You said so."

"I'm sure he knows to stay away from them," Jolie said.

But the child obviously wasn't ready to stop worrying. T.C. looked at Jolie. "We could stop by the big house. Easier than going for a trailer, coming back for him, then going back again."

But he would do that, Jolie realized, if it would ease Emma's mind.

"I'd like to do that anyway," he added, looking at her steadily, "if you're up to it. Start as you mean to go on and all that."

She knew what he was saying. That she had a right to be there now, and it would be good to establish that at the start. On one hand, she was tired of all the high drama and would like nothing more than normalcy for at least a few days. On the other, he was a Colton, and high drama seemed to follow even the "good Coltons."

Besides, wouldn't showing up at the big house be a good test of Whitney's sincerity? It was easy to apologize to someone who might never set foot in your home again.

"Is Fowler there?"

"Sunday afternoon, afraid so. But so are the good guys."

She smiled in spite of herself. "Piper?" she asked; she had always felt a kindred bond with the young woman who'd been orphaned at a young age, just as she had.

Something darker flashed through T.C.'s eyes for an instant, but he only nodded.

"Then let's go."

T.C. smiled, and she had the feeling he was proud of her answer. She smiled back, liking—no, loving the feeling.

He opened the corral gate and led the big horse out.

"Home," he said, and let him go with a slap on the powerful hindquarters. Flash snorted, tossed his head and took off at a rapid trot. It was clear he knew exactly where he was going, and Jolie found to her own surprise she was relieved at that, which told her how Emma must be feeling.

Jolie belted the girl into the car seat. "We're going to go to the ranch house, to be sure Flash gets there okay."

That seemed to mollify the child, and she settled in willingly. And squealed with delight when halfway there they spotted Flash, mane and tail flying, topping a rise headed for the ranch at a long, easy lope.

"He's beautiful, running free, isn't he?" Jolie said, turning to look at her daughter.

"Makes it even more amazing he works so well for us, doesn't it?" T.C. said. Jolie smiled at him, liking the observation.

She'd been smiling more today than she could remember in a long time. What had begun as one of the darkest moments in a life peppered with them had turned into the brightest, sunniest day she'd ever had.

And now she was headed toward the scene of the darkest day. Only this time she had T.C. at her side, and she knew she could face anything.

Even Fowler Colton.

Chapter 33

When they got to the house, T.C. honked the horn lightly twice. Jolie glanced at him, but he said nothing as he got out. But when he opened the car door for her this time, it was with exaggerated grace and even a small bow, as if he were a king clearing the way for his queen arriving back at the palace.

The massive front door opened, and four people spilled out. The good Coltons, she realized, recognizing Piper first, then Reid, Alanna and even Zane, Marceline's much nicer if intimidating brother. As T.C. turned to get Emma, the four swarmed her with welcomes so vociferous she couldn't doubt her welcome on this front.

And none of them were surprised.

She glanced at T.C., who now had Emma in his arms, and realized the truth of those phone calls he'd made. He'd rallied the troops for her. And for Emma, who was staring at the small crowd, wide eyed.

"Oh, my gosh. Look at you, Emma! You've gotten so big, and you're so pretty," Piper cooed.

Emma giggled. Jolie smiled.

"I've got some money I'd like to donate to your foster program, Piper," she said, with a glance at T.C. She saw her meaning register, saw his slow, gratified smile as she made clear her utter trust that he would always take care of Emma.

Piper looked surprised, but smiled, as they all did as they headed back toward the door. It only took Jolie until midway up the six grand steps to realize they had formed a wedge in front of her, T.C. and Emma, as if to declare their allegiance for anyone to see.

Anyone meaning Fowler, who was standing in the foyer as they came in.

She hadn't seen the man since the day before the painful scene in the library four years ago, but even back then she'd wondered if he'd had something to do with it. If he couldn't act directly, Fowler had a habit of planting seeds of discourse in the right fertile minds and then sitting back to watch what he couldn't do himself happen anyway.

He looked as he always had, tall, imposing, his eyes as cold a blue as she'd ever seen. She'd wondered once how many custom-tailored suits he had, since he wore one every day, even today, Sunday. And of course the black Stetson he always wore. To remind all, he joked, who the black hat was.

Only Jolie had never, ever assumed he was joking.

"Well, well," Fowler said. "Look who's here. Still leading my little brother around by his...nose, I see."

Start as you mean to go on...

Indeed, Jolie thought. She glanced at Piper, who had

Emma looking up at her in apparent fascination. Piper met her gaze, seemed to read her intent, nodded, then reached down and took Emma's hand.

Jolie made her way through her protective guard, passing between Reid and Zane, both of whom gave her subtle encouraging pats on the shoulder. She came to a halt in front of Fowler, who was looking at her the same superior way he always had, when he'd bothered to register her presence at all.

"I would prefer peace," she said, pleased with how firm and steady her voice sounded, and knowing it was at least in part because she had a solid wall of Colton support behind her. "But if you want war, you shall have it."

Fowler's eyebrows rose. "So the little kitchen maid has grown up?"

"Even the kitchen maid saw you for what you are. She was just too afraid to say so."

Fowler sniffed audibly. "And I suppose now you're not?"

"Of you? Hardly." She said it with as much disdain as she could muster, and was surprised both at how thoroughly scornful it sounded, and how surprised Fowler looked. "You and Tiffany make quite the pair. Two master manipulators. At least you're not making two other innocent people miserable."

She wanted to add a sarcastic "Your mother must be so proud," but in light of her recent promise to be civil with T.C.'s mother, she held it back. Besides, she was busy trying to figure out what it was she'd just seen in Fowler's eyes when she mentioned Tiffany. Something quick, darting, that had almost looked like fear. Was it what T.C. had told her, that he was afraid they might suspect his long-suffering girlfriend of his father's abduction and possible murder, and thus was trying to implicate somebody else, anybody else? Including her?

To her shock, Fowler looked away. He pretended it was to focus on T.C., but Jolie had seen the wariness, as if he were afraid she'd seen too much.

And then it hit her. Fowler wasn't afraid Tiffany would be suspected, he was afraid she'd actually done it.

Well, now, wouldn't that just be the perfect case of like finding like?

A scheme worthy of Fowler himself, executed and used against him. It would have made her smile with appreciation at the justice of it, if it hadn't been for the fact that T.C.'s father was still missing, and despite everything she wouldn't wish for that. She loved T.C. too much, and knew at the core he did love the man despite butting heads with him so often.

"It's up to you, Fowler."

His gaze snapped back to her, and she wondered if it was at her temerity, to use his first name. To the little kitchen maid he had always been Mr. Colton, preferable spoken with an undertone of fear. Well, he would find no more of that in her, she told herself firmly, and stared him down.

"War? Or peace?" she asked steadily.

For a long moment he stared at her, and she thought she saw a glimmer of respect in his gaze.

Then his expression changed to his patented impatient look. "I don't have time to waste on the likes of you. I'm expecting someone."

He turned on his heel and stalked into the study and shut the door with more vehemence than it required.

Cheers went up from four Coltons. The fifth, the one

who mattered most, pulled her into his arms and kissed her, eliciting another, rowdier cheer.

"Welcome to the family," Alanna said warmly.

"Such as it is," Reid put in.

"I think," Zane added, "it's just improved."

"Definitely," Piper agreed, lifting Emma in her arms. The girl was looking around wide-eyed, and Jolie knew they had a bit of explaining to do, about the new situation. But the chorus of welcome had warmed her to the core.

Much later, after a pleasant reunion with Bettina—who promptly took Emma off to help her make cookies—and both Aaron and Moira Manfred, who to her surprise remembered her quite fondly, and a long, meandering walk down to the livestock barn, Jolie found herself sitting on a bench outside the barn office with T.C.

"I still can't believe Flash actually beat us here," she said with a smile.

T.C. smiled. He loved that horse, and he didn't care who knew it. And that made her love him all the more. "He knows all the shortcuts, and can take them."

"I think Emma would sleep in his stall with him if she could."

"Speaking of sleeping arrangements," he said, "Your place is small for three, but we can make it work if you want."

She stared at him. T. C. Colton, living in her tiny apartment, in a neighborhood far removed from the opulent luxury of Colton Valley Ranch? But she saw the truth in his face; he would, if it was what she wanted.

"But if you think you can stomach it here, we can have my rooms redone however you want. The sitting room is kind of my office here, so I was thinking we could take over the guest room next door and have our own living room. And there's a single room on the other side for Emma. We can redo it any way she likes." He grinned. "Horses, I suspect. We can put a door in between us and her, too."

He'd obviously thought this all out, and Jolie was a bit taken aback.

"Or," he went on, "if that's too close to Fowler and Tiffany, and my mother, whose conversion is still suspect—" she was glad he'd said that; she had her own doubts "—we could do a couple of other things. There's room down at the main barn for a nice-sized apartment, a good safe distance from here. Emma would like that, I think. Or," he said with a sideways glance at her, "we could build something of our own, something modern, at the refuge. I have an even greater liking for the place now."

She knew he was thinking of those fevered moments in the shed, and she felt the heat burgeoning inside her at the thought that there would be more, many more of those moments to come. She hoped they would go back to the refuge, now and then, no matter where they ended up.

He leaned over and, as if he'd read her thoughts—as he probably had, she admitted—whispered, "I can't wait to make love to you in an actual bed. And sleep with you in my arms. And wake up in the morning with you. Every morning."

A shiver, a delicious one, went through her. "I love you," she said, because it was the only thing she could think of that appropriately answered everything he'd said.

And this time she kissed him, losing herself in the luscious feel and taste of him, loving the way he made that low, growling sound in his throat, as if he were slipping the leash for her, just for her.

Eventually, with promises of more to come, they

headed back toward the house to check on Emma. Bettina met them at the back door, looking anxious. Emma, was Jolie's first thought, but the kindly cook shook her head.

"It's just awful," she said to T.C. "I can't believe it."

She seemed beyond words and waved them inside. The moment they stepped in, they could hear raised voices from the front of the house.

"Maybe your place would be best," T.C. muttered.

"Less drama," she agreed.

But when they followed the voices into the foyer, the scene they found was the absolute last thing Jolie ever would have expected.

Piper, sweet, loving Piper, with her wrists handcuffed behind her back. Being led away by a uniformed officer while another man with a vest labeled CSI followed, carrying a large paper envelope. To one side stood another man, with a triumphant-looking Fowler.

Piper? Impossible, Jolie thought.

"What the hell is going on?" T.C. demanded. "Sheriff?"

"I told you it was her!" Fowler was crowing like four-year-old Emma, Jolie thought with disgust.

T.C. told his brother to shut up with an obscenity she'd never heard from him before. But he kept his gaze on the dark-haired man in the county uniform, who didn't seem happy for a guy who had apparently just made an arrest.

"We've found some pretty damning evidence," the man said, sounding reluctant.

Fowler couldn't resist chiming in. "They found a charm from that silly bracelet she wears, with her initials on it, right outside the window."

T.C. didn't even look at his brother. "They found it now? Three months later?"

"It was buried, it seems," the man said.

"The gardener found it," Fowler said. Jolie found the glee in his voice repugnant. This was his own sister he was condemning. But then he, and Marceline, had never really considered Piper their true sister, had they?

"A bit suspect, isn't it?" T.C. said, echoing her own thoughts. "All this time and now this conveniently turns up?"

"If it was buried, couldn't it have been there much longer?" Jolie asked. Fowler glared at her. She ignored him. She was going to be part of this family now—not an altogether pleasant prospect—and she was never again going to be intimidated by Fowler, or his parents. If he —and T.C.—still had two of them.

"It's not just that." A second man joined them, younger, with blond hair and light blue eyes. He was in plainclothes, but he had the same air as the sheriff, one of cool command. She guessed this must be the investigator T.C. had referred to, Kidwell.

"They found one of the old man's shirts wadded up in the back of her closet," Fowler crowed again. "And it's all bloody."

T.C. never looked at Fowler, but he frowned. "Piper's not that stupid."

"The evidence will be analyzed, of course. If it's not your father's blood—"

"Of course it is," Fowler interrupted.

T.C. whirled on his brother then. "You take a rather repulsive amount of joy in the thought that it's your own father's blood!"

Fowler looked taken aback for a moment, as if that idea had never occurred to him.

Charming brother-in-law you're going to have, m'girl.

But right now she was noticing T.C.'s clenched fists and wondering if he was going to deck his brother right here in front of two law enforcement officers.

"He's got it coming," she whispered to him, "and when you deliver it I'll hold your hat, but this might not be the best time."

T.C. turned his head to look at her. A slow, wide smile changed his expression from anger to a pure sort of happy that vanquished any last, tiny, lingering doubt she'd had.

He looked back at the sheriff, once more ignoring his brother, who had wisely backed out of reach. "She'll have the best attorney in Dallas, and bail as soon as it's set."

The man nodded. He flicked a glance at Fowler, and Jolie wondered if he was as suspicious of his motives as T.C. was. She hoped so.

"I'm so sorry," she said when they were alone again. "I don't believe for a moment Piper had anything to do with this."

He put his arm around her, pulling her close. "She didn't. Fowler's desperate, just like he was with you."

"Maybe you should have punched him."

His mouth quirked. "I'm glad you stopped me. Piper needs me able to help, not locked up beside her for assault."

"And you know Fowler would do just that."

"I have no illusions left about how far my twisted brother would go."

"I'm sorry about that, too."

He turned to face her. "It doesn't matter anymore. He doesn't matter. Nothing does, except that I have you back in my life. And Emma."

"She already adores you."

"I'll be the best father I can be to her, Jolie." His mouth

quirked again. "After all, I've had a great example of what not to do."

Jolie laughed, both at his words and the light tone. "Yes, you will be. I'm glad you're not letting this drag you down."

"I can face anything the Colton Fates throw at me, now," he said.

"Good," she said wryly. "Because then you can help me do the same."

"You'll have a lot of help, if you want it. But I don't think you'll need it. You stood up to Fowler in a way few do." He lifted a hand to her cheek. "I love you."

"I know," she said.

"Then that's all we need," he said.

The slow smile that curved his mouth and lit his eyes filled her with an entirely different kind of warmth. The kind that never wavered, that filled all corners of not just her body but her life. The kind of warmth she'd only ever felt with him, the kind she knew would endure through any trial, that would matter even when nothing else did.

Together they headed for the kitchen to find their daughter.

* * * * *

MILLS & BOON®

INTRIGUE
Romantic Suspense

A SEDUCTIVE COMBINATION OF DANGER AND DESIRE

A sneak peek at next month's titles...

In stores from 20th October 2016:

- **Landon** – Delores Fossen *and*
  Navy SEAL Six Pack – Elle James
- **The Girl Who Cried Murder** – Paula Graves *and*
  In the Arms of the Enemy – Carol Ericson
- **Scene of the Crime: Means and Motive** –
  Carla Cassidy *and* **Christmas Kidnapping** –
  Cindi Myers

Romantic Suspense

- **Runaway Colton** – Karen Whiddon
- **Operation Soldier Next Door** – Justine Davis

Just can't wait?
Buy our books online a month before they hit the shops!
www.millsandboon.co.uk

Also available as eBooks.

MILLS & BOON®

Why shop at millsandboon.co.uk?

Each year, thousands of romance readers find their perfect read at millsandboon.co.uk. That's because we're passionate about bringing you the very best romantic fiction. Here are some of the advantages of shopping at www.millsandboon.co.uk:

✱ **Get new books first**—you'll be able to buy your favourite books one month before they hit the shops

✱ **Get exclusive discounts**—you'll also be able to buy our specially created monthly collections, with up to 50% off the RRP

✱ **Find your favourite authors**—latest news, interviews and new releases for all your favourite authors and series on our website, plus ideas for what to try next

✱ **Join in**—once you've bought your favourite books, don't forget to register with us to rate, review and join in the discussions

Visit **www.millsandboon.co.uk**
for all this and more today!